Mason's laugh was throaty

It was full of gravelly undertones like his voice. The lines at the corners of his eyes deepened and crinkled in a way that made Anna want to laugh with him. Except he wasn't laughing with her—he was laughing at her.

"Nice swing, but oh, man. You don't know me very well if you think that's the bribe that'll get me into your movie."

She was stung. She had misjudged, which didn't happen often. "That's the point of the movie. No one knows you. We should."

He shook his head, suddenly serious. "No. You don't want to know me. The guy you want? Mason Star, lead singer of Five Star? That guy doesn't exist anymore."

He rubbed his hand back and forth in his short hair, leaving the front sticking up in messy points. "Matter of fact, why don't you put that in your movie? Mason Star died. RIP."

"People deserve to know what happened with the crash and afterward. They deserve the truth."

"I don't know what you think you know. But here's your truth. I'm not that guy anymore and digging all that up won't do any good for me or anyone else."

Dear Reader,

I always start my projects with a character. *His Secret Past* began from an argument I imagined between Mason and his teenage son, Christian. Even though they were fighting, the love between them was so achingly real I had to find out more. I fell in love with this guy who wanted to be a good dad, a good man, but didn't trust his instincts. All I needed was a woman who could challenge him but also realize how much he had to give. Hello, Anna! I had a lot of fun writing her quirks and her quick sense of humor. I hope you'll enjoy reading about Mason and Anna's journey from suspicion and secrets to love.

People have asked why I set the book in New Jersey—it's not the most obviously romantic state. Growing up in Pennsylvania, I vacationed "down the shore." (For those in other parts of the world, this means a town on the Atlantic coast, most likely in New Jersey or Maryland.) There's a magic feeling about the shore and a mythic tradition about the music that's played in the bars and clubs of shore towns during summer's long, hot nights. (Bruce Springsteen, anyone?) Although *His Secret Past* was originally set in Seattle, the romantic possibilities of a Jersey boy were too delicious to pass up.

I hope you'll enjoy this book. I'd love to hear from you! My Web site is www.ellenhartman.com, or send e-mail to ellen@ellenhartman.com.

Ellen Hartman

HIS SECRET PAST

Ellen Hartman

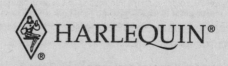

HARLEQUIN®

TORONTO • NEW YORK • LONDON
AMSTERDAM • PARIS • SYDNEY • HAMBURG
STOCKHOLM • ATHENS • TOKYO • MILAN • MADRID
PRAGUE • WARSAW • BUDAPEST • AUCKLAND

ISBN-13: 978-0-373-71491-9
ISBN-10:   0-373-71491-2

HIS SECRET PAST

This edition published by arrangement with Harlequin Books S.A.

® and TM are trademarks of the publisher. Trademarks indicated with ® are registered in the United States Patent and Trademark Office, the Canadian Trade Marks Office and in other countries.

www.eHarlequin.com

Printed in U.S.A.

ABOUT THE AUTHOR

Ellen has been making a living as a writer since she graduated from Carnegie Mellon and went to work for Microsoft writing documentation for Word. (In those days the company had 5,000 employees, windows were glass things you opened to get a breeze and Bill Gates was still single.)

She met her husband while he was living in Hoboken, New Jersey, and they lived there together as newlyweds. They share great memories of meals at Amanda's and late nights listening to music at Maxwell's.

Currently, Ellen lives in a college town in upstate New York, where she enjoys writing romances, horrifying her husband with her musical "taste" and watching movies, old and new, with her sons.

Books by Ellen Hartman

HARLEQUIN SUPERROMANCE
1427–WANTED MAN

This book is dedicated to my sister, Anne,
and my best friend, Stephanie. They keep me sane,
share my unhealthy eating habits
(another chocolate chip cookie, anyone?)
and are always willing to take to the dance floor
at the first hint of "Dancing Queen."
As always, my hat's off to my writing group,
Diana, Leslie, Liz and Mary. They kept after me
when Anna was eluding me and helped me
find her spark. Thanks!

CHAPTER ONE

April 2007

GNOCCHI. ANNA shook her head as she dropped her hoodie on the arm of the sofa. *Food bribes? How easy did they think she was?*

Her stomach growled as she narrowed her eyes at the big pasta bowl, full and steaming on her brother's dining-room table.

Something was up.

Anna eased the front door closed and slid the key into the pocket of her track pants. She considered the table with its cheerful centerpiece of daffodils and the wine-glasses she'd bought Jake and his partner, Rob, for Christmas last year. She tugged the holder off her ponytail, freeing her curly shoulder-length hair. *Someone had gone to some trouble here.*

Because Rob swore that making gnocchi gave him flashbacks to his grandmother's cooking lessons punctuated by her uncomfortably sharp tongue and handy wooden spoon, he made the pasta dumplings only on special occasions. Anna's birthday. Jake's birthday. The anniversary of his *nonna*'s death when he washed the gnocchi down with homemade wine he

bought from the Italian men's club at the end of the
rapidly gentrifying street.

Whenever he or Jake wanted to bribe Anna.

She let the aroma of Rob's secret family recipe spaghetti
sauce wrap around her, pulling her toward the kitchen.

"Honeys, I'm home," she called out as she walked into
the brightly lit room, the first Jake and Rob had remod-
eled since buying the dilapidated Hoboken brownstone
three years ago.

Jake was leaning on a stool at the island, one leather
loafer on the brass foot rail, his elbows propped on the
dark soapstone counter. He turned with careful nonchalance when she came in.

Anna lifted a hand, not committing to a hello before
she knew what was up. Staying with her brother and Rob
had its ups and downs. On the one hand, she loved
spending time with them. Eleven months out of twelve
she was on location or flying back and forth to locations
for Blue Maverick films, the production company she
and Jake ran. If she had anything she'd call a home base,
it was here with them.

On the other hand, this was their home and not hers.
And because the couple were renovating the place themselves, progress on the brownstone had slowed as Jake
was kept busy with the steady stream of film work. She
stayed in the cramped guest room, sleeping on a foam
chair that folded out into a twin-size bed. Her clothes
were stowed in a footlocker Rob had had since college.
She rarely bought books or CDs or clothes, or anything,
really, because she didn't have anywhere to keep them.
Although she relished her skill at living light, carrying
your entire life in a duffel bag had limitations.

"Gnocchi, huh?" Anna said as she propped a hip on the stool next to Jake. The two sat side by side under the cobalt-blue lamps, staring at the cherry-wood cabinets in front of them. "Where's Rob?" she asked.

"At the gallery. He's bringing dessert back later."

"Dessert, too? You're pulling out all the stops, little brother."

"What's that supposed to mean?" Jake asked as he got off his stool and stretched in that maddening way little brothers who outgrew their older sisters by eight inches stretched when they wanted to make a point. *Point taken.* Six feet tall, sporting a reddish stubble that was a shade lighter than his dark auburn hair, thirty years old, Jake wasn't so little anymore. But younger siblings never get the advantage, no matter how tall they grow. That was a universal truth.

"Rob made gnocchi so you can bribe me," Anna said.

He didn't even flinch. "You want to eat?"

"Chicken," Anna said.

"Gnocchi," he countered.

"*You're* a chicken. Spit it out."

Jake sank back down onto the stool and folded his hands in front of him. He opened his mouth to speak and then closed it again. Oh God, he was actually scared to tell her whatever this was. Up to that moment she'd been fooling around. Fun over, she asked quickly, "You're not sick, are you? Is it Rob? Jake? *Say something.*"

He shook his head. "I'm fine. Everything is fine. Actually, that's the thing."

They'd been business partners for close to nine years and siblings for thirty. Anna knew when Jake was struggling with the truth. Their perfect parents had been all about putting on a front in their shrink-wrapped Long Island home, appearing normal at all costs. That life of lies was what had driven her toward making documentaries. She liked the facts, not the spin. She and Jake had a hard rule that they wouldn't lie to each other. But it was difficult sometimes.

"You're scaring me and the gnocchi's getting cold, so just say it. We'll deal with whatever it is."

That seemed to be the permission Jake had needed because he blurted, "Rob's boss is selling Traction. He offered Rob the right of first refusal and he, um, we, decided to take it. The deal's final in August."

Anna nodded, encouraging him to go on. Rob managed Traction, a gallery on Hoboken's main street. She knew he'd wanted more control and now he'd have it. So far she wasn't sure what the problem was.

"I'm going to put up half the money, Anna. Not because Rob needs it, but because I want to. I'm tired of never being home, tired of the schedules and the budgets. Living other people's lives instead of my own. I loved Blue Maverick, you know that, but I can't live like that anymore."

Can't live like that anymore. Anna felt the room spin. Whatever she'd thought Jake might say this wasn't it. *He was talking about their company in the past tense.* "But Blue Maverick is finally solid. The schedules and money and the crazy stuff, they won't be as bad now. We can get an assistant full-time."

"The only way it will be easier is if I'm less involved and I can't do that. I can't 'take a step back' and know that someone else is making decisions for my movies. I need to get all the way out. I can't do halfway."

Neither of them could. It was part of why Blue

Maverick had come so far in such a short time. They'd started with one documentary financed with credit cards and loans from friends. They'd parlayed good reviews from that film into corporate work, political commercials and issue films for nonprofits. Another documentary in wider release had led to TV work and steadier corporate gigs. In the past two years Blue Maverick had started to feel viable.

"How can you walk away now? We can pick our next project—finally do what we want. We've spent the past four months brainstorming, for Pete's sake. Were you faking that whole time?"

Jake put his hand over hers. He was the one in their family who was easy with physical affection, where she and her parents were apt to stiffen up. Came from being the baby, probably.

"Whatever this last project is, I'm in. Rob agreed to run the gallery solo so we can do one more together."

"One more? That's it?" Fine for Jake—he had plans for *after*. But what did he think she'd do? Blue Maverick had been her life ever since she graduated from college.

As if he'd heard her thoughts, Jake said, "You still love it. Living with other people, digging into their stories and then moving on. But I want to settle down. Here, with Rob. I can't do that and Blue Maverick, too."

She pulled her hand out from under his and stepped back. "And I can't run Blue Maverick without you."

"Anna," Jake started but she stopped him with a look.

The finality of his announcement hit her. No Jake. No Blue Maverick. Everything she had worked for... She had to think. Was there a way to go on without Jake? Did she want to? "I have to get out of here before I say something

I'll regret. Tell Rob congratulations and thanks for the gnocchi."

She spun and walked out. She grabbed her sweatshirt from the back of the couch before yanking the heavy wooden front door open. Closing it behind her, the scent of Rob's sauce was abruptly cut off. Life would change just that quickly when Jake quit the company. Without her brother she couldn't do what she did. And if she couldn't make her films, what would she have left?

HOBOKEN, NEW JERSEY, was one mile square. Anna had jogged the perimeter many times during her visits. Tonight she ran blindly, veering off the curb because it was easier to dodge cars in the narrow streets than pedestrians on the sidewalks.

As twilight descended, she gradually came out of her fog. Trotting tiredly past the green spaces of the Steven's Tech campus, she became aware of the people around her again. Just up the block two boys were horsing around on the stoop of an apartment building. They wrestled over a basketball and before Anna even recognized the danger, the ball was in the street and the smaller boy darted between two cars after it. The driver of a black SUV coming down the street slammed on his brakes and his horn at the same time. The kid stopped dead and then sprinted for the sidewalk where his friend had gone still. The driver rolled down the window and yelled something at the boy before rumbling off.

Anna closed her eyes and took a breath. When she opened them again, the bigger boy had the younger one in a headlock and was giving him a good-natured lecture. If the car hadn't stopped, if the kid hadn't stopped…but they had, thank God, and everything was normal again that fast.

One more film.
One more shot.

Anna remembered the fax she'd gotten but left lying on her desk all week. *One more film.* Was it time to put her ghosts to rest? Go back to the night when her life had changed in one minute? One argument, one bad decision and nothing was ever the same again?

Shaking off a chill as her adrenaline receded, Anna turned down Sixth Street, heading back toward Traction, the gallery Jake and Rob were buying. It was smack in the middle of Washington Street, Hoboken's main drag.

As she approached the gallery, the display in the wide storefront window across the street twinkled and shifted. A clever combination of lights, reflective surfaces and electronics created the appearance of a waterfall cascading down the window complete with a foaming spray at sidewalk level. The word *Traction* appeared randomly in the spray. In the middle of the effect was a display space for a piece from whatever show was currently on. Anna had badgered Rob until he explained how it all worked and then she'd promptly forced herself to forget what he'd said because the illusion was so cool.

It was almost completely dark outside now and the gallery lights glowed brighter. Rob wanting Traction made sense, but Jake? That was a surprise. She knew the complications of their hectic life on the road had started to feel like a burden to her brother. Early on he'd gotten as much of a kick as she did out of starting life over with every project, finding a house-sitting gig or crashing with friends, exploring new towns and meeting people. Making intense connections and then moving on.

But when he and Rob bought their house, Jake had

started looking homeward more than ahead. She'd figured once Blue Maverick was more solid Jake would want to scale back. Turned out she'd been partly right, but instead of scaling back he was scaling *out*.

Rob appeared behind the window and Anna crossed the street. He turned when he heard the door open, and then tensed when he realized it was her.

Rob Parker was slightly shorter than her brother, blond, slender and good-looking in a hot-librarian way. He was the guy in high school who anchored the debate team and then got "discovered" by the cool crowd when he sprouted six inches senior year. His dark-framed retro glasses and longish sideburns fit with his job at the gallery but also looked natural when he was up to his neck in sawdust at the house.

"What would your *nonna* say if she knew you were prostituting her gnocchi?"

Rob relaxed when he realized she wasn't angry. "Nonna was the master of the food-for-favor exchange," he said. "She'd be proud of me for once."

Anna appreciated that he didn't even try to pretend the gnocchi hadn't been a bribe. He gestured to the upholstered chairs set under the photos on the east wall. "Want to sit?"

The show, photographs by an artist who'd grown up in Asbury Park, the nearby shore town where so much rock history was made, was opening the following night. Anna could almost smell stale beer in the black-and-white photos of dive bars and shore bands.

She moved closer to the pictures. The one on the left was a close-up of Mason Star, lead singer of Five Star. His long hair was plastered to his neck in sweaty streaks and his eyes were closed, but there was no mistaking that he was meant to be behind the microphone. Five Star was, after Bruce, the most famous band to "grow up" on the Jersey shore. If she had ever believed in signs, this would surely be one for the ages.

"I'm not staying," she told Rob as she looked at the next photo. This one showed Five Star walking out the back door of a bar in Wildwood, instrument cases slung over their shoulders. "I need to call Jake but I went out without my phone." She tried to keep her voice from shaking as she thought about what she was going to do.

Rob pulled his phone out of the pocket of his jeans and held it out to her. "Are you going to yell at him?"

She was touched by his concern for her brother. "Not unless he ate all the gnocchi."

"You didn't have any?" And now she heard concern for her, which touched her again.

"I couldn't eat." Anna met his eyes. "But if Jake agrees to my plan, I might feel better. If all goes well I'll be looking for a hearty breakfast."

Rob shot her a half grin. "That, Nonna would like. She loved gnocchi cold for breakfast."

Anna turned back to the photo of the Five Star concert. She stared at the faces in the crowd, knowing it wasn't the show she'd attended but looking anyway.

Jake answered on the first ring. "Rob? Have you seen my sister?"

"It's me," she said, cutting him off before he could say something she didn't want to hear. "I stopped at Traction to borrow Rob's phone."

She took a steadying breath as she gathered her courage. Jake said he'd do one last film. One last chance to work with him to find a true story and tell it. Before tonight she'd been lobbying hard for them to make a film about a girls' hockey team from upstate New York. The competing expectations for on-ice aggression and off-ice femininity created tension for the girls. Overinvested hockey parents with their cowbells and fistfights were a compelling backdrop.

She wanted to tell that story, but if she only had one more project, that wasn't the one.

"I thought about what you said," Anna told him as she touched the frame of the picture. "One more movie."

"The hockey thing is fresh," Jake said.

"It's good, but it's not what I want for our last film."

"Anna, stop saying 'last.' You can get someone else. With your reputation and the commercial work we have lined up, you can keep going. Colin Paige would work with you in a heartbeat and he's not the only one."

She nodded. "You're right. But Blue Maverick is me and you. Maybe I can keep making movies without you and maybe I can't. Either way, it won't be Blue Maverick. So I want our last project to matter."

"You have an idea?" The familiar surge of interest in his voice made her grip the phone tighter. She'd miss the perfect connection she had with Jake.

"I got a fax two weeks ago from a band. They're making a new album, first one in fifteen years, and they want a promotional film. Something they can show on TV to help sell the album."

He was hanging in but he sounded confused when he said, "But that's commercial work."

"It was Five Star."

There was a long silence. Anna put her hand over her mouth, forcing herself to give him time to think. "Is that a joke?" Jake finally said.

"I make movies to tell stories no one's ever heard. The truth. I want to tell what happened to Terri that night on the Five Star bus."

"What happened to Terri was a tragedy but there's no story there. It was an accident."

"The crash was an accident. But no one ever said why she was on the bus or who she was with or anything. It's like she was just a body and whatever happened to put her there didn't matter."

"Digging into that isn't going to help the way you feel about Terri. It wasn't your fault she got on the bus."

"Jake, she was seventeen and she died in that horrible crash surrounded by strangers who couldn't even be bothered to explain what she was doing on the bus after she died. She deserves to have her story told."

"So if we do this, if we go after this and find out what happened, what does that get you?"

"The truth."

He waited for a second. "We shouldn't do this on the phone. Come home."

"No. I know this is the one."

"But you said they want a promotional film for a new album. The tour bus crashing and Terri and those other people dying practically wrecked their band. They're not going to talk about that when they're releasing a new album."

"Jake, please," Anna said. She straightened and paced to the door, looking out at the well-lit street. "Getting people to talk about stuff they don't want to? It's our job. We're good at it. Let's end Blue Maverick the right way."

"I'll do what you want, Anna," Jake said. "But I want

you to be sure this is the one. I'm in if you want it." He paused. "Make sure you want it."

"I want it."

Jake's quick "okay" made her miss him more.

She said goodbye and then handed the phone back to Rob. "See you in the morning for cold gnocchi."

"I'm sticking with Wheaties." Rob pulled her into a quick hug. "But thanks for not hating me."

Anna patted him awkwardly. "See you."

Back on the street, she turned downtown, heading for the Strand, Hoboken's art house movie theater. *Red River* was playing. If Montgomery Clift couldn't distract her, nothing could.

She'd look for Terri's story—her last shot to find it—starting tomorrow. But for tonight, she'd escape.

Anna handed her money to Stephen, the Strand's owner/ticket taker/projectionist/popcorn maker, at the ticket window where he perched on a wooden stool.

Stephen had been a friend ever since he screened Anna's senior film here.

"No date tonight?" he asked.

"Too many offers, didn't want to hurt anyone's feelings." Stephen liked to tease her about her love life, maybe living vicariously since he'd been in what he called a "dry spell" as long as she'd known him. She didn't want to find out what that felt like. Her situation was different. She'd broken up with her last boyfriend, Boring Bob, on purpose.

"Maybe if you put some effort in you'd get more men," he said as he surveyed her well-worn track pants, black T-shirt and grey hoodie disgustedly.

"How do you know this isn't my best effort?" she shot back.

"I'm in a dry spell, not blind. You're hot under all that I'm-a-bad-dresser camo." He handed her a ticket, a box of popcorn and a large Diet Coke. "Just once I'd like to see you in a dress."

"Dream on," she said, laughing. In fact, Anna didn't own a dress. She had two suits, exactly identical, one navy, one black. The navy she wore to business things and any time she had to film a dress-up event. The black she wore to funerals.

She pushed open the door to theater one and found a seat halfway back on the aisle. The lights went out and the familiar darkness flowed over her. The projector clicked on, dust dancing in the light streaming toward the screen. Anna was home.

She made movies to tell the truth. She watched movies because they made her forget the truth. She was sure, deep in her bones, that she wouldn't be able to keep making movies without Jake. He was the only person she trusted enough to be as open and vulnerable as she needed to be to find the stories. Jake made her life work. He was her business expert, her partner, her friend, her home base. If she wasn't making movies, what could she do? If she didn't have her movies to fill her life, what would she have?

All that uncertainty loomed over her life outside. Here, in the dusty darkness of the Strand, Anna forgot it all and let the story carry her away.

CHAPTER TWO

August 2007

MASON STAR PROPPED his putter on his shoulder and glared at his son, Christian, but his heart wasn't in it and they both knew it. When Christian's cell rang somewhere in the hall outside his office, Mason was glad for the reprieve. *Coward.* The name fit. Made him feel guilty. But the fact was, he was tired. Tired enough that for the first time in years, he wished there was another parent on the scene. Not Christian's mother, but someone stable and responsible. He needed a break.

Christian barely acknowledged the ringing phone, ready to keep on arguing. Give the kid credit, Mason thought, reluctantly admiring the dogged stubbornness of the seventeen-year-old.

He shrugged a shoulder at the door and put his head back down as if the interrupted argument mattered even less to him than the putt he'd lined up with the coffee cup across the room. "Get your phone. We'll finish this conversation later," he muttered as he swung the putter and then watched the ball miss as Chris disappeared down the hall. His long game sucked and now he'd lost his short game, too. Mason hoped Christian's call would be an important one. Long, distracting, all-consuming. Possibly lasting the next three or four years.

He dropped the putter on the floor and slumped in his desk chair with his feet up on the oak file cabinet. The walls of his office were covered with photos of former Mulligans residents, interspersed with the golf course signs people had given him over the years.

The first sign had been a housewarming gift when Mulligans opened its doors ten years ago. The community he'd founded to provide a base for people starting over, using their second chance, was named after "taking a mulligan," golfer slang for a do-over shot. No harm no foul. That first sign read Course Re-seeded. Please Respect the Greens. He kept that one over his desk to remind him of why he'd started the place. Back then he'd been newly sober and doing everything he could to be a man worth respecting.

Mulligans had seemed like a perfect name for the community he'd envisioned where the residents would support each other to remember the past, but not live in it. That mantra was essential for his peace of mind.

The six homes, former railroad workers' cottages, faced onto a parklike yard and the larger community-center building. Mason and Chris lived upstairs over the community center.

Ten years after he'd opened this place, life was screwing with him, trying to tear him apart again. It had taken almost this long to feel as if he knew what he was doing, knew how to live this life right. And now it was all messed up.

He picked up the letter he'd been reading before Christian came in.

The Lakeland zoning board requests your presence
at a hearing to examine the extension of zoning
waivers for Mulligans. The waivers are delayed
pending a hearing to allow public comment from
neighborhood groups opposing the extension.

Mason put the letter back facedown. It rattled him to
know neighbor groups had formed under his nose and he
hadn't heard a word about it.

He jumped when, out in the hall, Christian let out a
whoop that could only mean one thing. Mason closed his
eyes and leaned his head back against his chair even as
his son yelled for him.

"Dad, we got it. Alex booked us to open for the Shreds.
The Shreds, Dad!"

Christian skidded around the doorway, his unruly, dark
brown hair flying back from his face. His hazel eyes, for
once not obscured by his ridiculous long bangs, were lit
up. They both knew this changed things, gave Chris
power over his dad in their yearlong argument. Which
meant Mason had to do something, say something, fast.
Before he lost the fight and his kid quit school and was
out the door on the road with his band.

But man, Christian was happy. Happy didn't come
that often these days. Maybe when he was alone or with
his friends Chris still cracked a smile. Here? At home with
his dad? Happy was rare enough that Mason couldn't
shut it down.

So he climbed to his feet and smiled. Tried to keep
some pissed-off dad in his expression, but there was his
kid. And this was big. Chris was happy and wanted
Mason to be happy for him.

Crossing the room, Mason put his right hand on Chris's shoulder. "Your band is good. We both know it. Looks like the Shreds know it, too."

Christian pumped his arm, the way he used to when he scored in soccer back before his band became the only thing he cared about. Mason missed soccer.

"I gotta call Drew," Christian said.

"Want me to take you all out for ice cream?"

Christian stared at him, unsure if he was joking. Mason wasn't sure himself—maybe he just wanted to keep this connection open, have it feel like old times.

When Christian didn't answer, Mason said, "What? I always took you for ice cream when you won in soccer."

Christian gave him one of those looks—the one that meant "my dad is a total loser." Used to be an offer of ice cream made you the cool dad. But the rules had changed and Mason was, once again, fumbling to catch up.

"Thanks, Dad," Christian said, and then his voice rose, "but we're going to be onstage at Madison Square Garden with the Shreds!" He looked dazed. "It's so awesome."

Christian's arms, skinny, ropy with muscle earned from hours playing the guitar, moved disjointedly by his sides. The kid had a lanky, almost six-foot frame.

Mason had been skinny, too, at that age, but in his case he hadn't had access to three square meals a day. Or any square meals a day. As lead singer of Five Star, a notoriously hard-touring, hard-living band, his diet had consisted mainly of Maker's Mark and whatever drugs happened to be in front of him. His mother hadn't been concerned with his diet, choosing to concentrate on her share of his earnings and his Maker's Mark.

Remembering what his life had been when he was

Chris's age prodded him on. Being a good parent some-times meant you had to be a bad guy…although not quite as bad as his son's mother. Ten years ago she'd dumped the scrawny, scared seven-year-old on his front porch with little more than a hissed "He's yours now" and a birth certificate listing Mason as the father.

"Getting this gig is a huge accomplishment, Chris. Recognition from a band like the Shreds is fantastic for you guys." He paused. The Shreds were a great band. Opening for them *was* huge. Mason knew better than most what this gig meant and he knew Chris and his band deserved the spot. Pride and fear sat uneasily next to each other in the pit of his stomach. "But this doesn't change anything. You're finishing high school. You're not taking your band on the road until you have your diploma."

Christian's hands balled into fists. Mason hated that he'd wiped the joy off his kid's face and replaced it with disgust. "That's completely unfair. Just because you screwed up doesn't mean I'm going to."

He was gone before Mason could call him on the attitude or the insult. Not that he had the energy anyway. Holy hell. If living with this particular incarnation of a seventeen-year-old pain in the ass was penance for his own misspent youth, well, Mason wished for the nine mil-lionth time he'd been a better person.

He slammed a hand on the office door frame before pulling the door shut. His open-door policy was one of the founding principles of Mulligans, but he had to put himself back together. Chris and the guys had no business touring at seventeen. What father in the world knew that better than one who'd been on the road at sixteen and in rehab at twenty-three? If his mother had done her job and said no once or twice, maybe his life would have turned out different.

Maybe if he hadn't been so young, hadn't latched on to David and Five Star so hard, he wouldn't have sunk so low when it ended.

He'd protect Chris. Keep him home as long as he needed to until he was sure his boy was ready to face the crap waiting out there for him.

He glanced at the door. Anyone who wanted him bad enough would knock. He picked up his putter, but he couldn't even line up on the ball.

Mulligans and Christian were all that had kept him sane and sober these past ten years. Now there was this zoning "opposition," whatever the hell that meant. And Christian was determined to skip out on the normal, middle-class life Mason had worked so hard to put together for them. *Crap.* He'd never been much of a thinker. Give him a job and he'd get it done. But there was nothing concrete here, nothing he could pin down.

He flicked open his e-mail. He highlighted five stock tips, two penis-enlargement messages and three other messages that looked like spam, and started to push delete when he saw the name. David.Giles@fivestar.com. He blinked.

Just looking at the name made him sick, remembering the last time he'd spoken to David, fourteen years ago. Mason had been begging. Been so far out of it, wasted didn't even begin to describe it. Somehow he'd gotten it into his mind that Five Star would take him back if they heard the song he had been working on. He'd been singing, or doing what his hollowed-out brain thought was singing, and David cursed him out.

David Giles. The guy had been like an older brother

once. The most important man in his life. The man who screwed him up so much he almost didn't make it.

Mason opened the e-mail, but his finger hovered over the delete key.

Mason,

Hey man. Been a while. I guess you know me and the guys are still touring. Not the same without you. Guess you know that, too. We're in the studio now, cutting a new album. Sounds amazing. You should come up. Bring your songs. Give me a call when you get this. (212) 555–2413.

David

So that was what it looked like. The invitation had finally come but it was fourteen years too late.

There'd been a time when this was all he'd wanted. Five Star, the guys he thought of as his family, had reconsidered and invited him back.

Still touring. Yeah. With his songs and his name. *Not the same without you.* That would have had more pull if they hadn't been the ones who booted him out of the band with no warning, no time for talking and not one single look backward. *Bring your songs.* As if he owed them one more thing.

Mason felt a satisfaction all out of proportion to reality when he pressed the delete key. He refused to admit he also felt a twist of panic when he closed the door on Five Star again. He didn't want that life back. But that didn't mean that it wasn't unnerving to say no to the offer when the life he had here was falling to pieces.

"DAVID GILES WOULD GET cut in the *auditions* for *American Idol*," Jake said. He was standing behind Anna, watching the monitor over her shoulder as she ran some of the footage they'd shot during the recording session earlier that day. Five Star's rented studio was a converted warehouse in Jersey City. The band had given them a small room to use as an office. It was windowless and with enough lingering scent of Lysol that Anna suspected it had formerly been a janitor's closet. Still, it was privacy, which mattered. She'd never worked on a project where she felt so uncomfortable with the subjects. Even the politicians they'd worked with for campaign ads had more integrity than this group. The only one of the four band members who didn't set off her liar warning system was Harris Coleman, the keyboard player. As far as Anna could tell in the two months they'd spent with the band, he didn't talk. Ever.

"Blue Maverick rule number 4, Don't Make Fun of the Documentary Subject," she said absently to her brother, eyes on the screen, mind running over all the problems with what she was watching.

"I'm stating a fact. That's allowed." Jake turned the volume on the monitor down slightly. Anna slapped his hand away and shot him an annoyed look. Jake's my-sister-is-a-big-fat-meanie expression hadn't changed since he was three years old. "It's hurting my ears," he said.

Anna paused the video and turned off the monitor. "This is serious. If they keep sucking this much there isn't going to be an album to promote, much less a film."

If the album had come together, Five Star might be almost finished in the studio and the movie would be well on its way to complete. As it was, the music was so bad, Anna was sure the footage they had was as useless as the session tapes.

Although the band and their managers had agreed to let her include some archival footage and do new interviews—she'd explained it as framing for the story—she'd gotten nothing about the crash or Terri. Chet, Nick, even the normally silent Harris, had all given her the same noncommittal answers. Hard show, late night, everyone bunked down, no idea how the driver lost control. No one knew Terri or why she'd been on the bus. The only interesting thing she'd heard was when every one of them asked some form of the same question. *Did you talk to David?*

David. He told several stories about heroic crew members pulling Mason Star out of the bus after the crash, several more about his own injuries, which as far as she could tell consisted mainly of a fat lip and interrupted sleep. Then he said if she wanted to know about the crash she should talk to Mason. So everyone pointed to David and then he turned right around to point at Mason. In Anna's experience, when fingers got pointed it was because there was something to point at. Somewhere in the intersection of David and Mason there was something to know. Her instincts told her that something was Terri's story.

"You know what David told me? Mason's mom was a dancer—in nightclubs. She changed her name legally to Sierra Star. Isn't that wild? Imagine being a boy, growing up with a stripper name?"

Suddenly the door opened behind them and David Giles walked in. He hadn't knocked, of course. David played bass and had taken over as lead singer when

Mason left. He was larger than life with an outsize ego and the mistaken belief that he was irresistible.

It looked as if David had drawn a line in the sand, daring age forty to touch him. His shoulder-length blond hair was highlighted, teased and sprayed to cover the fact that he had passed "thinning" and was well on the way to "bald up top." His fake tan was more Sunkist than sun kissed and, while his skinny jeans were probably the same size he'd worn in his twenties, considerably more of David Giles's middle spilled over the waistband than seemed comfortable.

"Anna!" He came up behind her and rubbed her shoulders, more irritation than massage. "How's my beautiful director today?"

Jake answered, "I'm great. Thanks for asking."

"Oh. Ha. Ha. You wish you were as good-looking as your sister here. Look at this hair—it's just begging to be touched."

Anna's curly brown hair had been exasperating her for the past thirty years. The way David obsessed over it and felt free to touch it was making her crazy. He was pushing her closer than she'd ever been to breaking Blue Maverick rule number 18, Don't Punch the Client. She shifted and rolled the chair to the left, temporarily out of punching distance.

"Going over the film?" David's high, excited voice grated even when he wasn't singing. "Does it look as good as it sounds?"

Jake crossed his arms and said, "Yep."

Anna lifted her shoulder and turned her head, hiding her mouth in her sleeve so David wouldn't see her smile.

"We're jazzed about the stuff we have down," David went on. "It's gelling. Organic, you know?"

Anna kept her eyes on David—if she looked at Jake she'd laugh. The music was organic in the same way half-cured compost was organic. "We're glad you're feeling good."

David shifted, touching his hair with his fingertips, a habit she'd noticed shortly after meeting him. It was as if he was reassuring himself the hair was still there, while making sure not to move it even slightly. It was a tic so delicate and unconscious and heartbreakingly desperate she might have found it sympathetic in a person she liked even the littlest bit. In David it made her clamp her jaws shut so she wouldn't tell him to get over himself.

"You want to run through some of the stuff you shot of that last session? We were really working that one."

Jake bent deliberately to tie his shoe.

"We don't show raw tape to anyone, David. We've discussed this before."

"But this is me. Let's see a bit, sweetheart, huh?"

She was saved from having to answer when the closet/office door banged open and Nick Kane, the Five Star drummer, pushed his way in followed shortly by a furious Chet Giles, the guitarist.

"You're not seriously thinking about changing the name of the band, David. Even you can't be that stupid," Nick yelled.

Anna instinctively reached for her camera and swung it to her shoulder, adjusting the wide-angle lens so she could see all three bandmates. Jake stepped back out of

David's light. He quietly adjusted the shade on the desk lamp to erase the shadows on Nick's face.

Chet stepped up to Nick. "That was a private conversation. You weren't supposed to hear it," he said.

David held up his hand. "Okay, Nick. I didn't mean for you to find out this way, but yeah. I brought up a name change to management and they agree. There's four of us, not five. Mason's not around but we're still using his name. Five? Star? None of it fits anymore."

"The G-Men?" Nick sputtered.

David looked irritated. "It was just an idea."

"What about this idea? We're Five Star. Besides, Mason's coming back. You got in touch with him. You said he's got new songs. Right?"

Only years of practice at keeping still and silent during shoots kept Anna from reacting. *Mason Star was coming out of hibernation?* She wanted to look at Jake, be sure he was hearing the same things she was, but she didn't dare look away.

"We need a plan B," David said. "He might not say yes."

Nick looked startled. "Mason was crushed when we kicked him out. He had no idea what happened. Of course he'll say yes. You said he was working on stuff already."

"I told you not to worry about this, Nick. You need to back off and let David do what needs to be done," Chet said. He reached out and poked Nick's chest. "Got it?"

Nick was the oldest member of the band; he'd turned forty-seven earlier that year. Right now with his dark eyes narrowed and his heavy jaw set, he looked dangerous. And pissed. "You did not just poke me," Nick growled.

"I certainly just did," Chet growled back.

Anna focused in on Nick's face as it tightened and

colored. He stared in furious disbelief from Chet to
David. Anna mentally scoped out the desk behind her,
ready to do what she could to protect the equipment if
the brawl brewing in front of her bubbled over in the
small space.

"You know what? Go to hell. I should have walked out
the day you cut Mason loose. That was wrong then and
this is wrong now. If he comes back tell him to call me."
Nick spun on his heel and left the room.

Chet turned on her. "Turn off the camera." Then he
walked out.

David put his hand up as if he was going to run it
through his hair, but he stopped himself, fluttering his
fingers off the crown instead. "Drama, huh?" he said.
"He'll be back. Nick'll be back, you'll see." He moved
toward the door. "We're not definitely changing the name.
G-Men was just an idea. When Nick comes back we'll
straighten this out."

Anna and Jake nodded.

BUT DAVID WAS WRONG. A week later he came into the office
where Anna was at the desk wolfing down a container of
leftover risotto she'd brought from home. David said he was
shutting down the studio and the movie. Nick was holed up
on the farm he owned outside Princeton and he showed no
signs of returning to the studio. The album was on hold until
the rest of the band figured out what they wanted to do,
either find a new drummer or wait for Nick to come back.

Anna's mouth dried up and she put her fork down.
She struggled to keep her voice even as she spoke.
"David, we have a schedule. You committed to the
movie. How can we—"

"Music doesn't have a schedule, Anna," David inter-rupted her. "You gotta let it flow. Organic, you know?"

Anna thought fast. She couldn't let him go. She hadn't gotten what she needed yet. "If you're taking time out of the studio that's perfect for the movie. We can do more interviews. Get the historical and background pieces down."

"Listen, sweetheart, as much as we love spending time together, we're closing down. If you want to meet up, there's a club on Sixty-fourth—"

"No," she snapped, the thought so repulsive she couldn't even keep her client manners in place.

Obviously irritated by her quick refusal, he said, "We're out of here at the end of the day. Take anything you need."

She reached desperately for something to keep him talking. "Have you heard from Mason? Is he coming back?"

"He has our offer. That's all I can say."

"What did Nick mean when he said it was wrong to let him go—"

"I told you, we're shutting the movie down," David said, cutting her off. "No point in answering questions right now." Abruptly he turned and left.

It took her seven seconds to go from stunned to furious.

She dumped everything out of the desk into her work duffel. Let them shut down the studio. This wasn't their movie anyway. Never had been. So what if she hadn't had the guts to pursue it on her own at first? She did now.

She was through wasting time. Finished waiting for someone to hand her Terri's story. Blue Maverick was better than that. Anna was better than that.

She was already working on her to-do list as she locked the door behind her. Number-one priority? Track down Mason Star and make him talk.

CHAPTER THREE

LESS THAN A WEEK after Mason was blindsided by David Giles's e-mail, he got knocked on his ass again by his friends and neighbors from the Lakeland Neighborhood Association.

There was a reason Mason would never be a politician. Actually, there was more than one reason, and the fact that he definitely had inhaled wasn't even in the top twenty. The primary problem was he just couldn't understand why so-called normal people had this need to ban anything and anyone the slightest bit different than themselves. It was yet another rule he hadn't learned growing up the way he did, where the only thing that mattered was if you had the rent or most of it come the first of the month. Maybe if he'd grown up middle class he'd get these people better. Because the fact was, Mason just didn't get them.

Take this zoning hearing.

Take Roxanne Curtis.

Take her to the top of the Empire State Building and drop kick her off.

Roxanne had been rubbing him the wrong way ever since Christian was the only kid left off her daughter's birthday-party guest list in second grade. The reason his kid wasn't on her kid's list? At the Mulligans Opening Day ceremony right before school started, Roxanne confessed her teenage crush on Mason's teenage self and suggested they re-create the sex-on-the-hood-of-the-Firebird scene from Five Star's *Dirty Sweet* video. Mason turned her down flat—wrong time, wrong place, wrong memory. And definitely wrong person.

A month later, Christian had come home from school crying, crushed by social disgrace. Using a seven-year-old kid as a pawn in revenge for a sexual rebuff was every kind of wrong.

Now Roxanne was after his other baby. Maybe it was the hearing so close on the heels of David Giles's e-mail, but he was having serious déjà vu. When he'd bought his property, refurbished the buildings and built the community center, it had been next to impossible to give away real estate in Lakeland. But the real estate boom had pushed even the upper middle class out into formerly scorned suburbs. Home prices in Lakeland, a twenty-minute train ride to New York, had skyrocketed and suddenly Mulligans was an unsavory, unwelcome neighbor in a town on the way up.

When Five Star, the band he'd helped build, had kicked him out he'd been a kid. He'd been so hurt and lost he hadn't fought back. He'd made a mess of things back then and the consequences came down on him hard. This was different. He wasn't letting Mulligans and all the people living here and taking their first vulnerable, fragile steps into rehabilitation get kicked out without a fight. The *point* of Mulligans was to make a community that would support everyone to get back on their feet. Everyone who lived here contributed what they could to help the others make it through the next step. He was ready to fight every one of the wannabe real estate moguls in this room before he let them touch his place.

Roxanne was standing in the aisle, one hand on the back of the chair in front of her. She was one of the native Lakeland "ladies" who were determined to ride the current wave of real estate money into a whole new set of friends and circumstances. She'd learned quickly, he'd give her that. She'd replaced her wardrobe of Kohl's bargains with designer knockoffs of just high enough quality to help her pass for upper middle class. She'd cut out her bad perm and tinted her hair that particular shade of blond that meant high-end shop job, not a drugstore box on the bathroom sink. And then, in her final coup, she'd remarried, a banker or broker or some money guy who worked in the city and rode the train home every night. Roxanne was on her way up and she was not taking no for an answer.

Tonight her crisp blue shirt was casually and calculatedly untucked over soft, narrow black pants. She was dressed to impress the zoning board with her values and citizenship.

Of course, he'd done the same thing. He understood that costuming supported image and that's why he was in a gray suit with an understated blue stripe, a dark blue dress shirt and a low-key tie. His clothes said serious, upstanding and smart. Respectable but not desperate.

Mason leaned toward his lawyer, Stephanie Colarusso, who was sitting straight-backed in the chair to his left, her angular face a picture of polite attention. An athlete her whole life, Stephanie's body language was always carefully controlled; she didn't make accidental gestures.

Right now her stillness and slight forward lean looked polite and professional to the other people in the room. He'd been friends with her long enough, though, to read irritation in the tension of her jaw muscles and stubbornness in the uptilt of her chin. "I need a crossbow, not a lawyer," he whispered.

Stephanie didn't look away from Roxanne as she whispered back, "She's going down, Mason. Make no mistake."

"In the ten years since this facility opened, our neighborhood has put up with more than enough," Roxanne said. Mason's hands twitched as he considered strangling her with the strap of her imitation-leather messenger bag.

"My neighbors and I have been more than generous," she went on, "letting these people live among us, letting their children go to our schools. We, the tax-paying citizens of the Lakeland Neighborhood Association, ask you to consider our needs. This facility should never have been allowed under our existing zoning codes. Now that the ten-year waiver has expired, we're asking the zoning board to withdraw the permits for Mulligans. It's time to admit what's been going on behind the fences. Specific objections are outlined in the document you have before you. Thank you."

Mason clasped the sides of his plastic chair so hard he was surprised it didn't crack. How dare she sit there saying "these people" and "expose" and "burden" about Mulligans? *Social-climbing suck-up.*

"Mr. Star?" Larry Williams, the zoning board chair was looking his way. "We're ready for your statement."

Stephanie gave him a quick nod. They'd agreed that he would do the talking. After all, this was supposed to be a neighborhood issue and he was the neighbor.

Mason stood and nervously crossed his arms. He shouldn't be this worried. This was only Hearing Room A in the Lakeland Town Hall. But the room was packed. How many years had it been since he'd been in front of a crowd of strangers? He used to know how to do this, but he realized now he'd forgotten the tricks. Besides, he knew what people saw when they looked at him. He knew what Roxanne meant when she said "these people." People like him, who'd made bad choices and couldn't be trusted not to make them again.

When he noticed no one at the zoning board table was smiling, he dropped his arms to his sides and forced himself to relax. *Focus, Mason.*

"I'm at a loss how to respond to Roxanne's statements," he said with a wry smile as he hefted the twenty-page document she'd passed out. He made eye contact with Roger Nelson, an overweight board member with a comb-over, who'd rolled his eyes when Roxanne passed out her "notes." Roger rolled his eyes again and winked at Mason. *One,* he thought. Maybe he could do this.

"Despite living near us for the past ten years, I think Roxanne may have a wrong idea about what Mulligans is, who we are. She mentioned 'facility,' but Mulligans is a community. Everyone who lives there does so voluntarily. We're all regular people with regular lives. We've chosen to live together to try to make things easier on all of us, but in every other respect we're just like the rest of you."

He gestured to the round table in the front of the room where he'd put up his table display about Mulligans. The three-panel poster included shots of the ninety-eight people—kids, adults, seniors—who'd been part of Mulligans over the years. He loved that display.

Brian Price, his manager, used it in presentations to social service agencies. The faces of so many friends who'd managed to get on their feet and move on gave him confidence. How could anyone feel threatened by those people?

Roxanne Curtis now had her arms crossed and her mouth was compressed to a thin, irritated line. She didn't look appealing or charming, Mason was pleased to see.

If she thought she could win this by tossing out insults about Mason and his friends and making sour faces—and typing up pages of innuendo—well, she had another think coming. He started to get into it. Roxanne had never been on the cover of *Rolling Stone*. She'd never had an entire stadium howling for her to give them *more*. She had no idea the depth of charm Mason could pull out when the occasion required. So what if it had been fifteen years since he'd last entertained a crowd? He'd start with the board. There were only nine of them.

Ducking his head, he looked up at the board table with a glint in his eye and the you-love-my-delinquent-self smile that he knew made women wish he'd throw them down on the closest bed, Firebird or zoning hearing room table. Two of the women at the table uncrossed their legs, one recrossed hers, and the last one fiddled with the second button on her shirt. *Two, three, four, five.*

"Mulligans provides low-fee housing and community support to a wide array of people. Everyone who lives there has been down on their luck, but with help, most of them make it back on their feet and go on to lead independent lives. We do provide financial assistance, but the main goal is to provide for the material and physical needs to help our residents reclaim their dignity and sense of purpose. For some people, that's safe, affordable child care. For some of our seniors, it's transportation and a feeling of safety during transitional times."

A neighbor, Dan Brown, was on his feet. "That's all very sweet, but the fact is, Mulligans is a flophouse. It's full of addicts and alcoholics. It's a magnet for crime and trash and a drain on our community's resources."

Mason realized he'd clenched his hands into fists. He knew for a fact that Dan Brown used his leaf blower to relocate leaves from his lawn into his neighbors' yards, called the police when people left their recycling bins out overnight and gave out apples, not candy, at Halloween. Being mean as spit apparently qualified him as a spokesman for the newly gentrified neighborhood.

"Mulligans is an intentional cohousing community, not a halfway house, Dan," Mason explained. "And you know it. You know who lives at Mulligans. Normal folks with normal lives. Like me. People who wanted to live in Lakeland when a lot of other people were calling it undesirable."

The woman sitting next to Roxanne stood up. "I'm new to Lakeland so I don't know anything about this stuff you're talking about. All I know is, I'm living on the same block as an institution with a ten foot fence and no financials on public record."

Mason hadn't met this woman before, but he was determined to placate her. "Mulligans is privately funded. We don't have to publish our financials."

"Privately funded by whom?" she asked.

"Me." Before he could add anything else, she'd turned to the board.

"Which is exactly my point. The information I know

about Mr. Star is far from encouraging. He's doing God knows what behind that fence."

Mason was stunned. Did this lady really think his money was tainted? By what? His reputation? Gossip? The history he'd never been able to shake?

Stephanie cleared her throat. He kept his mouth shut.

A voice from the crowd called out, "Property values are low because of Mulligans. Lakeland needs higher standards."

Mason wasn't sure who'd said that. Comments were coming rapid fire from all around now. He sat down abruptly when Stephanie tugged on his wrist. His head spun and for one second he was back in that hotel room in Chicago listening as David, Nick, Chet—even his own mother—yelled and threatened and finally told him to get out. He bit down on the inside of his cheek, using the pain to center back on this room, this crowd, which was all that mattered now.

Larry banged on the table, trying to settle people. Mason stared straight ahead, wishing he couldn't hear the insults and lies coming at him from all sides. What the hell had happened?

Of the four board members who'd wanted to screw him five minutes ago, three wouldn't meet his eyes. Three of the men were glaring at him. Roger, his comb-over askew, was shouting at someone in the audience, and Larry wouldn't stop banging long enough for Mason to get a read on him.

Stephanie pushed past him and went up the aisle to bend down next to Larry Williams. She whispered in his ear and Larry looked relieved.

The chairman hollered over the din in the room, "I

move that we table the discussion of Mulligans until our next meeting!"

The one woman who still wanted to screw Mason seconded and then looked quickly at him. He managed a grateful nod. Stephanie gathered the poster display and followed him outside.

"I apologize, Mason," she said. "I had no idea this was going to be out of control. I should have anticipated it."

"There's no way you could have known. I live next door to them and I didn't know. It's been an underground revolution." He shook his head. It was the same as Five Star—he hadn't seen that coming, either. "I had no idea they thought we were running a flophouse."

"That hearing wasn't about what Mulligans is or isn't. That was about people and their money—flat-out greed."

Mason ran his hand over his short-cropped hair. "I don't know. Some of it sounded pretty personal."

"Not everyone's going to be your fan."

"I'm not looking for fans," Mason protested. "It's Mulligans. I can't believe they don't see what Mulligans does."

"Clearly we have some work to do," she agreed.

While they walked slowly to her white, 1968 VW bug, she dug in her purse for her keys. He stood watching while she got in and buckled her seat belt. She started the car and then leaned out the window. "We'll beat this, Mason. Suburbanites don't frighten me."

He nodded. He trusted Stephanie. She was book smart, street smart and, after him, she was Mulligans' biggest fan. Plus, next weekend she was marrying Brian Price, the community manager, and then she'd be living at Mulligans, his companion in homelessness if they lost the zoning fight. Failure wasn't a word anyone associated with Stephanie Colarusso. That was good.

He went back toward where he'd parked his black Pontiac Firebird. It was the last thing remaining of his rough living Jersey-boy days—he'd never been able to trade it in for a Subaru. He rested the poster display on the hood while he leaned on the car, patting the pockets of the suit jacket he'd worn in the hopes it would make him seem trustworthy. He might as well have worn camo.

Just when he pulled out a pack of Marlboros and his silver lighter, a breeze kicked up. He turned his shoulder as he put a cigarette in his mouth and flicked the lighter. He dragged the smoke deep into his lungs and held it there, eyes closed, feeling the burn and savoring the scent.

"Smoking's not healthy."

Startled, Mason released the smoke before he was ready. A woman was standing in front of him. He'd been so absorbed he hadn't heard her come up. She was about Stephanie's height, a little less than shoulder high, but that was the only thing the two had in common.

Where Stephanie was all neatly contained planes, this woman curved and swerved. Her light brown, gently curling hair was streaked liberally with dark gold and tumbled down her neck, with smaller curls springing around her face. Her eyes, golden brown with a dark circle around the iris, tilted at the corners, contrasting exotically with her small, slightly upturned nose. He thought he'd recognize her if she was from the neighborhood—the way she filled her jeans was hard to overlook—but he'd better be civil on the chance she was one of *them*.

"I only take the one drag a day."

"What?" The woman's eyes widened in surprise and her expression was almost studious, like she was taking notes. She shoved quickly at the soft curls the wind had blown into her face, twisting and pushing them behind her ear. Mason caught the flash of chunky silver rings on slender fingers as her deft hands quickly and decisively tamed the curls. Woman 1, Wind 0.

"One drag," Mason said. "I kicked the six-pack-a-day habit but I miss it. The smell of it, the taste, the fire." He flipped the top of the lighter back and flicked the wheel, smiling at her through the flame. "If the day really sucks, I take two drags."

He took a second long drag and then carefully ground the cigarette out on the edge of the trash can next to the Firebird before tossing it in. "Haven't had to take three yet, though."

The woman studied him intently, seemingly unconcerned that he had no idea who the hell she was. Again he thought surely he'd have remembered her if they'd met before. And okay, she was round and sexy with her curvy hips and the black V-neck T-shirt shaping itself to her, but he didn't pick up strangers on the street. He grabbed the display, intending to cut this encounter short. She could be an old fan, but this woman with her sharp gaze didn't seem awestruck like a fan.

"One drag," she said. "That's a fascinating detail. Peculiar and vaguely masochistic, but fascinating." She stuck her hand out. "Anna Walsh. Nice to finally meet you, Mr. Star."

Ambush number three. Suddenly that third drag wasn't so far out of the question.

CHAPTER FOUR

HE WALKED AWAY. Anna should have expected that. He'd hung up on her just the day before after ignoring almost fifteen messages she'd left during the week.

He seemed taller than the six-one quoted in his bio and he was moving fast down the street. She appreciated walking with someone who moved as quickly as her for once. His hair was shorter now than it had been when he was with Five Star; more military than rock and roll. But the front was gelled with short, careless swoops that kept it south of severe, hinting at some leftover not-ready-to-settle-down.

Rocker Mason had been a pretty boy. At thirty-five, grown-up Mason was a man, shoulders broad and muscular, the planes of his face set and defined. He was saved from looking flat-out intimidating by the deep laugh creases at the corners of his eyes and the sprinkling of freckles on the tops of his cheeks and bridge of his nose. She hadn't known about the freckles and she found them oddly arresting.

She'd thought her mammoth teenage crush on Mason had died that night with Terri, but despite her wish to remain professional, the attraction had come barreling back five minutes ago when she watched him light his cigarette.

Her fingers twitched as she thought about getting his

face in front of a camera. How long would it be before she could sit him down and ask him questions? Because answers were all she wanted from Mason, no matter how pretty his green eyes were.

"Where are we going?" she asked.

"I need a drink," he answered. He strode forward, his long legs working effortlessly, the sexy swagger in his hips reminding her of the Five Star videos she'd sighed over in high school. His voice was gravel over dark chocolate when he said, "I don't need company."

"I need a drink, too," she said, pretending indifference. She'd read about his drinking and other addictions and knew they'd been the reason he got kicked out of Five Star. Listening to him speak about Mulligans in the zoning hearing she'd been surprised to feel grudging respect for the man. For a few years after he'd left the band, Mason had bounced around the celebrity scene and she'd found plenty of tabloid evidence that he'd elevated hedonism to an art form. Then he dropped out of sight. She knew he'd spent time in a rehab place run by Craig Jordan, a former session musician from Nashville. After that there wasn't much. She'd been lucky to stumble over the notice for the zoning hearing tonight.

She hadn't expected to see Mason. The best she'd hoped for was a word with his lawyer. She'd figured Mulligans was some tax shelter anyway—he lent the place his name and showed up for a charity function twice a year. But she was pretty sure from what she'd heard that he actually lived there. So what was he doing heading out to a bar?

If she'd been hoping to get the inside story on Mason Star, this was certainly a start.

Halfway down the second block he turned abruptly and

pulled the door of a shop open. Not a bar. Putting Pete's? Was it possible she'd just followed Mason to a golf shop?

He held open the door with one foot, looked up at the sky with a dramatic sigh and then waved her through. "No point in being ruder than I've already been," he said. "It's like you're missing the 'take-the-hint' gene."

"Occupational hazard," Anna answered absently, too busy observing him to take offense. She was glad she'd gotten this far, but she needed to concentrate. She'd surprised him tonight and probably wouldn't get a second chance. The gambit she and Jake had come up with to persuade him to participate in the movie was the best they had, but she wished she was more confident it would work.

"I thought you said you were getting a drink."

"I said I *needed* a drink. Not the same thing," he replied.

"Hey, Pete," Mason said to the man behind the counter. "You get that Ryan putter?"

Pete waved to the back of the store. "It's in the rack. We're closing in half an hour."

"Got it." Mason headed down the aisle. The entire back of the store was a fake putting green built up on a platform. A panoramic poster on the wall behind it gave the impression you were standing on the eighteenth hole of some golf course.

Anna was flying by the seat of her pants, way out of her depth.

Mason held out the poster from the hearing. "Grab this?"

It was an awkward size and she bobbled it when he handed it off. His hand flashed out to steady it. "Careful," he said. "That's my baby."

The way his eyes crinkled even as he cautioned her made an odd combination of brusque and friendly, vaguely insulting but genuinely good-natured. She couldn't decide which was real but the story hound in her was intrigued.

She got a hold on the poster and then stepped back to watch as he pulled a putter out of the rack and moved a bucket of balls close to the line. He stepped up on the platform and with absolutely no self-consciousness proceeded to sink five balls in a row. He moved with confidence, the same way he had when he'd owned the stage, she thought, comfortable in his body and his surroundings. He'd looked like that in front of the zoning hearing until chaos broke out and then he'd crumpled.

"You're good," she offered, confident in her assessment after a childhood of weekends spent at her parents' country club.

"The platform's a funnel. Pete wants to sell these stupid expensive clubs so he makes you feel like a hall of famer." Mason cleared the balls out of the hole and went back to the line. With his head down, concentrating on the ball, he said, "I don't suppose you tracked me down to ask me about my golf game, although I'd like to state for the record I'm a scratch golfer on a good day."

"If you're a scratch golfer, I'm Tiger Woods!" Pete hollered back from the front of the store.

"Jealous," Mason mouthed to her pointing at Pete. He'd stopped hitting and was gauging her reactions as surely as she was studying him. Performers did that, she knew, waited to see what the audience wanted and gave it to them. She'd need to be careful because she didn't want a line, she wanted the truth.

In the file she and Jake had compiled on Mason were pictures from when he was with Five Star, his magnetic personality obvious even in fifteen-year-old photos. Pictures couldn't do justice to the color of his eyes, though. Blond glinted at the temples of his rich, dark hair. His thick lashes were chocolate brown and his sculpted eyebrows a shade lighter. All that dark framing made the green of his eyes startling. Mason's eyes weren't a messing-around color like hazel. They were green like a beer bottle.

She'd never been sure if, given the chance, she would have gotten on the bus with Terri that night, if she'd have fallen under the rock and roller's spell. But the man standing in front of her would have no trouble persuading most women and a heck of a lot of men to do whatever he wanted. Anna's imagination strayed to what he might want, how he might ask for it in his smoky voice. Was this what Terri had felt? Was this why she'd made that fatal decision?

Mason Star had *lived* his life and he had the laugh lines and care lines to prove it. What had made him smile often enough to make those deep crinkles? What had put the care in his eyes? What combination of experience and personality and family had created this man who couldn't seem to help being polite to a stranger he wanted nothing to do with? What was he like when he was with people he *did* enjoy?

Stop it, Walsh. She needed to remember what she was here for. *Who* she was here for. She wasn't a seventeen-year-old kid with a crush on a rock star anymore.

She wanted his story because it might give her Terri's. Period.

"I want to make you an offer," she said. She and Jake had done their research looking for his vulnerability. She hoped they'd chosen the right hook.

"No," he said and then casually knocked another ball in the cup. He quirked his lips, though, in almost a smile, softening the rejection. Progress. She wished she had a camera to film his mouth. It was decadent, sculpted lips with little lines at the corners that weren't quite dimples but then again, definitely were.

She leaned back, took her eyes off his mouth, thought about Terri. "You don't even want to hear what I have to say?"

"You left fifteen messages. I heard. A movie. Five Star. My story. No." He sighed. "Oh, all right. I'll be polite. Make your offer." He cocked an eyebrow and waited.

"I assume you're not familiar with my work." He shook his head. She felt a twinge of disappointment, which surprised her. Why did she care that he hadn't even taken a second to Google her? "My brother and I make documentaries, but we have to pay the bills, so we do other things, too. Campaign spots, travel pieces, commercials, music videos."

Mason leaned on the club, waiting her out. If she'd expected him to react, she was disappointed again.

"Can I try?" she asked, stalling, unable to take the plunge.

He handed her the putter, taking back the poster display. She tested the weight and balance of the club before kicking a ball into place. The last time she'd held a golf club she'd been seventeen, playing in a father-daughter tournament at the country club. After Terri died and her relationship with her parents fractured, they'd barely spoken, let alone played golf.

While she lined up her shot, she went ahead with her pitch. "Our music videos are top notch. We've won video-music awards. The one we did for Del Sweeney was on

TRL for fourteen weeks straight." Which wasn't bragging but salesmanship. He needed to believe she knew what she was doing. "You agree to be in my movie and—" she swung the putter smooth and easy and waited until the ball sank "—I'll shoot a video for your son's band free of charge. I guarantee he'll love it."

She hadn't expected laughter. His laugh was throaty and full of gravelly undertones like his voice and she wondered how many years he'd smoked. The lines at the corners of his eyes deepened and crinkled in a way that made her want to laugh with him. Except he wasn't laughing with her, he was laughing at her.

"Nice swing, but, oh, man. You don't know me very well if you think that's the bribe that'll get me into your movie."

She was stung. She and Jake had misjudged, which didn't happen often. "That's the point of the movie. No one knows you. We should."

He shook his head, suddenly serious. He leaned one forearm on the railing around the platform and his face was closer to hers than was comfortable, but she forced herself to hold still. "No. You don't want to know me. The guy you want? Mason Star, lead singer of Five Star? That guy doesn't exist anymore."

He rubbed his hand back and forth in his short hair, leaving the front sticking up in messy points, and then looked at her, his head cocked to the right. "Matter of fact, why don't you put that in your movie. Mason Star died. RIP."

She held the club tighter, pressing her thumb into the grip. She needed Mason. What would motivate him? "People deserve to know what happened with the crash and afterward. They deserve the truth."

"What?" He looked more engaged than he'd been.

"There's more to the story of what happened. A story like that can't be left untold."

"I don't know what you think you know. But here's your truth. I'm not that guy anymore and digging all that up won't do anything good for me or anyone else."

"David Giles told me to ask you about the crash."

Mason's face settled, the light left his eyes. "You talked to him? No." He shook his head. "Forget I asked that. I'm living here now." He gestured around the pro shop, but she knew he meant Lakeland. "Five Star is history for me." The corners of his mouth turned down, the not-quite dimples deepening, communicating disgust. About her? The crash? She couldn't tell.

They'd misread him. He was slipping away. She had to think fast and find the right thing.

"Mason…" she started to say, but he shook his head.

"The last thing I need right now is for people to remember I was in a rock band."

She noticed the protective hold he had on the Mulligans poster. "Your neighbors aren't too thrilled, are they?" *He'd called it his baby.*

"You were at the zoning thing?"

"Stalking you. Sorry."

"Witness to the execution," he said wearily.

"I can help." She put down the club and stepped off the platform. She tapped the poster, focusing his attention.

His eyebrows lifted. "You bribe zoning boards?"

"You and your charming smile were doing okay with the board. It's the neighbors that killed you. Ms. Tidy Pants and the PTA brigade."

His shoulders slumped. "Roxanne Curtis and her

upwardly mobile assassins. If they'd come over and see Mulligans. Get to know us."

"Watch the movie I make about it."

"Watch the…?"

"You agree to speak on camera about the Five Star bus crash, I'll make you a kick-butt film about Mulligans I guarantee will not only solve your zoning problems, it will have your neighbors eating out of your hand."

"You *guarantee?*"

"Here." She reached into the inside pocket of her jacket and pulled out two DVDs in plastic sleeves. "Go home and watch these. Then call me and I'll start making one for Mulligans right away."

He shifted the poster and took the DVDs but didn't look at them. "I appreciate the offer, Anna, I do. And I can honestly say I admire your confidence. But I'm not going to talk about Five Star. Not to you. Not to anyone." He backed up, cradling his poster carefully under his arm. He put the DVDs in his pocket, though, she noticed.

"Can you at least think about it?" she asked as she followed him to the front of the store.

"I think about that crash every day."

She'd meant the movie, but he'd misinterpreted her. Deliberately or not, she couldn't tell.

When he turned left outside the shop, she let him go. She hoped that last offer had been the right one. The way he'd looked when she mentioned the zoning board made her think she had a shot at least. She never would have expected him to be as involved as he seemed to be in Mulligans.

She knew quite a bit about getting people to discuss things they wanted to keep to themselves. There was a time to push and a time to back off. Mason needed to stew over her offer before she gave him another nudge. And she needed to deal with the feelings he'd stirred up in her.

CHAPTER FIVE

MASON STARED at the screen. He couldn't believe he'd ever been the kid who was standing center stage singing the hell out of "Stage Fright." He'd been twenty when this movie, *Five Star Rising,* was shot. It was mostly a concert video, intended to support the *Five Star Rising* album during what ended up being his last tour. Tonight he was fast-forwarding through all the backstage coverage. Couldn't stand to see the bottles and women and himself wasting his life as fast as he could.

He *never* watched this movie. Damn Anna for making him seek it out. He'd come home expecting to clear up some paperwork and get to bed, but he'd been too restless. Angry about the zoning board, pissed off at David and his e-mail and really mad about Anna's offer. What the hell was David thinking talking to anyone about the crash? Telling her to come here?

Without the zoning fiasco, he'd never have given her offer to make him a movie another thought. But the hearing had been bad. He knew Stephanie would do her best, but people, not just Roxanne, a lot of people, were really upset. He used to be able to get people on board with his plans without even trying. But he'd lost something after Five Star. Now he couldn't even get a suburban zoning board to leave him alone. The last time people turned on him and he couldn't fix it, he'd lost everything. What if he couldn't fix this and this time Mulligans was the price?

Anna had said her movie would save Mulligans.

But he'd have to talk about the crash. She'd said people wanted the truth about it. He'd never told the truth. He'd had his reasons then and he still thought he'd made the right decision. What did Anna know or think she knew? He was pretty sure he and David Giles were the only ones who knew what really happened that night. David had his own reasons for keeping quiet. If he agreed to talk to her, how much would he have to say? What would she be able to figure out?

Those questions had led him out to the video store and then here, to this place in his past where he didn't like to go, thinking about the tour that led to the crash…and everything else that happened.

He had all the lights off and was sunk deep in the leather couch in the small room he and Christian used as a private family room above the common rooms where the residents ate communal meals several nights a week, did their laundry, conducted meetings and held functions.

This room had always felt safe to him. Seeing his old life in the midst of this real one was jarring.

Before he moved into Mulligans, Mason had never lived anywhere permanent. With his mom there'd been a string of trashy apartments and sketchy trailers. With Five Star he'd been a hotel nomad. He hadn't had much furniture here at first, but after Christian moved in, he'd needed to fill the empty spaces. He'd hired a decorator because he hadn't had the first clue about how to change a room into a home. He'd wanted Christian to feel normal and fit in, but Mason hadn't known what "normal" looked like.

The couches and chairs were deep and comfortable, large enough to handle his tall frame and durable enough to resist the energetic boy Christian had been. The natural-cherry bookcases lining two walls were crammed with his books and CDs, Christian's outgrown picture books and paperbacks, board games and puzzles.

Photos of him and Christian, their friends, Mulligans, everything he held close were framed in black metal and hung up on the third wall. He looked back to the screen when he heard the boy he'd been launch into the second verse.

"Stage Fright" was a cover but it suited his voice and had always set up the audience perfectly for Five Star's own soaring ballad, "Live." The screen flashed as the spotlight swung off him and out over the audience. In the brighter light, he caught a shadow and realized his son was standing behind him. He hadn't heard Christian come in. He turned the volume down and the room fell abruptly quiet.

"You don't think I've seen that before?" Chris stayed behind him.

Of course, Mason should have known Chris had seen the movie. But until that very second, yeah, he did think the kid wouldn't have seen it. Sometimes parents were the dumbest people on earth, brains dulled by loving their stupid children too much.

"I never showed it to you."

"It's on Netflix."

Was it too late to tighten the parental controls on Chris's Internet connection?

He tried to think of something to say, but everything

he came up with seemed awkward. He was half-afraid he'd blurt out something about ice cream again. Most of what passed for conversation between him and Chris these days was uncomfortable small talk strung together with uncomfortable silence, spiced up with occasional bouts of yelling.

He rolled his head on the couch cushion and saw that Chris hadn't moved. "You want to sit?"

He was careful not to react when Christian came around the back of the couch and settled deep into the cushions next to him.

"Why are you watching it?" Christian asked. The movie ran on, Five Star's music sounding small.

"I had a bad night. Zoning board. The neighbors put up a roadblock. Your friend Angel's mom is the ringleader."

"Roxanne Curtis?"

Mason held up a warning finger. "Do. Not. Say. That. Name."

Christian grunted. "She's just a woman, Dad."

"Satan spawn," he said, referring to Roxanne. Mostly.

Chris gestured toward the TV where the song was winding down. "So does this relax you?"

What was the word for the opposite of relax? "No."

Christian kicked his sneakers off and moved the DVD case over so he could put his feet up on the table.

"I like this picture," he said, holding up the *Five Star Rising* movie box. "Sort of doesn't leave you a leg when you complain about my hair, though."

Mason surprised himself when he said, "I hate that picture. The whole band hated it."

On the screen Five Star kicked into "Live." His younger self was holding the microphone close, singing with his eyes closed. He used to hang on to the stand like that when the spins got bad.

"Yeah?"

"See how the stylist put me so far out in front it almost looks like the rest of them are in a different room? Pissed them off. None of them believed me when I said I didn't care."

"You guys fought a lot."

"I was a lot younger than them. They were together five years before I started playing with them."

"Your mom met them, right?"

Slept with David Giles. He hadn't known that until later. His mom had been fifteen when he'd been born— barely thirty when she met David. "She was waitressing at a bar they played when their singer quit. She talked them into giving me a tryout."

He shrugged, pushing aside his uncomfortable memories. "Guess you and I got the bottom of the mom barrel. Too young. Too poor. It must have sucked for her." Not as bad as being her kid had sucked, but close.

"Too bad there wasn't a Mulligans for you guys."

"Yeah." Not that she'd have applied anyway. She'd enjoyed her addictions—booze, men, risk—too much.

"Want to turn it back up?" Chris asked.

"No," Mason said with no inflection. He didn't think he could stand to have Chris in the room with that. Watching the parts onstage would be bad enough, but the rest…

"How come you won't talk about it with me?"

"I tell you about it all the time."

"Just the crap, the drugs and the scary stuff and the fighting." Christian gestured to the TV. "We never talk about what *that* felt like. You and your guitar and the audience. When I watch that movie it's like I'm seeing someone who's not even you."

"You've seen it more than once?"

"Dad. Every guy in America who's in a band has watched it more than once."

That was depressing—he'd been so careful to keep Five Star out of Chris's life.

What could he say that wouldn't make the kid even more determined to take his shot with his own band?

He must have hesitated too long because Christian leaned forward again and picked up the plastic sleeve holding Anna's DVDs. "What's this?" he asked. *"City at War?"*

"Someone recommended it."

"Huh." Christian finished reading the back and then tossed the disk back on the table. "So you're not going to tell me why you're sitting here in the dark watching a movie about yourself that you had to *rent* and a documentary about Toledo public schools."

"Detroit, not Toledo."

Chris looked at him directly for the first time since he sat down, and the familiar anger was back. "Whatever." Before Mason knew what happened, his son was off the couch and halfway out the door. "You can't ever let anything go, can you?" Chris spat before he left the room.

"At least I'm not always pissed off!" Mason shouted just as Chris's bedroom door slammed. He clicked the volume back up and watched as Five Star scooped up seventy thousand fans crammed into the aisles at Giants Stadium and carried all of them along through "Live" and straight into "Beating Down the Door" and "Dirty Sweet."

He had no idea what he should have said to Chris. That he'd never felt better than he had when he was onstage with those guys and those songs and his guitar? That he'd been so drunk most nights that he wasn't sure what was real and what he'd made up? That he didn't watch this video because it made him ache, literally hurt, with wishing he hadn't missed so much of it? That he wasn't sure he'd done a good enough job, made Christian strong enough to resist what he'd find out there? That he'd never forgive himself if he let his boy go before he was sure he'd done everything right to protect him?

He hit the remote, cutting the credits off. He punched the open button on the DVD player and slid *City at War* in.

A haunting violin piece played over the opening credits, black-and-white footage of an inner-city neighborhood and then what could easily have been Lakeland but was most likely a Detroit suburb. Kids' faces flashed by, on the streets, reflected in the windows of a school bus, and in classrooms and school hallways.

Mason settled back into the couch, arms crossed, prepared to find flaws. Nitpicking would suit his mood right now. Unfortunately for him, Anna's confidence had been on target. By the time the forty-five-minute film was over, Mason would have been prepared to write a check to support the school bond if it hadn't already passed by a seventy-three-percent margin.

Why did it have to be this person making the movie? He wanted to say no. But what if she could help save Mulligans? What if everything he knew to do and Stephanie and the rest of his team knew wasn't enough and he had turned down the offer that could have saved them?

What if he didn't turn her down?

Anna had gotten under his skin in a way he didn't enjoy. There'd been something about her. He thought he'd seen something in her face, in the shadows of her eyes, when she was talking about the crash.

Whatever that thing he'd seen was, it couldn't be good for him. He'd left all that behind and didn't want to go back.

Pushing himself up off the couch, he stretched, feeling the pop in his neck. He'd take her idea and find some other capable, competent filmmaker to do the movie for Mulligans. He'd send the DVDs back to her with a polite thanks but no thanks.

He lay in bed awake for a long time. He'd made his decision but he was still unsettled by Anna, the way she'd watched him, like she knew things she wasn't telling. Like she knew the truth.

MASON PUSHED another board in place and leveled it with his knee while he banged two nails in to anchor the opposite end. He had Metallica cranked on his head-phones and an entire dance floor that needed hammering. He'd stopped actively picturing Roxanne Curtis's face on every nail head an hour ago and now he was just enjoying the banging.

"Mason." Stephanie took one of the earbuds out of his ear, and he jumped, narrowly missing his hand with the hammer.

"Good God, Stephanie, don't creep up on a guy."

"You were so wrapped up in your manly work you didn't hear me the first two times I called."

Sitting back on his heels, Mason took out the other earbud and paused his iPod as he looked to Stephanie's companion, Mulligans's manager, Brian Price, for support. Brian opened his hands in a "who me?" gesture. "She did try."

"Stuff it, Price. Next time build your own damn dance floor."

Brian didn't answer, just picked up another board and shoved it into place. He and Mason were used to each other's rhythms.

Brian had been one of the first applicants for a spot at Mulligans when they opened. He'd been an addict and a drunk, much like Mason but without the glitzy rock-and-roll mask.

He'd been working as a mechanic for the University of Washington for six months and hadn't had a drop to drink or a whiff of drugs in over a year. He'd barely been making the rent on his apartment, though, and had been losing hope that he'd be able to go back to finish his college degree.

Mason had seen a lot of people turn their lives around but not many made the total transformation that Brian had. He'd gotten his degree and then a master's in social work. Last Christmas he'd asked Stephanie to marry him. If Mulligans had a poster boy, Mason was pretty sure Brian was it.

Brian came into his own when he started managing Mulligans. He and Stephanie were planning to make their home here after the wedding. Damned if Mason would let the Lakeland Neighbors Hate Squad wreck any of that for them.

"My contract clearly states I do the brain work and you do the heavy lifting," Brian said.

"Yeah, well, maybe I'm amending your contract." Mason banged the last nail into the board and gestured toward the stack behind Brian. "Hand me another one, will you?"

Brian leaned down and passed the board to Mason who knocked it into position with his knee and then set the first nail. "What if we made a movie about Mulligans? Think it would help with the neighbors?" He drove the nail in to emphasize exactly how little he cared about their answer. Exactly how much he wasn't counting on Anna's quietly confident guarantee that the movie would make the neighbors cave.

"Where did that come from?" Stephanie asked.

"Someone mentioned something about it," Mason mumbled.

Brian looked intrigued. "You mean, like a documentary?"

"Not a whole big thing. A shorter film. People do them for community awareness and fund-raisers and stuff."

Stephanie nodded and put her hand in Brian's. "One of the banks I did some work for when I interned made something like that to sell a merger to their board of directors."

"So, what?" Brian turned his hand to clasp Stephanie's. "We invite Roxanne Curtis over for popcorn and change her mind?"

Mason put another nail in. "I don't know exactly how it would work. But it's not Roxanne Curtis so much as the neighbors as a group. If we get enough of them to defect to our side, Roxanne's revolt will collapse on its own."

He leaned back again, trying to project nonchalance. He was exhausted, had been up the night before with intense, crazy-making dreams of Five Star, Roxanne Curtis and Anna Walsh all mashed up together. "It's just an idea."

Stephanie nodded. "It's an excellent idea. Who do we need to talk to? A film company?"

Mason shrugged. "I'm sure we can find someone."

"We have to find someone good. If it's bad it will be

worse than not doing it at all," Stephanie said. "As soon as the wedding is over, we'll look into options."

Brian nodded with the same goofy grin on his face he wore whenever anyone brought up the wedding. Mason had never really considered marriage for himself. In his early twenties he'd been getting sober and after that he'd had Christian and Mulligans and they'd been enough to consume the lives of four or five men.

In fact, he'd never had a real relationship. Before he came to Mulligans, he'd never even *seen* a real relationship. He'd sworn off the women who wanted him because he was Mason Star the day he'd sworn off his other addictions.

He wanted what Stephanie and Brian had. They worked hard at their relationship, but the result, two people who knew each other inside and out and stuck with each other no matter what, that sounded right to him. He'd never figured out how to go about getting it, though.

Anna's hands swiftly subduing her wild hair were in his mind. She seemed like someone who knew what she wanted and wasn't afraid to fight for it. What would happen if he dated a woman like her? He bet she wouldn't be scared off by his past. But then, it was his past she was after. And the secrets he'd buried there weren't his to tell.

"I can't thank you enough for letting us have the wedding here," Brian was saying as he put an exploratory foot up on the half-finished dance floor.

Mason shrugged. "You live here. I'm not going to tell you you can't get married in your own home."

Stephanie shot him a look. "Does that make you the father of the groom?"

"Brian's not pretty enough to be my kid."

"Speaking of your kid, we'll see you tonight for dinner before the gig, right?"

Mason went back to banging. He focused his impatience on Roxanne Curtis, carefully ignoring any feelings about his lack of a love life, Anna Walsh or Mulligans.

A SUDDEN LOUD bang startled Anna. She rolled over and almost fell off what Jake called his guest bed, a foam chair that folded out into a flat, saggy twin mattress. It was lightweight and tipped easily, as Anna knew from painful experience. To maintain her precarious balance all night she'd learned to leave some brain cells on. It wasn't the most peaceful sleep but at least she wasn't sporting bruises every morning.

Another loud bang came from the room next door. Pulling the pillow over her head did nothing to drown out the pounding. Then she heard Jake asking Rob to turn up the music and Mason's rich voice growling the opening lines of "Dirty Sweet" came throbbing into her room. She wasn't getting any more sleep. That was clear.

Wearing the cotton tank top and pajama bottoms she'd slept in, she stumbled into the hall and pushed aside the plastic sheeting hanging where the bathroom door had been when she went to bed. She couldn't tell exactly what Rob and Jake were up to, just that it was messy and loud.

Rob saw her in the doorway and lit up like a four-year-old who'd caught sight of his birthday cake.

"Did you meet him?"

Anna nodded. She wanted to be excited but she wasn't sure she'd gotten through to Mason. And she wasn't sure what Jake would say about the Mulligans movie—would he count that as his last project? Would he be in for the

Five Star movie, too, even though that would push his re-
tirement plans out by several months?

"Is he still hot?" Rob asked. Mason's voice thrummed
through the iPod speakers set up on the vanity shelf.

Jake, who was standing on a ladder scraping the
ceiling paint, reached down to thump the top of Rob's
head. "Unprofessional."

The drums kicked in on "Dirty Sweet" and Anna
pictured Mason as he'd been in the video, super-sexy-de-
linquent hair and eyes, leaning in slowly over the girl
spread on the hood of the black Firebird. Anna's heart
beat in time with the drums. Last night when she'd seen
Mason leaning against that car in his suburban-dad suit,
the combination of society and sin was so hot she'd had
to take a deep breath.

"I'm not a professional," Rob said. "I'm a fan." He put
his hand over his heart. "Spill. Is he still hot?"

Rob ducked when Jake swiped at his head again, and then
he punched Jake's foot. "Stop hitting me. You worry about
what you're doing and let me worry about the rock star."

The song ended and Anna's mind snapped back to the
dusty bathroom. Watching her brother's scuffle with Rob,
she wondered how it had happened that she was forced
to spend her life with *boys*. "What are you guys doing?"

"Remodeling the bathroom," Jake said.

"Excuse me, I asked a question," Rob said. "You met
the man I've been in lust with since I was twelve. Tell.
Me. If. He's. Hot."

When Rob said lust, she pictured Mason's eyes and his
lips. *Lust, indeed.* She pretended to examine some paint
flakes on her foot as she waited for the blush to fade from
her face. "He's hot." Her voice sounded normal, thank God

for small favors. She had to stop reacting like this. Not only was it unprofessional, it was wrong. If only she hadn't dated all those boring duds. The first slightly—okay, wickedly—exciting guy she met was making her nuts.

"I knew he would be." Rob's smile was so triumphantly juvenile that Anna smiled with him despite her discomfort.

Jake's professional interest trumped his annoyance with Rob. "He'll be good on film? When he was a kid he had that magnetic thing going."

"Oh, he's still got the magnetic thing." *Control, Walsh. He's just a man. The subject of your film.* The fact that he was buckets of hot couldn't matter except that it might attract viewers to the movie. "Any chance you'll be finished remodeling the bathroom soon so I can take a shower?"

Jake scraped energetically. "Give us two weeks."

"I meant like sometime in the next hour."

Rob had fallen suspiciously silent and Jake's expression reminded her a little too much of the times he'd wanted to gloss over the truth about his report cards. "We turned off the water. It's going to be a while."

"Turned off the water?" she asked.

"I forgot you were here. We were up early and I guess we just…started."

Anna wanted to say several things. None of them were nice. But the fact was, she knew Rob and Jake were more than generous to let her stay with them for so long. Usually when she crashed with them it was for a week or two at the most, but this time, with Five Star local, she'd been in their house for more than six weeks. Now with Mulligans, she wouldn't be leaving any time soon.

"All right, it's the Y for me," she said.

"Don't, Anna," Rob said. "Give us a few minutes to clean up and you can get in here. I'll put the water back on if your brother won't."

They all stared around the bathroom, which was covered in dust from the tiles Rob was prying off the wall with the claw end of the hammer and the paint Jake was scraping from the ceiling. Plastic sheeting draped the floor, the window and the sink. Anna had lived in a lot of what could kindly be called bohemian circumstances, but this was just plain nasty.

"I'm fine at the Y."

Jake stopped her. "Wait, certain people got sidetracked by lust. You didn't tell us what he said about the movie."

"I offered him the music video and he laughed at me," she said.

"Doesn't he like his kid?"

"He didn't say. I made a second offer."

Rob sighed dramatically. "Fine. If I have to do it for your art, I'll let him have his way with me. What time will he be here?"

Jake swatted him again, harder, if Rob's wince was real. "Ahem, Rob. You're not single."

"So? You want in?"

Jake looked at her over Rob's head, ignoring his leer. "What did you offer him?"

"His place, Mulligans, is having zoning trouble. I said we'd bring him the hearts and minds of his neighbors."

Jake nodded. "One man's misery is another man's opportunity to make an issue film."

"So you're okay with doing this movie while we wait on Five Star?" Anna watched her brother carefully. Even with their no-lies rule, she knew he might pretend more enthusiasm than he really felt because this mattered so much to her.

He didn't even hesitate. "I'm okay with it. I promised Terri's story would be the one. If this is part of that, I'm in."

Anna swallowed. She wished she could hug him, just impulsively reach for him. But that wasn't her. Something must have shown on her face, though, because Jake hopped off the ladder and wrapped his arms around her. She hugged him back, ignoring the paint chips and the mess, grateful to be understood. She let herself lean into him and then pushed back. "The menu at the Shannon said Denny's making meat loaf tonight. You guys want to meet there tonight?"

Jake looked at Rob then they nodded in unison. So she'd be the third wheel as usual. At least there'd be mashed potatoes.

CHAPTER SIX

MASON WAS UNCOMFORTABLE.

It wasn't the restaurant. The Shannon was utterly familiar to him, the cramped and well-used interior of the bar on a side street in Hoboken in no way reflecting the brilliance Denny brought to the menu of home-cooking staples. Two years ago Denny and his brother Sean had allowed Christian and his band, ACD, to play their first-ever gig here. The boys had played the Shannon the first Saturday of every month for a year until their reputation outgrew the cramped stage and dance floor. Tonight they were coming back for a special appearance.

It wasn't the people making him feel weird, either. Brian and Stephanie were his oldest friends. The three of them had sat at this very table more times than he cared to remember. Which maybe was the problem. He'd encouraged Christian and his buddies, had sat through practically every show they'd ever played. He knew as well as the Shreds did that ACD had the chops to go somewhere.

It made him simultaneously proud as hell and scared to death. Would a normal parent even have let their child be in a rock band? How was he supposed to be a good dad when he didn't know exactly what that meant?

Stephanie paused between bites to squint at Mason over the edge of her bread stick. "You okay?"

"Fine. Great," he lied. She gave him a look.

He lifted the glass of water next to his plate. "Here's hoping the two of you are blessed with health, happiness and a great life together."

Brian and Steph raised their drinks and joined the toast.

He glanced at the door, wondering when Chris and the guys would show up and instead he saw *her*. Anna and two men had just walked in. Okay, this was ridiculous. Was she stalking him? If he found out she was here because of Christian's band...

She turned to scan the room and her eyes met his. Either she was a great actress or she was honestly startled. Her eyebrows shot up, hidden by the curls tumbling on her forehead, and she lifted a hand hesitantly, her chunky silver rings catching the light over the door.

"Who's that?" Stephanie asked even as Mason nodded in reply.

"Anna Walsh," Mason said, trying to sound offhand. He picked up his bread, willing her to stay away.

The shorter, blond man nudged the redhead and inclined his head toward Mason. All three started forward.

"Anna Walsh the filmmaker?" Stephanie poked Brian. "Is that her brother? Remember we saw them speak at the festival at the Strand last year?" She turned back to Mason. "How do you know them?"

They were at the table before he could answer.

"Mason? Hello." Anna and her two companions were poised next to the table. Mason stood, even as he wished he'd turned his back on her when she waved. She was wearing black again tonight, another V-neck T-shirt with a pair of jeans and those same beat-up boots from the other night. On someone else it might have been boring, but Anna's crazy curly hair, her wide eyes, not to mention her very attractive curves, pushed the package toward gallery owner or funky landscape designer. Or, he supposed, documentary filmmaker.

"Anna. These are my friends, Stephanie Colarusso and her fiancé, Brian Price."

Anna shook Stephanie's hand and then Brian's. She turned to the redhead beside her. "My brother, Jake, and his partner, Rob Parker."

Mason put his hand out and got a firm, friendly shake from Jake. Rob smiled at him and pumped his hand several times more than was necessary as he said, "I've wanted to meet you since I was twelve!"

Anna bumped Rob with her elbow. Her brother rolled his eyes. "We sometimes think he's still twelve."

Stephanie stood and motioned to Sean who'd just come from the kitchen. "No problem. Mason doesn't mind." She pushed out the empty chair next to her. "Why don't you join us. We love your work."

Mason wanted to head this off, but what could he possibly say?

I'm allergic to strangers?

Excuse me while I jump off a bridge?

I can't have this woman within fifty feet of my life.

Before he knew it, Sean had brought more chairs and menus, and Anna, Jake and Rob were seated at their table.

"So," Stephanie said, "how do you know Mason?"

Perfect.

ANNA WOULD have to be blind not to have noticed Mason was uncomfortable. He was as gorgeous as she remembered, in a warm brown dress shirt with an open collar and a pair of jeans, but he looked ready to jump out of his skin.

She'd almost refused the other woman's invitation knowing Mason didn't want this, but she had to take the chance. If she had the opportunity to persuade Mason to take their offer, she had to do it. It couldn't matter that his green eyes were panicked as he looked from her brother to Rob, who was practically salivating, to his friends and then to the small stage at the back of the restaurant.

Oh, no. She realized now why the sign out front announcing ACD—Live Tonight! had jogged her memory. It was his kid's band. He was going to think she was stalking him.

"We wanted his help on a project," Jake answered Stephanie before Anna could think.

Mason's friend Brian leaned forward. "That's such a coincidence. Mason was just telling us this afternoon about an idea he has for making a movie, but he doesn't know who to talk to. Maybe you can give him some pointers."

"But Anna already offered—" Rob started and then stopped with a wince. Jake must have stepped on his foot, but the damage was done.

"Anna offered?" Stephanie asked, her expression confused, and then her mouth tightened. "Anna Walsh offered to make your movie, Mason, and *you turned her down?*"

Mason was so miserable at that point, Anna almost took Jake and Rob and walked away. But she couldn't. She needed him, and if she had to use his friends to force his hand, she would.

"He hasn't turned us down yet," Anna said. She opened her eyes wide, innocent. "Right?"

"I didn't even get a chance to think about it," Mason protested. He glared at Brian. "I was just talking this afternoon. Not making a plan."

Stephanie recovered her poise. "I'm sorry, this isn't something we should be discussing now. Clearly Mason has some questions." She gave him the look Anna's mother used to use when one of her children forgot to say please. "Which he'll no doubt ask after he's had a chance to think about this amazing opportunity that any non-profit would kill for." She paused. "Let's enjoy our dinner. Have you been to the Shannon before?"

Anna had to admire Stephanie's aplomb. The woman must be the boss at work—hers was not a taking-orders personality. In the breathing room while Jake and Rob answered questions about their house and how long they'd been in Hoboken, Anna studied Mason. Watching Stephanie chastise him like a badly behaved five-year-old had been another revelation. So many of her expectations about him had been wrong. Where was his ego? And he was clearly at home in the Shannon. She'd never deny the food was great, but it was hardly the kind of place she'd expect him to hang out. Yet here he was. Eating meatloaf and mashed potatoes in a comfortably shabby restaurant. And? The man was miserable. She'd caused that. How much could she afford to care?

She couldn't. She couldn't back down. Not now.

THE DINNER WENT surprisingly well. Stephanie steered the conversation away from Mason and pulled a surprising number of details out of Anna and the other two. Brian compared notes with Jake on the Mets and Knicks, and Anna and Stephanie bonded over their shared dislike of fur coats, stockings, oil companies and the tolls on the Garden State Parkway.

Not a bad dinner, if only he wasn't constantly on edge wondering what Anna planned to spring on him next. Just as they finished dessert, Christian and his bandmates, Alex and Drew, started their sound check.

Rob had been watching the boys set up and now he asked Brian, "Are you staying for the band?"

Brian shrugged. "Have to. It's his kid."

Rob's swift double take as he scanned the stage and then looked back at Mason was almost funny. "Oh. The one with the guitar? He looks like you."

No way Rob was faking surprise about the band. If Anna had come on purpose because of Christian, she hadn't told her friend. Which meant she probably wasn't stalking him. Which meant…exactly nothing. She still wanted to make that Five Star movie and he still didn't want her to.

ACD launched into their first song, "Cover Me." Christian had written it when he was fifteen—it was one of the first full-fledged songs he'd ever written—and it was still one of Mason's favorites. The poppy melody was dissonant with the lyrics, a love-gone-wrong tale. People moved closer to the stage, blocking Mason's view, but he could still hear Christian's voice and still feel the pride in knowing his kid did something extremely well.

Anna leaned over to say in his ear, "They're awesome."

And if someone was that happy listening to your kid's band, it got a lot harder to keep the walls up.

When the band went on their break, Mason thought Christian would come over, but the three boys filed off the back of the stage and out the fire exit. He shoved aside thoughts of what they were doing out there. He was sure they weren't stupid enough to do anything illegal on the street outside the Shannon.

He picked up the water pitcher and filled everyone's glasses. "So you think they were awesome?" he asked Anna.

"I loved them. I would go see them again in a heart-beat." She put her hand on the V-opening of her shirt and Mason liked the way the silver rings looked against the pale skin showing at her throat.

"Do you like music?" he asked.

Jake and Rob started laughing, and Anna gave them a haughty look. "Ignore them," she said.

"No, really, Anna, tell him some of your favorites."

She pretended to ignore them, but Mason's curiosity was piqued. "Is there a story here?"

"No story," Anna said. "I have eclectic taste and that seems to amuse my feeble-minded brother and his friend."

Jake spoke to Stephanie and Brian. "You have to understand, in this alternate universe, eclectic is another word for god-awful."

A faint blush spread over her cheekbones and Mason decided that an embarrassed Anna was not a bad thing.

"How about one?" he prodded. He couldn't resist a music conversation, no matter how stupid it was to get to know Anna.

Rob's shouted The Partridge Family was drowned out by Jake's Rod Stewart. And then Rob added, "She has 'I Got You Babe' on autoreplay on her iPod."

Mason stared, half appalled, half knowing they had to be kidding. No one could have taste that horrible. "Sonny and Cher? Seriously?"

Anna, in a dignified voice, said, "Seriously, my all-time favorite song is 'Dancing Queen.'"

They all looked at Mason. Stephanie gave Anna a thumbs-up and whispered, "That's a great song."

"I'll give you that one. It's a solid pop song. Not horrible."

"Okay, Mr. Musical Taste, name some of your favorites," Anna challenged, brown eyes glowing with good humor.

And then it was his turn to be embarrassed as Brian and Stephanie shouted, "Don't ask him that."

"Don't," Brian repeated. "He's a music geek. We'll be dead of boredom before he finishes his Top 5 All-time Songs with Pedal Steel Guitar Leads or whatever picky thing he's obsessing over right now."

Stephanie had her hands over her ears. She raised one tentatively. "Is it safe? Is he speaking music-techno-babble yet?"

Mason crossed his arms. "Anna and I need friends who appreciate us better."

"We appreciate you," Brian said. "We just don't appreciate the lists."

"Or the lectures," Stephanie chimed in.

"Right."

They both nodded.

"I like popular music, too. I gave her 'Dancing Queen.'"

"Quick," Brian said. "You have two seconds to name one band you like that anyone else at the table has even heard of."

Mason smirked. "Garth Brooks."

Anna clasped his forearm. "I love him."

Even as his skin prickled with awareness of her small, cool hand, he shook his head. "I was kidding."

She met his eye, her hand still on his arm. "I wasn't."

But then the boys were back from their break and the music started again and she moved her hand. He missed it. He wished she'd left it there. He wished he didn't wish that. He wished he'd had a chance to name a band so he didn't look like a snob. But, he checked out of the corner of his eye, she didn't look hurt or upset. Maybe Anna was one of those lucky people who didn't care what others thought about them.

ACD wrapped their show with a cover of the Styx song "Renegade." Everyone in the place was on their feet singing the chorus, including Anna. As the last reverb died away, he leaned down. "'Maggie May.' That's one I like— the Rod Stewart version."

She cocked her head. "Are there other versions?"

He held in a sigh and she patted him again, too briefly. "Kidding. I have eclectic taste, I'm not clueless."

Stephanie stood up. "I have to get Brian home. His pre-wedding jitters are screwing with his beauty rest."

Brian rolled his eyes. "Nice to meet you," he said to Anna.

Jake and Rob went back to the kitchen to see if they could sweet-talk Denny into packing a few brownies to go.

Mason and Anna were left standing together. She leaned back on the table, stretching her legs out in front and crossing her booted feet. "So what's with the name? ACD?"

"It's their initials—Alex, Christian, Drew." Mason lifted his shoulders. "They were fourteen when they started playing together—it's boy humor."

"Oh, I think it's funny. I was just wondering where it came from."

The way she said it, he could tell she meant it. She wasn't what he first thought. He'd seen her driving for a deal, single-minded and brash. But tonight she'd been sweet with her brother and Rob, funny, self-effacing and comfortable in her own skin. She was easy to be with and didn't even seem to notice all the little ways she drew people out. And now she thought his son's juvenile-joke band name was funny, which he actually did, too. Definitely a different person than the one he'd first met. Or no, a different side of the same person. He couldn't afford to forget that she still had a goal and it still included him and Five Star.

"Hey, Dad." Christian's long bangs were swept to the side and sticky with sweat so Mason could see his eyes. He radiated the afterglow of playing for an audience. "You see these things?" Christian thrust a wrinkled piece of paper toward him.

As Mason took it, Christian lifted his chin and said "hey" to Anna. Mason cocked an eyebrow.

"Anna Walsh," he said, "meet my son, Christian, who knows how to greet people politely but chooses to speak in monosyllables."

Anna said "hey" back in exactly the same nonchalant, teenage-stoner voice. She and Christian shared a grin at his expense while he looked at the paper. Community Meeting was the headline and it went on to describe the opportunity Lakeland had to "rid itself of a drain on the resources of our community." There was a date and time for a planning session above Roxanne Curtis's address.

"I'd like to rid the neighborhood of Roxanne Curtis," he said.

"Those are all over Lakeland, stuck in windows," Christian said. "She's really serious, huh?"

Chris had developed a terminal case of cool around the time he turned fifteen, which meant no emotions should be shown in public, particularly to a parent. He hadn't heard his son sound nervous about anything in years. Mason realized that for everything Mulligans meant to him, it was Christian's home—the only place the kid had ever felt safe and settled. Roxanne was *not* taking that away from them.

"She's not going to do this, Chris. I promise."

For a second Christian looked at him the way he used to when his mom had first left him, like he wanted to trust but couldn't make the leap. As fast as that look crossed his face, it was gone again, replaced with the familiar don't-care cockiness. "I gotta go help break down the stuff."

Mason watched him go and then remembered Anna. She was still next to him, pointedly *not* looking at the notice, giving him his privacy. He saw the curiosity she was fighting and realized what that meant for her. She wanted the story, wanted it badly, but wouldn't take it unless he offered.

Was that small respect enough to go on? Could he trust her? If he told her what happened on the bus, what he'd done, what he'd seen and what he'd not done, where would she go with that? If Christian found out or his neighbors did, would he lose everything that mattered anyway? Could he lie? Again?

He didn't have an answer to any of those questions. All he had was Anna. Her intelligence and good humor. The clear affection she had for her brother and Rob. She'd even managed a connection with Christian. Stephanie approved of her—he'd seen that in the first five minutes. Plus, she had the experience and the reputation to make the Mulligans movie matter.

Decision made, he held the paper out to her. "If

we're going to work together, you better know what we're up against."

Her eyes never dropped from his face, never went to the paper. "We're doing the Mulligans movie?"

"You promised kick-butt."

"You'll get it." She put her hand on his arm again, making a bond even as she held his gaze. "Do I get the Five Star story?"

He felt his stomach seize.

"When we're done with Mulligans I'll give you what I can for the other one." Mason made sure she was paying attention before he went on. "I don't know what that will be though. There's stuff I'm not sure I can tell you."

She twisted the big silver ring on her left hand, studying his face. When she gave an almost imperceptible nod, his pulse jumped. He and Anna were going to do this thing together.

"First things first," Anna said before pushing her curls behind her ears and grinning wickedly. "Let's kick Roxanne Curtis's stuck-up butt."

ON THE WALK BACK to their place, Jake and Rob were ecstatic. They congratulated her on sealing the deal and complimented her on the way she'd seen through to the key to Mason's cooperation. All of it was true. None of it was new to her—making people talk was her business. So why did she keep seeing Mason's face when he was looking at Christian and promising to protect their home? She knew that was the tipping point that had given her the leverage she needed. She should be thanking whatever fates had sent Chris over with that meeting notice at that exact moment. Instead she felt sleazy.

Mason had basically admitted that he knew more about the crash than he'd let on. Ordinarily that kind of teaser would have kept her awake mulling over possibilities and angles. Instead she was awake thinking about the pain and fear she'd seen in Mason's eyes as he agreed to her terms. She felt dirty, knowing her insistence on the truth had caused his pain.

IF THE LAKELAND zoning board got a look at Christian's bedroom it was entirely possible Mulligans would be condemned, not just rezoned. He and Christian had a deal where he didn't complain about what went on in here and Christian didn't let his mess progress past the doorway. The deal kept them from arguing, but it also kept Mason out of the room. It had been several months since he'd done more than knock on the door to wake Chris up.

They used to paint the room every summer. Chris loved the mess and changing stuff and doing real work with his dad. Mason got a buzz from the fact that it was *his* place. His house where he could do what he wanted. For at least three years now, the walls had been the same green.

The room had been changed in other ways, though, and as Mason stood near the closet wondering where the hell Christian's old starter guitar might be, he was struck by the familiarity. He could be standing in *his* old room. From before he met David Giles, before they became Five Star, before he left the ratty trailer he lived in with his mom for life on the road.

Same heaps of dubiously clean clothes. Same stacks of music—his had been tapes and Chris's were CDs he'd burned. Same litter of flyers for gigs and spare amp cords and guitar picks. Chris had papered the wall around his bed with posters—the names were different but the substance hadn't changed. Chris even had a memo board on the wall near his bed covered with lyrics and song ideas. Had Mason told Chris he'd done that?

The shades were down and windows shut, keeping out the light and keeping in the unpleasant aroma of teenage boy. How many hours had he spent holed up with his Walkman in the near darkness of his own room?

Weird. He thought of their lives as so different, but his son's hopes and dreams were very close to the ones he'd had at sixteen.

Opening the shuttered doors of the closet, he shoved a bunch of empty hangers out of his way so he could get a look at what was piled on the floor. Mangy clothes and outgrown sports equipment mostly. But then he saw the neck of the guitar in behind a lacrosse stick. He put a hand on the overhead shelf to steady himself and leaned to grab the guitar. When he pushed himself upright he knocked a pile of sweatshirts off the shelf. A flurry of baseball caps came down on his head and shoulders and then, with a soft plop, Christian's teddy bear hit him in the face. Mason caught it before it hit the ground.

Polar Bear Peek. He hadn't seen the thing in years. Hadn't known Christian still had him. Granted, it looked as if Chris hadn't thrown anything out. Ever. But Mason was stupidly happy to see the toy. With the guitar under one arm, he backed out of the closet. He gave the bear a squeeze.

"Are you hugging Peek?"

His son stood in the doorway, staring.

"No," Mason said quickly. "He fell. I was looking for your old guitar." He held the instrument up as evidence.

"You were so totally hugging him." Christian shook his finger in gleeful mockery.

Mason put the tattered bear on the bookcase next to him. "What are you doing home?"

"Saving you from turning into a complete freak. What else do you do when I'm not around?" Obviously Chris was enjoying this way too much. "Let me see him." Chris held his hand out.

Mason tossed him the bear.

"I don't even know why I still have him," Chris said, and then looked around the room. "I should get rid of some of this stuff."

Mason's pulse jumped. The bear was the first thing he'd bought Chris. They'd gone to Macy's to get clothes. When Chris's mom left him with Mason there hadn't been much on the inventory besides one boy. He'd needed jeans, new sneakers, pj's, socks, a bathing suit…

Peek had been in the kids' department on the end of a display. He'd been an unnamed polar bear then, not Peek yet. Chris's hand had lingered on the soft white fur and Mason had thrust the bear at him, desperate to make some connection. Later he'd realized that seven was almost too old for stuffed animals, but in the moment Peek had helped to bridge the gap between a man and a boy who had no idea how to spend time together, let alone how to be a family.

"You can't get rid of Peek," he said a little too sharply.

"Okay, Dad. Calm down." Christian came all the way in the room, passing Mason, and sat on the bed. He put Peek down next to him, then toed off his sneakers and lay down on his back. "What are you doing with the guitar?"

"Louise wants to take lessons. I said she could have it."

"Isn't that dangerous?"

"Guitar lessons?"

"Yeah. What if she wants to do something with her music—you're going to have to hold her back with an iron fist, too."

How long did that take? From laughter to full-on sarcasm in three seconds flat.

"I don't know why you don't trust me to know what's best for you," Mason said. He didn't think he needed to let Christian know he had his own doubts on the subject.

Chris folded his hands under his head. "Dad, the problem you have with the band isn't about me, it's about you. *You* can't trust *me*."

"I'm ready to support your career after you graduate."

"Not this again." Christian closed his eyes, but it looked more as if he was willing Mason away than relaxing. He crossed his feet and somehow made even that look angry.

"My son is not going to walk away from high school without a diploma. It's just not going to happen." As soon as he said it, Mason knew it was wrong. Ultimatums were bad. Mulligans hosted the damn Parenting Your Teen lecture series twice a year—he'd listened from the back of the room enough times to know he was doing this wrong.

"You know what's weird?" Chris said quietly. "You don't even know if that's true."

"If what's true?" Mason asked.

"If I'm your son. My mom dropped me off and then split. You never had a test. Did you?" Chris's voice was surprisingly calm. He almost sounded as if he was asking an ordinary question like, "Did Metallica ever open for

Ozzie?" As if he wasn't ripping Mason's heart out and then prodding it clinically.

"What the hell are you talking about?"

"You never checked, did you? With a blood test?" Again his son's tone was so calm, detached.

He couldn't speak. Why would Christian even think about this? It made no sense. Sure, he was right—Mason never had a test. But only because he'd never needed to. He'd taken one real look at Chris, recognized the worry and the fear that was eating him up from the inside out, and he'd just known. Christian needed him. Mason had been ready to have someone need him.

"You have no idea if she was telling the truth," Christian went on. "She lied to me all the time. So she maybe was at your show in Pittsburgh. Probably eighty thousand people were there that night. How can you know? She's dead so you can't even ask her."

Mason was holding the neck of the guitar so hard the tuning pegs bit into his palm. "You're my son." It wasn't an answer, and yet, for Mason, it was the only answer.

"That's not enough for me. I want to have it tested. I want to know for sure."

Hearing him say those words, *not enough for me,* knowing Chris was that ready to throw away everything they had, it cut the legs out from under him. Mason's hands started to shake.

How could Chris lie there and say this stuff and not know what he was doing to Mason? But of course he did know. That's why he was doing it. Like most kids, he held all the cards. He knew his stupid father loved him too much to come back with anything this harsh. Feeling trapped, Mason's temper flared. "You want this damn test so you can get out from under me. Well, sorry, pal. Blood test or no blood test, you're my kid. I raised you and you're stuck with me."

Christian opened his eyes, furious. "I knew you'd say that. You always have to be right."

"No. God, Chris, I don't always have to be right. I've apologized to you about enough things that I think you'd know that by now. But about this? I am right."

"What part? You're right about how I should live my life? Right that I'm going to make every stupid mistake you made? Or right that you're really my dad? Seems like there's a pretty decent chance you're wrong about every single thing on that list."

Mason put a hand on the bookcase to steady himself. "Where is this coming from?"

Christian sat up, swinging his legs over the side of the bed. He looked younger with his shoulders hunched, and Mason wanted to go to him, but he didn't know what he could do that wouldn't kindle more anger. "I just want to know," Chris mumbled.

Mason's thoughts spun. He needed to put the brakes on while he figured out what to do. "I guess a test is something we could talk about," he offered, hating the words even as he knew he had to give Chris something, if only to hold on to him for a while longer.

"Whatever," Christian said as he slid his feet into his sneakers. "Alex is coming to dinner. I'll be downstairs."

Mason was alone again. Tires crunched on the gravel driveway and he glanced out the window to see Anna and Jake climbing out of a rusty blue Saab. He clenched his hands into fists and he actually took a step forward as if he would punch the wall. *God*. He had no idea what just happened with his kid. And now he was supposed to put on his stage face and go show these people exactly why Mulligans deserved to exist. He couldn't manage a conversation with Chris, how was he going to face Anna and her questions?

SHE HADN'T KNOWN what to expect. The inside of most social-services centers like this were institutional, down-at-heel and they always featured an homage to whatever benefactor provided the funding. She'd done some research to see where this place fit in, but Mulligans guarded its privacy as much as that of its residents.

The people at the zoning hearing had called it a halfway house. Mason had called it cohousing. But anyone who came in the front door of this place and mistook it for anything besides a home was blind or possibly deranged, because she thought even a blind person would be able to *feel* that Mulligans was home. The kind of home Anna'd always wished for when she was growing up in her mother's decorator show house.

The front door opened on a spacious, welcoming room, with a deep window seat piled with pillows, bookshelves crammed with books and games and two groups of overstuffed chairs clustered around scarred coffee tables. It was as far from institutional as you could get.

Jake nudged her. "Not exactly a rock star's lair, huh?"

"It's probably a front." Anna wasn't willing to admit Mason might be more than she'd expected or that this was anything more than a job.

Mason had said he'd meet them, but when he didn't show up after a few minutes, they followed the sounds of clinking silverware and conversation down the hall. Anna stopped in the doorway to the dining room and knew this scene would be central to the film. Floor-to-ceiling windows and French doors on the back wall let light stream in and pulled her eye outside to the bank of greenery separating Mulligans from the street behind. A middle-aged woman pushed open the double-swinging doors in the back corner and Anna glimpsed a kitchen.

Ten or so round tables and ladder-back chairs were scattered through the large room. People of all ages, from a sober-looking senior couple in the corner, to a baby in a high chair, sat around the tables as four people wearing white aprons moved through the room setting out dishes on the buffet counter and filling water glasses.

"Hey," Christian said. He'd been sitting at the table to their right and stood up when he saw them. He was wearing a black T-shirt with a red dog screen-printed on the front and the hems of his beat-up jeans hung ragged around the tops of his sneakers.

Anna smiled at him. "Hey, yourself. Good to see you again."

"My dad said you were coming." Chris slid his already full plate to the right and dragged another chair over from the table behind him. "You've got him all nervous. He's probably upstairs changing."

She didn't know what to say to that. Probably if Mason was nervous about something it was the zoning board and not her. She turned to Jake. "I don't think you met my brother, Jake? This is Mason's son, Christian."

Mason came through the door then and Anna couldn't help appreciating how hot he looked in khaki pants and a crisply pressed white linen shirt. She tried to look at him as a filmmaker, getting a sense of how he moved, but she'd be kidding herself if she didn't admit he kicked her pulse higher. And if her palms were tingling and she'd started to sweat just a bit, she hoped her reaction had more to do with the fact that her last boyfriend had been blander than white bread than it did with Mason in particular. After Artie, any man with half an ounce of personality would have piqued her interest.

Right. She really needed to practice lying to herself.

Mason was carrying a child-size guitar. "Glad you could make it," he said. He stood next to Christian but they didn't look at each other. Something was wrong. Anna noticed that his smile didn't quite make it to his eyes, but since he was putting effort into making his act work she played along.

"Your place is lovely," she offered. And then he did something odd. He looked, really looked, at the room. As though he hadn't been there before. The green of his eyes deepened and he nodded so slightly she wouldn't have seen it if she hadn't been watching him closely. Like he was reassuring himself. Or reassessing the place.

"I had a good architect," was all he said.

A little girl, maybe ten years old, hustled up to him, a skinny preschool-age boy close on her heels. "Mason, you brought the guitar!"

"Told you I would, Louise." His smile as he handed over the guitar was real. "Hey, Dante."

As soon as he heard his name, the boy lifted his arms. "Up," he demanded.

Mason scooped him up, settling him on his hip in a motion as practiced as any parent's. Years spent observing people through her camera had given Anna a sense of when they were performing and, despite the cheesy perfection of this scene, she didn't get a fake vibe from Mason. This was him, how he really was. He smoothed the girl's brown hair back off her face absently as he told her to bring the guitar by anytime it needed tuning. "Thank you!" Louise said and then she threw her arms around Mason's waist, knocking the back of his thighs with the guitar and bumping the boy with her head.

Anna watched his smile broaden at the effusive hug, the laugh lines at his eyes crinkling even as he spread his feet to steady himself. "Enjoy it, okay?"

"Spreading the guitar gospel?" Anna asked.

Christian snorted and spun away to sit down. Mason's eyes flicked to his son but he didn't say anything, just gathered himself before saying, "You guys ready for dinner?"

He gave the little boy a quick squeeze and then set him back on his feet. "Your mom's waiting for you, okay, buddy?"

As the boy walked away, Mason pulled out the chair next to Christian. Anna realized he intended for her to sit in it. She shot Jake a look that said *laugh and you'll die* and then allowed herself to be seated as if she were the country-club wife she'd sworn never to become. She kept her back carefully straight so she wouldn't risk leaning into Mason's hands, but she felt them anyway right there so close behind her.

"Do you have a group dinner every night?" she asked after Mason took the seat next to her. Professional questions would get her mind off his hands. Off his long tapered fingers and the lean but strong wrists visible under the turned-back cuffs of his shirt. The way his big black watch looked sexy smart. *Professional, Walsh.*

"Tuesday, Thursday and Sunday. The community contract says everybody eats here at least twice a week. Each household cooks twice a month and serves twice a month. That way we all get waited on and do the waiting. Keeps us connected. There's nutrition and budget education but it's low-key. For some people this is their first experience of this kind of dinner—napkins, sitting down, no TV. So we keep it casual, but it's part of the contract that you show up."

A second teenager slid into the chair next to Chris, his plate full from the buffet. Anna recognized him from the other night at the Shannon. "You should have come on a night when Mr. S. was cooking. His mac and cheese is, like, restaurant quality." The boy looked distracted and continued. "If restaurants served mac and cheese. Which more of them totally should because it's the perfect food."

Anna found herself smiling at the boy's enthusiasm. His blond hair was longer than Christian's and pulled back off his face in a ponytail. He shoveled food into his mouth as if he were starving.

Mason shook his head. "Anna, Jake, meet Alex. Christian's friend, Mulligans's unofficial boarder and my macaroni and cheese groupie, apparently."

"That's right. I never miss dinner at Mulligans when Mr. S. is cooking."

Christian rolled his eyes as he filled his glass from a pitcher of water on the table. "You never miss dinner no matter who's cooking, Alex."

The other boy shrugged cheerfully.

"You ready?" Mason asked. Anna found herself in line between him and Jake. Because they were here to start framing concepts for the movie, she was taking special care to observe everything she could. The fact that she was trying to ignore Mason two feet behind her was making her job difficult. And making her frustrated. The black leather belt with a wide silver buckle cinched low around his lean waist was drawing her eye and not in a professional way.

Anna grabbed a plate and concentrated on the buffet. *This* they could use in the movie. The dinner was simple but smelled delicious. Green beans in balsamic vinegar, baked potatoes steaming in foil pans and a choice of sliced roast beef or a seafood stew.

Jake turned to Mason as he waited for the woman in front of him to finish putting condiments on her potato. "Anna's favorite thing in the world is a buffet. She'll be applying for a spot here if you don't look out."

"We only take people who have nowhere else to go." Mason laughed. "Anna can come and eat whenever she likes, but she wouldn't qualify for a housing spot."

Jake turned back to the buffet, speaking over his shoulder. "Anna hasn't had a permanent address since college. You sure she couldn't squeak by?"

Her good mood evaporated in less time than it took Jake to make that offhand, unintentionally hurtful remark. The cheerful chatter, the delicious smells, even Mason's sexy belt were suddenly nothing compared to the sinking pit in her stomach. She was even more unsettled to find out how much the comment bothered her.

She glanced up and saw Mason looking at her. "My work. I move around for my work. It's what I do." She hesitated, thinking she sounded as if she was justifying her lifestyle, which didn't need justifying because it was *fine*. It was how she wanted it. "I like it this way."

Forcing a smile, she pointed to the sour cream. "I hope that's not low-fat."

If he didn't look entirely convinced by her fake cheer, well, she hadn't been fooled by him earlier so now they were even.

When they got back to the table, Christian and Alex were finishing their meals. Mason raised an eyebrow when his son pushed his chair back and started to leave. "You don't have five minutes to stay and talk?"

Chris sat down heavily and rolled his eyes. Alex scratched his nose. Mason took a long sip of his water. Jake buttered his potato. Anna stifled her own eye roll. *Boys.* And *men.* Why could they not master the art of small talk?

"So, you guys are juniors? Seniors?" she asked.

Alex spun his fork on the edge of his plate. Chris tapped his fingers. Mason glared at his son. "They're going to be seniors," he answered.

Alex's face brightened and Anna could practically feel his relief that he'd thought of something to say. "You make movies, right?"

She nodded. *Please don't let him ask if I know Lindsay Lohan.*

"Did you make any that I've seen?"

She sincerely doubted it. "Probably not. But, hey! I directed the video for "Rock On" for Del Sweeney."

It was as if she'd poked Chris with a needle. "That was you? That was awesome!" He and Alex were the opposite of apathetic now. "Remember that part where they're onstage and those things shoot up behind them like fireworks but they're really water or whatever? That was so cool."

Alex was nodding. "Remember we tried to figure out

how that worked so we could do it?" He looked eagerly at Anna. "How *did* you do that? Can you show us—"

"Hey," Christian broke in, "maybe Anna can come by practice sometime and watch us. Would you want to? Maybe bring your camera?"

"Christian. No." The sharp command in Mason's voice surprised her. "Anna's doing the movie for Mulligans. Besides, you guys don't need a video. Not yet."

She wasn't sure what was going on. Mason's reaction seemed out of proportion to Christian's overeager assumption that she wouldn't mind filming his practice. But then she saw Chris's face and she realized the two of them were locked in some argument only they understood.

"Fine, Dad. We stayed like you ordered. We chatted like you ordered. Which was totally useless, thank you very much. Now we're out of here."

Alex looked wide-eyed from his friend to Mason but didn't say anything, just followed Chris when he picked up his dishes and headed toward the kitchen.

Anna was embarrassed. Ordinarily she would have ignored Chris's attitude, but Mason looked sideswiped and she didn't think he'd be able to follow if she or Jake tried to change the subject. Besides, she felt as if it was partly her fault.

"He seems really tense."

Mason nodded, but then with a twist of his lips said, "I hope he's just really seventeen."

"I'm sorry I mentioned the video."

"It's fine. He and I are having an issue but nothing you need to worry about."

Which, Anna knew, was his way of saying back the hell away from my kid. Suddenly she didn't want to make small talk, either. She turned back to her dinner, taking a bite of baked potato and sighing.

Mason looked at her. "You okay?"

"This is delicious." Normal. Talk about the food. Which *was* delicious. She looked at the other people in the room, trying to sort them into family groups. "Do you have other visitors, besides us and Alex?"

"No. If someone wants to bring a guest, they're welcome. But usually it's just the residents. We have six houses, some of them are double units. Right now we're at pretty much full capacity with twenty-six people."

Anna savored another bite of baked potato. Jake had gotten the seafood stew and she was definitely going to get him to give her a bite. This was such a lovely place, wonderful food, nice atmosphere. She wondered what the people from the zoning hearing would think if they saw Mulligans like this. *Wait.*

Jake paused with his fork halfway to his mouth. "What, Anna?" He spoke to Mason out of the corner of his mouth. "You'll get to know that look. See how she's pushing her hair around? Twisting her rings? It means she's getting ready to push some person around, twist things to suit her. Here's hoping it's you and not me."

"Why do you do that?" Anna asked him.

"Do what?"

"Talk about me like that. Like you know what I'm thinking."

"Because I do," Jake answered as if it was the most obvious thing in the world.

Mason's head swiveled back and forth between them as though he'd never seen or heard anything so fascinating. When Anna pointedly turned her shoulder, shutting

Jake out of her line of sight, Mason said, "Don't stop on my account."

"Please." Anna said. "There's no reason to indulge him."

Jake snorted but didn't reply. Anna focused on Mason. "This is a wonderful experience. If I were you, I'd open the dining room to the larger community once in a while. Maybe on a set night every year. It would help break down the mystery about what you're doing."

"Told you," Jake muttered.

Mason leaned back in his seat and scanned the room again. He spoke slowly, as if he was thinking aloud. "We don't have anything to hide, but I don't see that we have anything to prove, either. If people want to talk, they're going to talk."

"That's my point. They're going to talk, so why not give them something to talk about. You start the conversation instead of letting them drive it."

Mason sipped his water. He didn't look convinced. "Mulligans is about people getting back on their feet. Mostly we're people who don't really fit into the whole middle-class thing on the outside. I'm not putting my friends on display like a science experiment."

"Okay," she said. "It was just an idea."

Anna sensed she needed to back off, but she wasn't giving up. She'd come back to this idea again because hearing Mason talk had convinced her even more that she was right. He was hiding out here behind the fences. The same way he was hiding what really happened that night on the bus.

WHEN THEY FINISHED eating, Louise's mother, a slender woman with dark hair and eyes came up to them, holding

Dante by the hand. Louise followed her, stumbling as she tried to strum the guitar and walk.

"I'll find you a case for that and a strap," he told Louise. "Maddie, this is Anna Walsh and her brother, Jake. They're the ones I told you are making a film about Mulligans." He paused. "Jake, Maddie will show you around the community center while I take Anna to see a home."

Louise piped up. "Can I be in the movie? I know all about Mulligans 'cause I've lived here for a whole year."

Maddie stroked her daughter's hair. "We'll see, baby."

Mason motioned to the hall door. "Be sure you show Jake the kitchen and the supply room? Okay?"

Maddie nodded and then she and Jake set off, Louise and Dante trailing them.

Mason and Anna went back down the hallway and out the front door of the center. "I asked the Hendersons if we could go through their place. It's the third one on the left."

The center yard around which the homes were set recalled the village greens she'd seen on a trip to Ireland. The six small houses all had front porches, which the community center's architect had copied in the deep, wraparound porch on that larger building. Climbing trees dotted the edges of the wide, open lawn spotted with worn brown patches that spoke of baseball games and hard play, not neglect. Anna saw a fenced garden on the left, with tall spikes of corn and staked tomato plants.

"I ran a Google search on Mulligans and got mostly golf sites," Anna said as they walked down the gravel path. "You don't believe in promotion?"

"We don't need it. We've been turning people away since we opened. Wish we could take more."

"Sounds like your neighbors need an education,

though. I mean, this place doesn't look much like a flop-house to me."

"Everyone who lives here has a need for community but no access to it," Mason said quickly. Clearly the explanation was familiar territory for him. "Everybody has something to contribute. We make each other stronger. Take the Hendersons. They're seniors. They owned a home in a rough neighborhood. George was mugged and they knew they couldn't stay where they were. They applied for Mulligans because they're safer here. In return they do babysitting, George teaches some woodworking classes and Helen runs a sewing club."

Anna purposely kept her gaze off Mason. His voice was so warm, he clearly cared deeply about these people. She didn't want to embarrass him into clamming up.

"What about Louise and her family?"

Mason glanced down at her and she met his eye. "No one's perfect. Right?"

"Right."

"Maddie had…substance-abuse problems. They were living on the street for about a year and then…social services took Louise and Dante…. Scared Maddie to death, she says. So she got in a program and got clean."

Anna nodded. This story was clearly hard for Mason to tell.

"When you…get out of rehab, if you're not a celebrity, it's hard to get your feet under you. Landlords want first, last and security. Employers see you as a risk. Day care for both kids cost about what Maddie could pull in from the jobs she could get. When life is that hard, when putting a meal on the table and a roof over your head takes everything you've got, making a lasting change is harder than ever."

"So Mulligans is like an extended family for her?"

"Bingo. We require a minimal rent but it's on a sliding scale and our day care is free. The community meals are free, too—which helps stretch the budget. In the community center, we have washers and dryers, a supply cabinet for cleaning stuff and school stuff and a clothing exchange. But you know what? I sound like it's about money—and part of it is—but part of it is having people care about you, you know?"

Anna wasn't sure she did, but he was on a roll, so she nodded.

"There's all kinds of people out there skating by with no one watching out for them. Here we're backup if your day sucks and you need someone to take the kids or you're dying for a drink and you know you shouldn't have one or you just want someone to talk to."

They'd reached the small house now with the lace curtains in the front window.

"It's not like the people who live here are going to disappear if Mulligans does. They'll just be left on their own again."

An elderly woman opened the door, holding it wide and beaming at Mason. "Were you planning to wait out there all night?" she asked.

Mason climbed the steps, providing introductions but letting Mr. and Mrs. Henderson—Helen and George before they'd finished touring the front room—take control. Anna listened carefully to the couple, taking in the substance of their words, but searching for the emotion behind them. Helen showed off the curtains her sewing group had been working on, prompting George to point out the simple bookcase he'd designed and taught in his own workshops.

"Who comes to the workshops? Are they required?"

George led them down a narrow hallway to a small kitchen. "Not required. Some folks don't come. But the folks who do come—and we've been doing this about five years—they all go home with something to be proud of."

Helen twitched a terry-cloth dish towel to straighten it. "Mason took my curtain class. Made a real nice set for the day-care center."

Anna watched a flush climb up his neck to his ears.

"Helen, I was auditing your class. I had to make sure you knew what you were doing."

The older woman shook her head fondly. "I saw your face when you finished them."

"This must be a breach of teacher-student confidentiality," Mason complained.

Helen took pity on him and ushered Anna outside to see her flowers.

Anna tried to pay attention, but it was hard because she was rapidly recalculating everything she thought she'd known about Mason. The man she'd expected would have been above this community, a figurehead. Anna had seen his real friendship with the Hendersons, based on mutual understanding, not economics.

Anna wasn't sure what to feel about that.

MASON WAITED on the path while Anna wished the Hendersons good-night. He stretched his back, looking up at the sky where the sun was fading to a deep yellow-and-pink haze. His muscles were so knotted he didn't know how he'd fall asleep that night. If the conversation with Chris hadn't been stressful enough, he'd had to shadow Anna on this tour, watching her parse and dissect the thing he'd built here with every probing question she asked the Hendersons. He was encouraged that the Mulligans movie would be as effective as she'd promised, but he was bone deep scared about having her turn that perceptive mind on him and the Five Star crash.

"You mind if I smoke?" he asked her as they walked toward the community center.

She tilted her head and looked at him. "You've been tense since we got here. Do we need to talk about anything?"

God, she spooked him—it was as if she could hear what he was thinking.

"I had a long day." He took out his cigarettes and tapped one out of the box, the scent of the tobacco calming him even before he lit it. He tilted the box to her, never expecting her to take one, but she plucked one out and put it between her lips.

"You smoke?"

"Nope. But when I'm filming I like to get into whatever my subject is doing. It gives me perspective if I share experiences."

He took out his silver lighter and kicked up a flame to light his cigarette. He held it out to her, waiting until she caught on and put her cigarette back between her lips. She leaned in and touched the tip to the glowing tip of his own, her silver rings catching the reflected flame as it burned hotter on her inhale. When she let it out, he felt her breath on his hand and thought about how long it had been since he was close to a woman he found attractive. Her wide, exotic eyes closed as she sucked in her first mouthful of smoke and he took advantage of that to watch her face, feeling stupid and turned on and unable to look away. He saw her roll the smoke and then release it and he wondered if she'd savor a kiss that same way. When her eyes opened again she caught him staring.

He took a drag, kept his eyes on hers, enjoying what he was feeling. It took him back to the old days when he hadn't known the meaning of careful. Cigarettes and lust and a gorgeous woman on a hot, dark night. Damn, it felt good. Which was bad. They weren't kidding when they said cigarettes led to more serious temptations. He needed to let his pulse settle. He held the smoke and then exhaled.

"That's one drag," she said. "One more, right?"

Was her voice unsettled? Was she feeling this, too?

"Two. That's the limit. How'd you like it?" he asked.

"Disgusting." She leaned down and stubbed the cigarette out on the ground and then put it in her pocket. "The fire was good, though. Wild."

Oh hell, she had felt something. Mason liked the way her face lit up, her nose wrinkled when she said disgusting but her eyes sparkled. *Wild.* Impulsively he handed her the lighter. "Why don't you take this."

She flicked open the lid and twitched the wheel. A flame shot up and she stared as if she was cataloging the colors. When she flicked it closed, her voice was back to normal. "That's cool. But I couldn't take it. How would you light tomorrow's cigarette?"

"I can get another one."

She held it out again. "Really. I try not to accumulate a lot of stuff."

He looked at the lighter. A lot of stuff? Or was there another reason she'd refused?

"Right. Jake said you travel light. How about you borrow it? Give it back to me when you're done with the movie."

"All right."

She changed her mind so quickly, he knew. She'd wanted it all along. She folded her hand over the lighter and slid it into the front pocket of her jeans. Slid…into the front pocket…

He took his second drag and then stubbed his own cigarette out. "What else have you tried 'cause someone on a project was doing it?"

"I did a river cleanup in Portland. We did a thing about voodoo for the Discovery Channel and I made altars. Oh, and Internet porn."

Mason choked. "Filming or acting?"

Anna grinned up at him. "I like to direct."

He stared at her.

"Don't you wish," she said. "I *read* Internet porn for a project we did about college students."

"And?" he asked.

"You'd be surprised," she answered and he *was* surprised. Surprised how fast he'd built a mental image of her alone in a room with a fast PC and a cable modem, looking at the screen, but maybe, just maybe, thinking about him.

"So…" He coughed. "What do you do when you're not taking other people's hobbies and bad habits for a test drive?"

"Plan projects that let me test-drive other people's hobbies and bad habits."

Jake met them at the bottom of the community center steps. They exchanged goodbyes before he had a chance to ask another question, but he wondered about what she'd said. He didn't think Anna was the kind of person who either put up with bullshit or handed it out. Was it true that someone as intense as her really didn't have a life outside her work? Jake had said she didn't have a permanent address. She didn't even want to take the lighter because it would weigh her down.

Hell, it didn't even seem as if she had her own hobbies. He'd gone on the road because his mother took him, but it's not as if he'd had anything worth hanging on to. What had set Anna off? Some trouble? Garden-variety restlessness? Whatever had launched her, he was sorry she hadn't ever slowed down. He knew what that kind of life did to you.

He couldn't afford to let her get hung up on him. Couldn't let her test out any more of the personal details of his life. She'd been starting to craft the Mulligans movie right there as she asked the Hendersons questions and followed up on their stories. Which was the problem. He should shut her out, but he couldn't. He needed to give her everything she asked for so the movie would be the best it could be.

Mason closed the community center door behind him and went down the hall to check on the dinner cleanup. He needed a project, some practical piece of labor, the harder or dirtier the better, that could take his mind off the fact that he was starting to think more about getting close to Anna than pushing her away.

CHAPTER SEVEN

ROB PARKED on the street and the three of them walked to the gate in the high fence surrounding Mulligans. Frothy rosettes of white netting anchored with baby's-breath nosegays decorated the gateposts. Brian's story was one of the narrative threads of the film. He'd been with Mulligans since the beginning and his successes were such a triumph. Today they would shoot some footage of Stephanie and Brian's wedding.

Rob held the gate open for them, Jake carrying the larger gear bag and tripod, Anna with her smaller Canon. Three steps inside the gate, she stopped in her tracks. Jake turned to her, the camera bags pulling wrinkles into the shoulder of his khaki suit.

She gestured. "Look," she breathed. The yard had been converted from a well-worn backyard into a picturesque wedding stage. The location was a gift to their film. Anna couldn't have designed a set more perfect to convey the idea of a caring, connected community.

Every porch was strung with a wide bunting of white netting secured with lush bouquets of baby's breath at each corner. Big, terra-cotta pots dripping with more baby's breath lined the steps down from the community center's front door. A pair of white ribbons outlined a path from the bottom of the steps to a simple wooden altar laid with a white cloth and tall candles in the middle of the yard.

Jake nudged Rob with the tripod. "She's going to cry."

Rob shrugged. "She always cries."

Weddings hit every one of Anna's vulnerabilities: family events, emotional moments and the shameful love of all things bridal she'd been nursing since she'd gotten her first Barbie in kindergarten.

"I'm supposed to cry at weddings," Anna said. "I'm a girl. Besides, crying guests make the bride happy." She pointed to the closest cottage. "Baby's breath is totally underrated. Look how pretty that is." When she imagined her dream wedding, baby's breath always played a central role.

Jake pointed Rob toward the rows of chairs near the altar. "Go grab a seat. Close to the underrated baby's breath. We're going to set one camera up near the entrance and then get a spot behind the altar." He raised an eyebrow to confirm that Anna was seeing the same things he was.

"Focus on Brian's story—he's the poster child. Mix in the other residents. We've got to show them working together. It's like a Mulligans graduation so we need a triumph."

Just then, Brian, his face red and sweating above his white tuxedo shirt, came up behind Jake. "God, am I happy to see you." He paused to catch his breath. "If I weren't getting married and my bride-to-be wasn't having an absolute, hundred-percent freak-out, I would never ask this…" Brian paused to suck in more air. "The video guy is stuck in traffic and he'll be here but not in time to get the 'bride-in-the-bedroom sequence,' which according to Stephanie is essential to the wedding-day video."

Brian looked as if he had more to say, but Anna cut in. "I'd love to. Where is she?"

Brian looked a little taken aback by her fast, emphatic agreement. Jake rolled his eyes but Rob put an arm around Anna's shoulders and squeezed as he said, "She's a *girl*. She gets this stuff."

"I was supposed to find her cousin but he's not around and I saw you."

"Brian." Anna spoke slowly. It was the proper thing to do with people suffering from shock. "Where can I find the bride?"

Brian blinked. "Right. The bride." He pointed over his shoulder at the community center. "Upstairs. The door on the right at the end of the hall."

The center was busy with people chatting in the foyer and milling in and out of the meeting rooms and dining room. This was the first time she'd been upstairs where Mason and Christian lived. The hall was quiet and Anna hesitated at the landing. This was Mason's home. The private space of his life. She took a long look around, but the doors on either side of the hall were closed. She hesitated, wishing she could poke into the rooms. A closed door was worse than a dare to her.

Ever since she was a little kid she'd been an unrepentant snooper. Finding out what made people tick. Looking for their secrets. *The things she'd discovered while babysitting.* She knocked on the last door.

"You better have a video camera in your hand," Stephanie called, "or you're dead, hear me? Dead."

Anna pushed the door open and went in. Her Fairy-Tale Wedding Barbie had nothing on Stephanie Colarusso. The woman looked fantastic. She was standing still in the middle of the large bedroom, her hands clasped in front of her. The dress she'd chosen was a creamy white. Embroidered daisies sprinkled the skirt, glinting with beaded centers. Her dark hair was pulled back in a simple comb with a half veil falling from a cluster of baby's breath. The fact that the comb was slightly off center did nothing to detract from her beauty.

Anna teared up, and then smiled when she thought of what Jake and Rob would say.

"Please tell me you're smiling with me not at me," Stephanie said.

"I'm smiling because weddings turn me into a chick. You look perfect. If I were casting for a bride, I'd pick you."

Stephanie sighed and her expression softened, which made Anna relax, confident she was finally in the company of someone who understood weddings. Gushing would not only not be frowned upon, it was expected.

"Brian said there was a video emergency. I'll get some footage and your guy can cut it in with his stuff later." She flicked the button, turning her camera on and lifted it. "Move one step to your right so you're not in front of the window."

The other woman looked horrified. "Brian asked you to do this? I sent him and Lisa, my maid of honor, out to find my cousin Ronnie."

"Please, Cousin Ronnie?" Anna scoffed. "I'm a trained professional. Let me have some fun." She gestured reassuringly. "Brides are my favorite thing."

Still, Stephanie hesitated. "You can't want to do this. It's a wedding video."

"Oh, I want to." She watched Stephanie through the viewfinder, her movements graceful and neat as she straightened her full skirt and fiddled with the comb holding the veil. She saw the minute Stephanie gave in.

"Swear you're okay with this?"

"Totally. Turn so you're facing the window and then look back at me." Stephanie followed her directions, but her body tensed. Anna needed to get her chatting so she'd forget about the camera. "The yard looks beautiful."

Stephanie didn't quite smile as she nodded, the comb sliding a bit. *Not quite relaxed.*

"When I played wedding with my Barbies," Anna went on, "I always had baby's breath. I stole it from a silk arrangement my mom had—it was the only flower small enough for those irritating little Barbie hands. Come toward me."

Stephanie smiled. *More relaxed. Better.*

"It's just pretty, you know?" Stephanie said. "It's not trying to be anything it's not." She stopped and Anna shifted left to find better light. Stephanie glanced out the window. "Thank God he got it all up."

"Was it a local florist?" Anna asked, not really paying attention, just keeping the bride's focus on the conversation instead of the camera.

"Mason did it."

If she'd been chewing gum she'd have swallowed it. "Mason?"

"Don't believe his shtick. He'll tell you he has no skills, all he does for Mulligans is pay the mortgage." Stephanie lifted the sides of the dress and the light caught the beads in her skirt. Anna adjusted the zoom. "But he's been out there for days. He built the dance floor himself. He and a work crew of kids put up the netting last night and then this morning they went back through with the baby's breath. It's what he does—takes care of everything."

Wow. Mulligans certainly wasn't the vanity project she'd expected. Clearly Mason's whole life was here. Maybe too much of his life, she thought, remembering the fence outside, designed to keep Mulligans in as much as to keep other people out.

"Okay, why don't we have you sitting down." Anna scanned the room. "Try the bed. I want to see how you look with that mirror behind you."

After a second she registered that she had pointed to a bed. A man's bed. Turning a quick circle, she realized this was Mason's room. A prickle of awareness crawled up her neck. This was his bedroom. And that exceptional four-poster in front of her was his bed. Where he slept.

She swept the camera over the rest of the room, Stephanie forgotten for the moment. Anna would never let her mother know this, but she'd overheard enough comparisons of decorating schemes and furniture grades in her childhood that she could instantly catalog the items in a room and give a rough guess at both their cost and quality. Someone with taste and money had taken trouble with Mason's bedroom, choosing pieces like the Stickley dresser and armoire.

But unlike the coldly "done" rooms Anna's mom had created, Mason's was personal. An acoustic guitar leaned against the wall. The big, complicated watch he'd worn the other night lay on the dresser next to three framed photos of Christian.

On the wall next to a door leading, she guessed, to a bathroom, were two ceramic handprints—Christian's no doubt. Anna turned a complete circle, sweeping the camera over each surface. There wasn't one thing in this room to indicate Mason had ever been in Five Star.

Not a photo, gold record or piece of memorabilia. David Giles's home theater was a shrine to the band. Where was Mason's ego trip? Where were the mirrored ceiling, the shag rug, the obvious signs that a rock star lived here?

Nothing. This room was *Traditional Home* not *Rolling Stone*. She could imagine Mason dressing for the wedding, untied bow tie hanging around his neck, as he deftly inserted his studs, the tux jacket spread out on the bed. She swung the camera back. That bed. Right there.

"So, uh, why are you dressing here?"

"It's easier. Mason's walking me down the aisle and we're starting from the community center. My folks passed on a few years ago, so this is my family."

"I'm sorry," Anna said.

"I miss them. Who wouldn't? But Mulligans is... I'm happy to have these people."

While Stephanie spoke, Anna had edged closer to the bed. The thick cotton comforter was a masculine combination of chalk blue, cream and brown stripes piped in contrasting black. Everything was pulled tight and tucked in tighter. She counted six pillows and the throw on the end was...she leaned in to let it brush her calf...cashmere. Someone liked to be comfortable.

"Damn it," Stephanie said, startling Anna backward. "Sorry. I hope bridal cursing doesn't offend you. This veil is killing me."

The comb holding the veil had lost its battle and was now in full flight toward the floor. As Stephanie got up, she said, "I have bobby pins in the bathroom. I'm going to anchor this sucker in there for good this time."

"You want help?" Anna asked.

"If I do it myself I can't blame you later when it falls out again. Don't film me, though. I don't want cursing in my wedding video!"

Stephanie disappeared through a door next to the armoire. Anna eyed the bed, huge and radiating comfort. The exact opposite of the lumpy foam thing she'd been sleeping on for the past few months. It must be a king-size. How long had it been since she'd slept in a real bed? The odd contrasts of soft and hard on Mason's intrigued her. What would she find out about the man if she…

But she shouldn't. She really shouldn't. It was his *bed*. *Exactly*.

She sat down. Gave the mattress a small, experimental bounce. Jake's ratty foldout would have tipped her off for that. This one barely registered the movement. Stable and strong.

"Thanks for doing this," Stephanie called from the other room. "I'm a huge goof about weddings. I think Brian thought I was actually going to flip out without this scene in the video."

Putting the camera down next to her, Anna brushed her hand over the comforter. Nice thick cotton. Good choice. Sensible but pleasing to the touch. She stroked it again as she said, "I love weddings, too. I spent hours planning mine when I was a kid."

She had to find out what it felt like. With a quick glance at the bathroom door, she lay down. Gently, so she wouldn't disturb anything. She'd put in so many hours on Jake's piece of junk that didn't deserve to be called a bed. She deserved this. She closed her eyes. Oh yes, this was a good bed. A very nice bed. Firm mattress. Firm pillows. *Firm. Mmm.* She liked firm.

She took a deep breath. Not because she was sniffing the sheets. Because she would never sniff the sheets. Not on purpose. She just needed some air. Because the room was hot. Or she was hot. Or something. But it was possible Mason's sheets smelled of lemon mixed with something spicy. She sniffed again. Yes, definitely lemon. And what was that spicy thing? Clove?

Anna stretched sideways, dropping one high heel off the side of the bed so she could tuck her toes into the soft cashmere throw. It had been years since she'd touched cashmere. Couldn't have imagined the luxurious feel of this one. For one second, she wondered what it would be like to lie here for real. Next to Mason, wrapped in his soft throw, touching his firm shoulders…

"You've never been married?" Stephanie asked, interrupting her fantasy.

Three bland boyfriends ago Chad had proposed. She might long for the dream day, but she couldn't say yes to a man who thought reruns of *Happy Days* were stimulating.

Anna would not live the kinds of lies her parents had. So why was she thinking of Mason *again* and what was that twinge of regret? She didn't *regret* not being married. She *reveled* in her freedom.

"Never been and probably never will," she said, perhaps too heartily. This bed was so comfy she could imagine staying here for a long time. She sank into it, pulling the cashmere up with the toes of one foot as she took a deeper sniff of the pillow. "I have too much to do, you know?"

"Like napping in my bed?"

Mason's gravelly voice touched every one of her nerve

endings. She sat up so quickly she almost fell on the floor. *Where the hell had he come from?*

His tie was still untied, the ends hanging down to the middle of his crisp white shirt. The spiked front of his hair was damp from the shower. He'd been in here recently, dressing, just as she'd imagined. *Lemon and spice.*

She fumbled for her shoe. *Where the hell was it?* "I was just, um, waiting for Stephanie. Because she had a veil problem. And she went in there. And I was waiting…" *Finally!* Her foot slid into the shoe and she grabbed her camera, standing fast. "You have a very nice bed."

For the first time in her life, Anna fully understood the phrase "to die of embarrassment." Unfortunately it was just a cliché and not an actual event. Dead would be better than still here in front of Mason. Stephanie saved her by coming out of the bathroom, glaring at him. "I sent you downstairs. This is a man-free zone."

He lifted one hand in protest. "I went. I forgot Christian's studs. I knocked." He looked at Anna again. "I guess you were both busy."

Anna discovered an urgent need to adjust the camera lens. Mason grabbed a small, black velvet box off the dresser and crossed to the door. Anna made the mistake of looking up and he was waiting for her, one hand on the open door. "Thank you," he murmured. "I like my bed, too."

He was gone before she could think of a reply.

"What's he talking about?" Stephanie asked, puzzled.

"Nothing," she answered. "Why don't you re-create the veil fixing here? I'll film you with no cursing." She and Stephanie indulged themselves for a few more minutes until Stephanie's maid of honor came back with the official wedding photographer in tow.

"I better go," Anna said.

Stephanie surprised her with a quick hug. "Thanks so much. I'm glad you were here."

Anna nodded, waiting for the other woman to release her. Stephanie pointed to an archway across the hall. "Back stairs. It'll be less crowded."

DOWNSTAIRS, ANNA DIDN'T realize she was passing Mason's office until she heard his voice. She tried to breeze past casually but one glance in and she stopped. She couldn't have looked away if she'd tried. She barely restrained herself from raising her camera.

Mason had his back to the door, his head bent in concentration as he tied Christian's bow tie. They were dressed identically in black, shawl-collar tuxedos.

Christian's head was tilted back to give his dad room. Anna watched, mesmerized by the combination of domesticity and masculinity. She'd just about made her legs move when Christian caught her eye. "Hey, Anna," he said.

"Hello again," Mason said without looking up. Without mentioning his bed. *Thank God for small favors.*

She edged into the office, knowing it made sense to avoid him until he'd forgotten about the bed, but irresistibly drawn by the scene. Mason's fingers moved deftly as he tightened the knot, pulling the ends precisely even. He held his bottom lip in his teeth as he worked and Anna knew then that whatever Mason had been when he was younger, he was completely a dad in this moment.

"Jake says tying a bow tie is harder than lighting a fire by rubbing sticks together," she said. "You ever think about offering classes in man skills?"

Chris stepped back and patted the tie, his hair falling

down over his eyes. He threw his dad a scowl that didn't hold any of the heat of his sullen looks the other night at dinner. "He'd do better with a girl-skills class. Accessories 101. He bought me studs because he said the rental ones were crap."

Mason put his hands on his hips, holding the edges of his jacket away from his slim waist as he scowled right back at his son. She remembered reading that a man's shoulder-to-hip ratio could trigger an instinctive cave-woman hormonal reaction if it was a particular number. Anna couldn't remember what the exact ratio was but the cave woman in her was pretty darn sure she was staring at a living, breathing example of it. *Get a grip.* Hormones were unprofessional.

"The rental studs *are* crap," Mason countered. "I'd have bought you a tux, too, if we didn't have to match Brian's rental."

"That'd be useful," Christian said, "'cause I'm going to dress like this all the time." He scuffed one patent-leather dress shoe on the wood floor.

"First wedding I was ever in," Mason said, "the tuxes were powder blue. The shirts had ruffles, also powder blue, and we wore white loafers."

Chris, in full teenage flight from paternal reminiscences, slipped past Anna toward the door. "Dad, the growing-up-Jersey stories scare people. You have *got* to keep them to yourself."

Anna saw Mason's eyes follow Chris as he left and knew there was a kid who hadn't walked out the door for the first day of school without a photo shoot. "You shouldn't tease him. You never wore a powder-blue tuxedo."

"First of all, it's my parental duty to tease my teenager

as often as possible. And second, this is New Jersey. I not only *wore* the blue tux, I *ate* the blue mashed potatoes."

She'd never seen Mason dressed anything but impeccably. "How old were you? Two?"

"Seventeen, maybe? It was Nick Kane's first marriage. Sheila was his girl from back home in Wayne. She picked the tuxes and Nick was too whipped to tell her we looked like a prom band."

"I can't imagine you agreeing to wear it."

Mason lost some of his good humor. "Five Star was my family. You don't say no to family." He shifted his feet and Anna saw him shove his memories aside. "You look...nice."

She was wearing her navy suit. She knew exactly how she looked in it. Invisible. Enveloped. Part of the background. The jacket had a high mandarin collar, buttons down the front, and hung in a shapeless-line past her hips. The skirt came to just below her knee and was neither slim nor full. She was a filmmaker, not a film star, she'd explained to Jake on the countless occasions when he'd tried to get her to buy something new. Her job was to observe, help people forget she was there so they'd relax on film.

So why was she happy she'd opted for the high heels she seldom wore? And was that her hand fiddling with the top button of her jacket? She shoved the rebellious hand into her pocket. Not that she would have unbuttoned the jacket anyway. She'd somehow lost her white blouse between the house she'd been sharing during her last film and Jake's. That morning she'd pulled on a T-shirt and buttoned up her jacket, figuring the stand-up collar would conceal the T-shirt.

"Do you care where we set up?" she asked.

"As long as you're not on top of Steph and Brian I'm fine."

"Okay. See you."

"See you, Anna," Mason said. Anna felt his eyes on her as she left the office. She refused to care if he'd noticed her shoes.

Then he called out from behind her and she realized he had come into the hall. "Save me a dance."

She turned and he raised his eyebrow again. Flirting? Challenging? Both? She wasn't sure. Her pulse skittered higher. She managed a short nod but didn't trust her voice as she continued toward the foyer. She'd decided to stop dating boring men, but that didn't mean she had to dive headlong into her client list just to spice things up. Even if her client smelled delicious and looked even better. Good thing she'd be long gone before the dancing started.

ANNA FILMED the beginning of the wedding but turned the camera off once the service started. She wouldn't use Brian and Stephanie's ceremony in what was essentially a sales pitch.

She slipped into a seat next to Jake and Rob near the front on the groom's side. After Stephanie and Brian exchanged rings, the priest stepped back. Anna winced when Mason and Christian left their positions flanking Brian to stand near the altar behind a set of microphones. Apparently she was the only one not exploiting the moment. This was what she'd been expecting all along. The ego that had been missing was about to rear its ugly head.

Rob leaned forward around Jake and whispered, "I can't believe he's going to sing."

"I can," Anna whispered back.

Jake gave them both the evil eye and they shut up, but

Anna crossed her arms, prepared to lose the little respect she'd developed for Mason.

He'd picked up a guitar and was watching Chris's face intently. At a slight nod from his son, Mason started playing. Chris sang the lead with Mason floating harmony behind him. The song was beautiful. The lyrics perfectly captured a man falling in love with his best friend, someone he feels completely comfortable with. By the time they'd gone through the chorus once and come back with a line about her sense of humor and being together all day and all night, Anna was sitting as openmouthed as any teenage fan girl.

Mason's hands on the guitar were as sure as they'd been tying Chris's tie before. He held the guitar as if it was an extension of himself, each chord strong and clear. His singing voice was a shade higher and smoother, all dark chocolate without the gravel of his speaking voice.

The way Mason looked at Chris and at Stephanie and Brian had Anna reaching for the tissues she'd hopefully stowed in her pocket. The four of them were family and Mason clearly didn't care who knew how he felt. His green eyes were unguarded as he looked long and carefully into the faces of the people he loved.

This song wasn't about Mason Star, it was a gift to Stephanie and Brian. A gorgeous, loving, lyrical present to them. Stephanie cried, Anna cried, every woman in the audience cried as Chris and Mason sang a love song for their friends.

Anna pressed her palms flat on the chair and watched Mason—he didn't look out at the audience, not once. He was singing but he was clearly not performing, and Anna was confused all over again. If he wasn't Mason Star, megastar, then who was he?

Once the rice was thrown, Anna packed up her camera. Jake and Rob had gone to get some footage of the guests and then they were meeting her at the car. She packed slowly, hoping someone would ask them to stay because she liked wedding receptions as much as she liked the weddings themselves. Anna was fascinated to study the ways people loved and let themselves be loved. Growing up as she had, with parents who had carefully constructed their image, Anna was a sucker for real emotions.

She edged around the group surrounding Stephanie and Brian. Ducking her head through the shoulder strap of the camera bag, she turned to go.

MASON HAD BEEN TALKING to Stephanie's cousin Ronnie when he noticed Anna packing up her camera. How he noticed her in that drab suit, he didn't know, except it seemed as if he was constantly aware of where she was. When she bent to lift the bag and he got a nice look at her sweetly curved ass, which even that hideous piece of old-lady costuming couldn't conceal, he excused himself and went to her.

"How are things going?"

She tugged the strap of the camera bag and it pulled the collar of her jacket open, giving him a glimpse of a hot-orange shirt. Damn. That was the first color he'd seen her wear. The jacket had to go. It was spoiling his view of Anna in her orange shirt. When she noticed him looking, she tugged her jacket back in place, patting it closed.

"We're going to head out," she said. "I think we got enough footage for what we need."

They weren't staying? Of course not. Why would they? Mulligans was a job for them. It didn't mean anything.

"Glad you got what you need." He heard how rude he sounded but he couldn't manage to be polite.

Anna looked as if she was going to say something but thought better of it. "We'll be back on Monday."

"Actually," Jake said as he and Rob approached, "Stephanie asked us to stay." He lifted the bag he was holding. "You have someplace we can stash our gear?"

"Please tell me you didn't ask them if we could stay." Anna whirled on Rob. "Tell me he didn't ask them."

"Jake?" Rob said. "Jake's much too well bred for that."

Anna looked relieved for a half second before Rob added, "I asked them."

"Oh, Rob. How could you? It's their wedding."

"And you love weddings. If you had to leave early you'd have moped all night. Plus, Chris said the band is great. It's all eighties covers." Rob patted her arm. "Stephanie said we didn't need an invitation. Apparently it was implied."

Anna hesitated, looking toward Stephanie and Brian as if she'd see something to help her make up her mind. She really did want to stay, Mason realized. That shouldn't have mattered to him. But it did.

"Besides, you owe me a dance." Mason grabbed Jake's bag, not giving her any more time to think. "I'll put your stuff in my office." He squinted at Anna. "You hot? Want me to take your jacket?"

Why did she look nervous when she touched the top button again and shook her head? All he knew was that jacket was going down.

LATER, AFTER HE'D MADE the toast and Stephanie cried all over him again and they'd all taken a turn or two through the buffet line, Mason came across Anna in the crowd watching Stephanie and Brian have their first dance. The evening was certainly warm enough that she could have at least unbuttoned the damn jacket, but it was still covering everything he wanted to see.

"I wouldn't have pegged you for a wedding groupie," he said as he came up behind her. Brian twirled Steph as the song went into the last chorus. Mason hated the prick of loneliness he felt seeing them married and so wrapped up in each other.

"I'm full of hidden depths," Anna answered with a shrug, a hint of her breasts moving under the jacket. He was well aware of her hidden depths. The thing that scared him was how much he wanted to explore them. He took another stab at the wardrobe-removal offensive. "Stephanie gave me the okay to take off my jacket. Apparently Emily Post has rules about this stuff, but Steph said the bride trumps etiquette. So it's safe, if you want to take yours off, too."

She didn't bite. Didn't even glance away from the dancing.

"Is this the first wedding you've held here?" she asked.

"What? Yeah. It was Brian's idea."

"You should do this more often."

"I'll see if we can interest some of the single residents," he answered, a little confused about her point.

"No. Have parties. Invite the neighbors in." She went back to studying the dance and he went back to studying her. He had no idea what she'd been doing earlier up in his room. All he knew was what he'd felt when he'd seen her rolling around on his bed.

He was attracted to Anna. *Ha. Attracted.* He wanted her. Bad. In his bed. Against a wall. Under him. Over him. Didn't matter as long as it was her and him.

Stephanie's face glowed as she and Brian moved together to the music. What would that feel like? To know you'd found the right person at the right time? He edged closer to Anna. The sleeve of her jacket brushed his wrist.

Anna was focused on the dance. "When they look at each other you can tell they're going to be together forever." She glanced at him finally. "That was a gorgeous song. The one you and Christian did. Did you write it for Stephanie and Brian?"

He laughed before he realized she was serious. "What?"

"I mean, for their wedding, or was it something you had that just fit?"

"Anna, that was 'Crazy Love.' Van Morrison recorded it on *Moondance* in 1970, and since then it's been covered by everyone from Helen Reddy to Rod Stewart to me and my kid."

The look on her face was priceless. How could someone as sharp as her be so hopeless about music?

"Seriously?"

And then he made a mistake. He meant it to be a joke but Brian and Stephanie finished the dance and everyone cheered around them and he had to lean close to hum the tune. Because of how close they were, how good she smelled, how much he wanted to plunge his hands into her hair, it didn't come out as funny. It came out as a come-on.

The crowd pressed forward, eager to start dancing. He was jostled against Anna. He watched as her expression changed from thoughtful to embarrassed to flushed—more because of the way their bodies were pressed together than because she hadn't recognized the song.

A smart man would have backed off. Hell, on any

other day, he would have backed off. But Stephanie and Brian were out there wrapped up in each other and he'd seen Anna in his bed. And he needed to get that jacket off her. Wanted her to wrap herself around him. He took another half step closer and slid one hand down her back, pretending to steady her.

"I never know stuff about music, I just listen to what I like," she said as she tried to back up. But there were people behind her and his hand was pressing her toward him and she didn't make it far at all.

He took another step forward and her heels were on the dance floor and he decided that what he needed to do right now was dance with this woman.

"I'm going to see to your musical education." Wearing the delinquent love-me grin that never failed him, he lifted her hand, and she didn't try to take it back. That was a clear enough sign for him. "This song, "Living on a Prayer," was recorded right here in New Jersey by a man named Jon Bon Jovi."

He'd maneuvered them all the way onto the dance floor. One more step and the crowd would close up behind him. "Regardless of what you or I might think about the depth of his musical gifts, Mr. Bon Jovi knows how to rock the crowd." His lips were close to her ear and his voice was a tight, rough whisper. "Ready for that dance, Anna?"

IT WASN'T THAT she didn't know what he was doing. Or suspect. She wasn't *stupid*. Mostly.

It was just the way he did it. One step at a time. Pressing against her the whole time. Not in a rude way. Not intruding. Only the gentle pressure of the warm length of him, impossibly handsome with the sleeves of his tuxedo shirt rolled back to expose his long, guitar-playing hands.

And then one of those hands was holding hers and the other one was on her back, pressing gently, exploring in a way that was deliciously, subtly thrilling. The tease of a touch that wouldn't progress but wouldn't end.

Her nerves jumped, making her hyperaware of him. The clean, lemon spice scent coming from his shirt. The muscles moving in his thighs. His firm stomach. Which reminded her of his firm bed. Which made her think about him in the bed.

But what the hell was she doing?

The dance floor was hard under her heels and the crowd pressed in tighter. He took her hand and the space behind him closed. The band started playing and the crowd was moving. He smiled and made that joke about Bon Jovi, which, if she was going to be honest, was a band she loved with her entire disreputable pop-music-loving soul.

He asked her to dance with that smile that spoke to every irresponsible urge she'd ever had and her brain said *run* in exact unison with her mouth saying, "Lead the way."

She might have bad taste in music, but Anna loved to dance. It wasn't often she'd danced with anyone who could keep up with her. But Mason wasn't a rock star for nothing. The man had moves.

Anna raised her arms and laughed out loud and let herself go. "Living on a Prayer" led into "Jessie's Girl" and straight on to a Def Leppard/Bay City Rollers combo that left her gasping for air. She couldn't remember the last time she'd danced with someone who had as much sense of drama and fun as her. Usually she had to hold back, tone it down, but Mason stayed with her and every time she thought he would bow out to sit down he turned it on a little more.

He moved his hips in a way that made Anna think about his bed again, so she moved her gaze to his shoulders, which didn't help because the white shirt was pulled tight, giving a wicked hint of lean muscles. Before she lost her mind completely and reached for him, she looked up and saw that his eyes were on her, watching her hips and her breasts. And, God help her, she put an extra shimmy in her ass just to make him sweat.

She pulled the front of her jacket away from her chest. She needed air. If only she wasn't wearing this damn T-shirt. The dancing had heated her up but she suspected that waist-to-shoulder ratio cave-woman thing was also playing a role. Could anything accentuate the perfect V of Mason's broad shoulders and tapered waist better than the stark white tailored shirt and black cummerbund and suspenders? Watching him grind his hips to the dirty intro to "Pour Some Sugar on Me," Anna thought she might, for the first time in her life, be the one to call it quits.

He leaned in close, one hand on her shoulder. "You have to be roasting. Take your jacket off."

She moved away a step and smiled mysteriously. Let him think she was hiding something worth seeing.

The music slowed and she recognized the opening line to "Hungry Heart," one of her all-time favorite Bruce Springsteen songs. The tricky thing, though, was it wasn't clearly a slow song and wasn't clearly a fast song. She didn't know if she should keep dancing or try to make her way off the dance floor.

Mason grabbed both her hands and the decision was

made for her. He pulled her closer and wrapped one hand around her waist while the other covered her fingers and held them against his chest.

"Bruce was really reaching on this one," he said, his lips stirring the hair near her ear, sending shivers down her spine. "The first line is good but then…"

"Then it stays awesome right through the last line," she countered.

He moved their joined hands slightly and Anna felt a tug on the top button of her jacket. His fingers twisted in hers and the button was undone. He was taking off her jacket. Without asking. Right now.

Holding hands with a man while he undressed her in public, the way she was both helping and helpless to stop him, was so unbelievably sexy Anna couldn't say anything, not even when he guided their joined hands lower to the second button. By the time he got to the third, she was practically panting.

This time he had trouble and their joined fingers pressed into the tender skin of her belly, the insistent rubbing sent sparks straight through her. She had to stop him. Move back, let go of his hand, slap his face.

One more button and then she'd stop this.

Leaning her shoulder into his, she twisted slightly to give him better access. When the third button came undone, he spun them in a lazy circle while Bruce wailed and Mason moved their hands lower to the last button. She wanted him to get it open fast so she could shove the stupid jacket off and have nothing between them but the thin cotton of their shirts. She wanted him to go slow so he'd keep his fingers there, low on her belly where she could keep imagining them straying even lower, still twisting and touching.

The button came free, her jacket opened and she sighed. Or he did. Or the crowd did around them. It was hard to think with the music and the heat. With his hand sliding up her side, under the jacket now, lifting it off her collarbone, tugging it down her shoulder and then sliding it slow and slower off her arm.

His eyes were on hers, that insane green sparking with a combination of passion and confidence and humor Anna had never seen in the eyes of any man. It was the sexiest thing in the world. And it was all hers. She forgot about keeping her shirt covered, forgot about the other people and drank Mason in.

He pulled her closer to take the other sleeve off. While she was tight against his chest, he leaned down to whisper, "Sorry. You looked hot."

She pressed closer to him, her breasts tight with desire. The song ended and the band announced they were taking a break. Mason's right hand slid farther down her back to press her ass and he brought their joined hands up again close to her chest, pressing her back while he bent his head to her neck. Her jacket fell to the ground unnoticed. She arched toward him.

He jerked backward, dropping her hand and breaking the contact. Anna felt the shift like a blast of air-conditioning.

Mason leaned closer to her breasts and then with his head still bent over them, peered up at her. "Does your shirt say Try Mama's Hot Sauce?"

He tried to look at it again but she leaned past him, recovering her jacket and shrugging it on. She started to button it back up, but he caught her hands in his and stopped her.

"One more peek." He was practically giddy.

She went for dignified. "I misplaced my blouse."

"You…" He had to put his hand over his mouth to stem the laughter. "You *misplaced* your blouse? What about a different blouse? Or a shirt that doesn't say Mama's Hot Sauce?"

He was so happy with that witty comment that he busted up laughing again.

"At least my shirt's not rented."

"Ouch, that hurts," Mason said insincerely. "I'm only wearing this because Stephanie made me. I have a tuxedo and three shirts I can wear with it. That way if I misplace one…"

Anna gave him a swat on the arm. "You're not that funny."

He pulled at the lapels of her jacket. "Let me see again because I'm starting to think it didn't say 'hot sauce.'"

Anna yanked away from his hands. "So I only own one blouse which I've misplaced. So I don't have a million shirts hanging in my closet. I don't even have a closet. I have a duffel bag. Which suits me fine because I'm not contributing to our nutso overconsumption."

He'd stopped reaching for her jacket and was listening, eyes on hers, not looking quite so amused any more. She was irritated but not mad. As a matter of fact, she was irritated because she was pretty sure he'd been about to kiss her neck. Which, at the time, had seemed like a most excellent idea. And she'd missed her chance and couldn't imagine being stupid enough to get in position for another round anytime soon.

"You want to get a drink?" she asked.

He nodded. She almost missed it but just before they

started walking, he glanced around. The same way her mother would have glanced around to see if anyone at the country club had seen Anna drop her fork.

"Is something wrong?"

"No. You're fine."

"I wouldn't want my shirt to bother Stephanie. Or anyone else."

"I said you're fine. Let's go." He smiled, but the spark was missing from his green eyes. This smile was an act through and through.

And that was that, Anna thought. From tear your clothes off to fake smile in two minutes. She thought that might be a record.

MASON WAS PISSED at himself. He'd taken off the damn jacket in the first place. And now she knew he was uncomfortable. He wished he wasn't. He knew he shouldn't be. It was just, he'd spent so many years trying to fit in, to be a normal, middle-class, suburban dad. And there were still times when he screwed it up. She thought it was about the shirt but that wasn't it. It was the whole thing. Her. He shouldn't have danced with her. He shouldn't have taken it so far. He wanted her to make the movie about Mulligans, get him his zoning waivers and then leave him alone.

But he'd been lonely, watching Steph and Brian and knowing he'd never have that. And there was Anna. She'd been smoking hot on the dance floor. Even in the world's ugliest suit, she could move, and he loved watching her do it. He loved knowing that he was pushing her on, that the two of them were throwing sparks. It all felt so good. Right.

But then he'd seen her shirt and, yeah, it was funny.

Nice for her for being comfortable in her own skin. But it wasn't normal. She broke all kinds of rules and didn't care who knew it. He couldn't afford to be connected to that.

It had been hard to figure out how to fit in in the suburbs. He didn't know the simplest stuff. Did dads join the PTA? How often did you mow the grass? If your kid was home sick, did you write "Dear Mrs." in the note or use the teacher's first name? There were rules on top of rules and he'd been on edge for what felt like years while he watched and mimicked his neighbors. He'd never become part of their circle or really gotten to know them, but he thought he'd gotten pretty good at faking he was one of them.

Anna wanted to disturb all that. Here, in his home, with Chris in such a vulnerable place. And he'd been so stupid that he'd gone dirty dancing with her. If he'd wanted to prove that he was still the same idiot he'd been when he was twenty, he couldn't have picked a better tactic.

God, he could shoot himself. He straightened his shoulders and plastered a smile on his face and escorted her over to the bar. He kept one hand lightly, politely, on her arm. He clamped down hard on his self-control, ignoring the warmth of her skin. He'd made one bad decision tonight, but that didn't mean he couldn't recover. He'd just have to be sure it didn't happen again.

Stephanie and Brian were standing at the bar. They were each holding a wine goblet filled with ice water and lemon wedges. Stephanie's face was flushed and Mason noticed she'd switched out of her heels and into a pair of Converse high-tops with baby's breath glued around the ankle.

He gestured down at her feet. "The flowers are a nice touch. Classy."

Stephanie passed a glass of water to Anna and a second one to him. Then she lifted her glass. "A toast. To Mason and his new career as a wedding planner." They all touched glasses. While Mason was still gulping water, Stephanie nudged Anna.

"That's a very funny shirt. Where'd you get it?"

"I made a commercial for Mama. It was a gift." Anna didn't look at him when she said it. She pushed her hands into her hair, in the gesture he was starting to realize meant she was feeling impatient, and twisted it back behind her ears. He remembered watching her do that the first night they met, before he even knew her.

She was still addressing Stephanie. "Before you ask, no, I don't have another shirt. I wore this one on purpose to your wedding."

Stephanie and Mason spoke at once.

"I wasn't going to ask."

"She doesn't have a closet."

Anna glared at him, but Stephanie looked at her with new interest. Brian lifted an eyebrow at Mason and shook his head discreetly, but the damage was done. Stephanie was on the trail of someone she could help. You don't become a public defender if you can pass up the chance to help someone.

"No closet? What, like you have a studio?"

"No, like I sleep on Jake's foldout bed."

Stephanie blinked. "Oh."

"She travels for work," Mason said quickly.

"Will you stop making excuses for me?" Anna snapped. "It's okay that I don't have a closet."

Jake and Rob walked up in time to hear Anna's protest.

"You want a closet?" Jake asked. "Does it have to be a whole closet? It's not as if you have any stuff."

"Jake. Stephanie. All you kind people, I do not want a closet," Anna said.

Mason wasn't sure when he stopped feeling uncomfortable and started to enjoy watching Anna fight off the well-intentioned prying of his friend and the not-so-well-intentioned ribbing of her brother.

"Why are you wearing that shirt?" Rob asked. He glanced from Stephanie to Brian. "She has a perfectly nice blouse she usually wears with the suit…"

"I misplaced my blouse."

"This is why you need to open the bank vault and invest in some stuff, Anna." He half turned to Stephanie. "If it's not made by Nokia or Canon, Anna pretty much has no interest."

Anna held up a hand and ticked the points off wearily as she said, "I don't have a closet or a house or an extra fancy shirt and I sleep on a foldout bed. I move around a lot. The shirt I'm wearing was a gift from a woman who sells hot sauce. And I'm happy with my life."

"You weren't so happy about the water," Jake put in.

Mason had always wanted a sibling. Watching Anna and Jake tweak each other was fun. He couldn't resist. "The water?"

"The water is your fault, Jake," Anna said. "It has nothing to do with my lifestyle."

"The water is so not my fault. It's Rob's fault. He's the one that cut the pipe."

Rob looked irritated now. "The schematic clearly said

the smaller one was the water. If things had been marked correctly—"

"If you'd called a licensed plumber," Jake amended.

"I *did* call a licensed plumber."

"After you cut through our water pipe with a hacksaw 'cause you thought it was an old steam pipe."

Mason hadn't enjoyed anything this much in a long time. He was almost disappointed when Stephanie reached out to clasp Anna's hands. "Feel free to say no, but if you want it, my house is empty right now. You can move in for a while." She included Jake and Rob. "You all can. Until the water's back on at least."

Anna was already shaking her head when Jake said, "That'd be great. We'd only be there a few days but maybe Anna would like to stay on. You've been at our house so long you're probably going stir-crazy, right?"

Anna was about to say she was fine where she was when she noticed the hand Jake had around Rob's waist. The way they were leaning on each other in exactly the same comfortable closeness that Stephanie and Brian were sharing.

They hadn't been alone in their place in the six weeks since she'd moved in. Privacy was hard to come by in cramped quarters set up for two but making room for three. It was time for her to move out.

THE RECEPTION WENT full throttle until close to midnight, but Anna felt a confusing mix of disappointment and disconnection. She hadn't talked to Mason after the jacket debacle. She'd danced some more, once with Jake and Rob and later with a group of women Stephanie dragged together. She was conscious of being an outsider in both groups, though, and didn't really enjoy it. She'd thought about asking Jake to take her home but that would have led to questions she didn't feel like answering. So she hung on, smiling and chatting and feeling utterly out of place.

This was exactly why she should have stayed behind the camera. She should never have agreed to dance with Mason. It was the way she'd felt her last year of high school—Terri was gone and everyone was whispering about what happened and they looked at Anna differently. She'd always been popular, her sense of fun and interest in other people making her a natural magnet for groups of friends. But that year she was an outcast. People said Terri never would have been on the bus if Anna hadn't teased her into going onstage.

She was sitting at a round table watching the groups of people laughing around her, picking morosely at a second piece of cake and wishing she were back at Jake's. Curling up in her pathetic bed was all she could think about.

Chris flopped into the seat across from her, and his friend, Alex, took the one next to him. They'd clearly been dancing. Both boys had shucked their jackets and Chris's shirtsleeves were rolled up to his biceps while Alex's ponytail glistened with sweat.

"Hey," Chris said. Anna "hey'd" him back.

"You don't like the cake?" Chris asked.

Anna poked her fork in deeper and twisted. "No. I like it fine. I'm just—" She remembered who she was talking to and figured it wouldn't be a good idea to tell Mason's kid she was sulking because she'd gotten gypped out of her kiss on the dance floor. "I've had enough." She poked the cake again. "What's up?"

Alex looked at Chris. They wanted something and Chris was the spokesperson.

"The other night at dinner, my dad said, you know, no videos."

She nodded, sure now that she should have left hours ago. This wasn't a safe conversation.

"I'll be eighteen in January. And if we're going out on tour, we need a video. So we wanted to know how that works, how we can, you know, hire you?"

Chris ducked his head, glancing sideways at Alex who gave him the least discreet thumbs-up ever.

As mad as she was at Mason for caring about her stupid shirt, she felt sorry for him. This kid was a heartbreaker, one minute an adult, the next a belligerent, prickly teenager. And the next as unsure of himself as a six-year-old stepping up to the plate in T-ball the first time.

Anna shoved the ruined cake away. "You guys were great the other night. I'd love to do a video with you. But my brother is quitting our company, I don't know if you know that?"

Chris shook his head.

"So we're down to our last two projects. The Mulligans one and then Five Star. After that, Blue Maverick is over." She still couldn't say that without a twist of panic in her belly.

Christian sat up and the nervous boy was gone, replaced by an angry man. "What about Five Star?"

Perfect, just perfect, Walsh. Mason was keeping secrets. Why hadn't she left? Would Chris believe she had sudden-onset laryngitis?

"We haven't started anything. It's —"

Anna hadn't seen him approaching, but suddenly Mason was there, his hands gripping the back of the chair next to Chris. "What's up, guys?" The tension in his white-knuckled grip gave the lie to his casual words. Obviously he'd heard what they were talking about.

"Nothing," Christian said as he shoved his chair back and stood. "I asked Anna if she'd take me for ice cream."

"Chris, wait a second," Mason said. But it was too late. The kid was gone.

Alex stood, too, looking confused. "I guess I'll go get more cake," he muttered before he slunk away.

Mason leaned over the table, glaring at her. The heat in his green eyes was pure anger, but the tight line of his mouth showed how hard he was holding himself in. "You and I have a deal. It's got nothing to do with him. Back off."

"Mason, calm down. I didn't—"

"Back off. That's all I'm saying. I don't care what you know or think you know. That's my kid and he's got no part in this."

She was shaken by the intensity of his reaction, but she knew the conversation with Chris had been wrong. Even if it hadn't been entirely her fault. "I didn't realize he didn't know. I'm sorry."

"I told you I don't talk about Five Star. Did you think I was kidding?"

No. She'd thought he meant he didn't talk about it to the press. It never occurred to her that he didn't talk about Five Star with Chris. What layers of lies were behind his silence?

"I'm sorry," she said. "I didn't realize."

He shoved himself upright. "I'm going to bed. Your stuff's in my office. The key is on the doorjamb."

She watched him walk off. He moved easily through the crowd but he didn't talk to anyone or even say goodbye to Stephanie and Brian. He looked utterly alone. As alone as she felt.

BACK AT JAKE'S finally, she pulled on her pajamas but left her suit lying on the floor. She gave the pile of discarded clothes a kick to move it closer to the top of the foam bed. If she tilted her head just right on the pillow, she could still smell the lemon-spice scent of him on her jacket. She drifted off imagining a strong arm wrapped over her, soft cashmere cradling her, holding him close and feeling him hold her.

CHAPTER EIGHT

SHE WAS PACKING her duffel bag when Jake knocked on the door frame.

"Got all your stuff?"

Anna nodded. The plumber had shown up that morning at Rob and Jake's and the water was back on, so she was moving into Stephanie's by herself.

"I saw you dancing with our client," Jake said as he leaned against the door, crossing his legs. "Is that a new service we're offering?"

"Shut up."

"Seriously. Did you kiss him? 'Cause it looked like more than dancing, if you know what I mean." Her brother wiggled his eyebrows in a dead-on imitation of a horny fifteen-year-old.

"Shut up, Jake."

"But did you kiss him?"

"He's a client. I can't kiss him."

"Can't isn't the same as don't want to."

"Oh God, who are you now? My middle-school diary?"

"Anna." He'd stopped joking. His brown eyes were so dear and so full of love she almost couldn't look at him. She pretended to focus on removing the last few T-shirts from the bottom of the steamer trunk. "You looked happy, Anna. You were dancing and you looked happy."

She wasn't sure what to say. "It was a wedding—I got carried away."

"What happened to rule Number 1? No lying?"

"Fine." She straightened up but kept her eyes on the shirts she was rolling to pack. "I find Mason attractive. He's fun to dance with. But I won't let it go further than that. I can't."

"You can if we don't do the Five Star movie."

She dropped the shirt she was holding. Jake was still leaning on the door frame but his posture was anything but relaxed. "What are you talking about?"

"I'm talking about you're my sister and I love you." He pushed off the door and crossed to put an arm across her shoulders. "For the first time in forever, you looked as happy as you do with a camera, except you weren't filming anything."

"It was just a dance."

"God, Anna, am I talking to Mom? Tell the truth."

She shrugged off his arm before she slapped her last T-shirt in the bag and tugged the zipper closed. "I'm not lying."

Jake waited.

Anna tried to hold his gaze but in the end she caved. She didn't have to say out loud that she'd been falling for Mason—Jake would know. She focused on the real problem. The only one she was willing to face. "I owe Terri."

"I know. But when I think about what you're willing to give up to get to the truth… You're so afraid of living a lie that you've almost given up living. Mason's moved on and he doesn't want to talk about the crash. Think about what this movie could do to Mulligans. Whatever happened to Terri is in the past. Maybe you need to think about the future."

Anna counted to ten. She counted to ten again. Didn't help. "You know what, Jake? You opted out of my future the day you quit Blue Maverick. If you want off the movie, tell me. But if you're in, be in, and forget about talking me out of it."

"I'm in. But being in on this project means the same thing it always did. If I see a problem, I'm going to bring it up. Right now I think it's possible we might have a problem. I'm not saying we should stop, but I do think we have to consider what we're doing and why."

"Fine," Anna said, sounding snotty even to herself.

"Fine," Jake answered just as snottily. But he grabbed her duffel off the bed and carried it downstairs for her. It wasn't an apology but it was him showing her he was still with her.

ANNA STUDIED Stephanie's house. It was tall, thin and covered in black shingles. The front door was painted dark, luscious lipstick red. Planting boxes hanging off the porch railing were filled with red and purple and white flowers. Anna thought the place looked mysterious, secretive and sexy, especially when compared to the characterless suburban castles on either side of it.

Stephanie had been passionate about the fact that she was holding out for a "real" offer. So far she'd been deluged with people wanting to buy the place as a teardown, but she wanted a buyer who'd love the house.

Anna picked up her duffel and the box of dishes and things Rob had insisted she take with her and started up the walk. Rob and Jake were coming out the next day with all her work gear, cameras, lights, editing equipment. She loved this part of her peripatetic lifestyle. Every possibility in the world existed from now until she opened the front door. The last time she'd had a place to herself had been a house-sitting gig in Seattle. She was looking forward to being on her own.

The key stuck in the lock, but after she twisted it hard, she felt the catch slip and the front door opened. The house was small, one room wide and three deep. Stephanie told her this had been the stationmaster's house when Lakeland had been a rail hub. Anna shrugged the duffel higher on her shoulder and started to explore.

She liked the lines of the rooms, tall ceilings and mullioned windows. Old-fashioned plaster walls kept the house cool and made her feel secure. The walls were white everywhere she looked. Stephanie'd told her she'd meant to paint them but never got around to it.

In the dining room, she stopped to examine the built-in china cabinet, which looked original to the house. The drawers were all exactly sized to serve a particular organizational function and Anna appreciated the craftsmanship, even if she shuddered at the idea of eating dinner with so many tools and the rules that inevitably accompanied them.

The kitchen was tiny, white again, and so clean Anna stopped at the threshold, poking her head around the door frame before putting Rob's box down on the floor. It wasn't often that she took the time to cook for herself. Kitchens, even tiny ones, intimidated her. She'd come back later and put away the things Rob had packed.

Back in the front hall, she went up the stairs. There were three bedrooms and a bathroom. Only the front bedroom, with a view of the street outside and a side window looking onto the yard, had a bed, so Anna dropped her bag in there. The bed was made up with a dark blue comforter, serviceable but plain cotton twill. Two plump pillows rested against the simple white-washed headboard of what, if she wasn't mistaken, was a queen-size bed. And it was empty. All hers. She took a moment to let it sink in.

She put one hand out to test the mattress and then sat gingerly, bouncing gently.

Oh good Lord, she'd died and gone to heaven. After those long weeks at Jake's, she had a real bed, with a mattress and box springs. She could roll over. Heck, she could have restless sleep or nightmares or even *thrash* if she wanted to. She could—oh, no, she was not thinking about *that*. Jake and his stupid horny innuendos. She lay down and lifted the edge of the lace curtain to check out the yard.

Dropping the curtain, she bent to untie her boots before kicking them off. Then she stretched out and bunched both pillows under her head. This was going to be okay. She had a good feeling about this place. She could be alone here and figure out what she wanted to do after they finished the Five Star movie. Because no matter what Jake said or what Mason wanted, she owed Terri and she would tell that story. She was sure now the truth hadn't been told before and she was also sure who had the whole story. She just needed to deliver his movie first.

THE ONLY TROUBLE with that plan, she realized the next week, was that Mason had apparently changed his mind about the movie. He wouldn't take her calls. He wouldn't take Jake's calls. His cell phone went straight to voice mail and his office phone seemed to be disconnected.

Ordinarily she and Jake would have strategized a plan of attack. But this situation was complicated. The Mulligans movie was both a favor and a bribe. If Mason didn't want to do it anymore then he didn't owe her the Five Star story.

Jake said to give him time. Anna agreed. Not because she thought it was the right plan but because her feelings about Mason had her so screwed around she was glad for the break. She decided she'd call once every day and a half, leave a message and wait for him to come to her.

She spent the week settling into Stephanie's house. The quiet was a gift and a burden and an intimidating challenge.

She made dinner for herself in the tiny kitchen every night. Her recipe repertoire was limited and mostly included foods whose name started with the word *frozen* or *instant*. The night she had to chuck the teriyaki chicken that tasted like nothing so much as a big bowl of salt, she almost caved and walked the six blocks to Mulligans for the buffet. Mason had told her they wouldn't turn anyone away. He didn't have to talk to her, just make sure there were enough baked potatoes to go around.

She resisted, though. If he came back, it would be on his own terms. He'd been spooked at the wedding and pushing now would make that worse.

On Wednesday she made her call to Mason and when that got her exactly nowhere, she made a mistake. She called her mother.

"Mom?"

"Anna." Her mother's voice was flat. "I already spoke to Jake this week." Which was her way of reminding Anna of the rules. Her parents spoke to Jake and he was meant to convey all important details to Anna. That way they didn't have to deal with the inevitably messy, one-on-one communication with Anna.

"I know," Anna fumbled. "I have a new place I'm living. I thought maybe you might be able to give me some advice. About decorating."

"Why would you waste your time decorating a place you have no intention of staying in? Where is it? Where are you?"

Why had she made this call? She knew how her parents made her feel. Her mom didn't even know she was living in New Jersey. Not even an hour from home.

"Nowhere. Forget it. I'm sorry. Tell Dad I said hi."

"You're not making sense, Anna. Why did you call?"

"I don't know," Anna muttered.

Her mother pretended not to hear that and they managed another two minutes of uncomfortable chitchat, long enough that her mother could pretend everything was normal. When her mother said goodbye, Anna shut her phone with a snap.

That had been stupid. She grabbed her sweatshirt and headed out the door. She needed to walk. She went downtown to the Lakeland shopping district. Boutiques and specialty shops bursting with fall merchandise lined both sides of three blocks. She fell in love with the colors in the window display in a knitting store and found herself inside with no idea of what to do next.

"Can I help you?" A woman in an intricately textured sweater of pale lavender had materialized at her elbow. Anna, who'd happily worn a T-shirt and jeans every day for at least a decade and had never had a hobby, suddenly wanted that sweater. She wanted color. She wanted change. She wanted something delicate and frivolous and gorgeous next to her skin.

"That orange yarn in the window, with the knubby bits? I couldn't walk by it."

The woman moved to a rack of wooden bins and picked out a bundle of the orange yarn. Anna reached out to pet it. It felt so soft and was exactly the shade of a late-September sunset. "That's the one."

"Do you have a project in mind?"

"No. I never did this before."

Anna walked out with her yarn and a set of bamboo needles wrapped in tissue tucked in a yellow bag along with directions for how to knit a scarf. She thought about showing Mason her scarf. She'd pretend it was no big deal—just something she knitted up on the spur of the moment.

She knew he thought she didn't have any interests outside the film. Well, now she did. She was a knitter, knitteress, person who knitted. Whatever.

She continued along the street for another block, thinking about knitting, when she saw a sign advertising a Lakeland Neighborhood Association meeting.

She tore it off the pole but then realized similar signs were posted in many of the shop windows. *Oh, Mason.* Her heart sank knowing that he must be hurt to see the neighbors gathering support. Why wasn't he calling? He needed her.

Anna scanned the street for notices she could discreetly remove. Two women with the blond-streaked pageboy cuts she associated with country-club pools stared at her when she took a sign off the bulletin board outside the post office. Anna gave them a wide-eyed look as she pointed to the sign on the board, Official U.S. Postal Service Notices Only. She smirked. "It's the law."

She got as much of a kick out of watching their faces pickle up as she used to when the golf pro at her parents' country club kicked her off the course for not wearing proper attire.

She heard slow clapping and looked across the street. A stocky man stood under a faded marquee for the Lakeland Cinema. She ripped one of the signs in half and he whistled. She waited while an SUV barreled past and then crossed the street.

"I take it you're not a member of the Lakeland Neighborhood Association?"

The man snorted. He had dark eyes and his hair was cropped close to his scalp. He pointed a thumb over his shoulder. "You don't see any of those signs on my place, do you?"

The doors of the theater behind him were chained closed. "You're not open today?"

"Not open period. I'm moving south to live with my brother. This place is on the block, waiting for a buyer."

"So what's your interest in the Hate Club?" She lifted the signs she still held.

"No interest in them. I know too many folks who've been helped out by Mulligans. No way I want to see that place closed down. My nephew, Stevie, he lived there for two years—moved out in April. Got himself a job with the county. First time he's ever had a job. Imagine that? First job in his life and he's got to be at least forty. Why they want to shut a place down that helps people get up and going, I just don't know."

Anna reached into her pocket and pulled out her wallet. She opened it to pull out a business card. "Is Stevie local?"

The man nodded.

Anna stuck out her hand. "Anna Walsh, nice to meet you."

"Manny Alvarez. Likewise."

"I'm making a movie about Mulligans—working with Mason Star on it," she said. "I'd love to talk to your nephew and maybe to you again, this time on film. You think he'd be interested?"

"I tell you what, you come by anytime and I'm ready to go. I'm down here most days sorting the place out. I'll get in touch with Stevie. He's in Montclair but he don't mind coming over to Lakeland once in a while—check out the old stomping grounds, you know?"

Anna briefly considered kissing the man. He'd just handed her the movie framework. She'd been looking for a hook and now she had it.

Family reunion. She needed to get Mason to give her a list of everyone who'd ever lived at Mulligans. The Lakeland Neighborhood Association would be hard pressed to misrepresent the good done by Mulligans if she lined up a succession of shining examples.

She tried Mason's number again while she walked and got voice mail. If he didn't call her soon he was screwed and so was she. Anna wasn't used to letting the clients dictate the schedule like this but she'd let it go. She had to. Right now he held all the chips even if it did seem as if the residents association was upping the ante.

STEPHANIE AND BRIAN left for Hawaii the Monday after the wedding. Mason had promised he would get in touch if anything happened with the zoning board but he lied. Later that day when the mailman delivered a letter informing Mr. Mason Star that the next zoning hearing about Mulligans was scheduled for November fifteenth he printed the date on his desk calendar and then moved his pencil cup until it was positioned precisely over the date. November fifteenth was exactly two weeks after Anna had promised she'd deliver her movie. The movie he'd been hoping would solve the zoning issue once and for all. The movie he hadn't given her the go-ahead to start. She had left a voice mail that morning, which he deleted without listening to.

On Tuesday, he got a letter from Lakeland High School informing him that his child hadn't filled out a course schedule for his senior year. When he confronted Christian, the kid told him he could fill the schedule out himself since he was the one who cared. In one of his finest parenting moments ever, he did not sign Chris up for cosmetology and Latin. He did, however, fill the schedule out, forge his child's signature and mail it back. If Chris didn't like the classes, well, that was why they had an add/drop week, right? Jake left two messages. He deleted them both and turned off his cell phone.

On Wednesday he was in his office trying to get his putt back in shape, when the phone rang. The caller ID didn't show Anna's number so he picked it up. *Bad* idea. A reporter from MTV wanted him to confirm that he was going out on tour with Five Star in October. He pretended he was the receptionist and then pretended to take a message.

When he answered the phone a second time, it was a freelance reporter with a different story—she said Nick Kane had told Five Star to find another drummer unless they took Mason back and did Mason have any comment on that? No, he did not, he informed her, because his name was *Jason Star,* not Mason Star. After that he unplugged the phone. He turned on his cell phone just long enough to delete a message from Anna and one from Jake.

Thursday he hit on a solution. He went golfing. Drove himself out to Long Island where a buddy he'd met in rehab was the pro at a country club. He played eighteen holes, no cart. When he was finished he took a steam and then a shower. He had his shoes shined. By the time he'd sampled every personal grooming service the club offered except the manicure, it was time for dinner. His buddy invited him to sit in a poker game in the smoking lounge and he killed the rest of the evening losing eighty-seven dollars while nursing a club soda.

He went back out to the club every day for the next week. His long game still sucked and his short game showed no sign of returning. He won back his eighty-seven dollars but lost a bunch more and stopped counting. It didn't matter anyway—he had plenty of money. What he didn't have was any clue about what to do next with the movie or Mulligans or Anna or Chris or anything. So he golfed, lost money at poker and tried like hell to stop thinking.

He made it through six days with his new all-golf-no-thinking lifestyle. But then Friday morning he stopped in his office to pick up an extra sleeve of balls and found brochures and an application from a paternity-testing service that Chris must have left on his desk. And there, in his chair, was Louise, chin wobbling as she held out a sign she'd found taped to Mulligans's gate advertising yet another community meeting for the Roxanne Curtis Property Value Support Team.

Mason read the notice and then, with great drama, balled it up and tossed it in the trash. He hoped she'd think that was funny and that would end it, but Louise hadn't lived the kind of life where problems disappeared because you wanted them to. She tracked the piece of paper with her eyes and then went back to staring at him. Her sneak-ered feet barely brushed the floor as she swung the desk chair from side to side.

Mason crouched down and turned the chair, holding it steady so he and Louise were eye to eye. "Sorry you saw that."

Louise looked at him. He could see she was hoping he'd tell her something to let her know how much she had to worry. She didn't have enough faith to hope he'd tell her something that would make it all better.

"It's people talking, not anything you need to worry about."

"No one can make us move?"

Which was a question he wished she hadn't asked. Because the fact was, the zoning board could make Mulligans move. Louise had been homeless right before her mom went to rehab. When she'd first come to Mulligans, he'd given her a backpack filled with school supplies. She'd asked him to write her name and address on a piece of tape instead of directly on the tag in the backpack. In her experience, writing your address with permanent marker just led to a whole lot of crossing out.

"The people who are having that meeting can't make us do anything. They're rude and wrong and they're acting crazy. But Brian and Stephanie and me are doing everything we know how to do to make sure the people who *are* in charge listen to us."

"Can you make them listen?"

His mom would have lied to him in a heartbeat. Hell, she would have told him to shut up and quit bugging her five minutes ago. He couldn't do that. The point of this place was that they helped each other to be better. Louise had asked him to be straight with her. She deserved a real answer.

"I hope we can. But no matter what happens, we're sticking together. If we do move, I promise we'll go together."

She searched his face but he didn't think she found what she was looking for, because when she jumped down from the chair she said, "It's okay, Mason. I understand."

He knew exactly what she meant. How bleak it was when you were old enough to understand but couldn't do a thing to change anything. If you were little and the adults around you let chaos happen, you learned to cope. You stopped trusting and stopped hoping. As long as you could keep half a step ahead of the mess, you felt as if you had something. His safety net had been a Mets backpack. Whenever his mom made them move, he'd put his important things in the backpack and carried it himself. He was sure Louise had her own bag somewhere and that she was getting set to pack it again.

She was almost out the door when he said, "I'm going to do everything I can to fix this, Louise. Every single thing."

He knew he hadn't given her enough. She needed to know for sure it was going to be okay and he couldn't tell her that.

He sat down in the chair and let loose a string of curses that would have singed Roxanne Curtis's ears if she'd been there to hear them.

But she wasn't there. No one was there but him. He'd started this place, let Louise and all the others move in here, and set down roots. He'd said it was safe to hope.

It was up to him to follow through. Even if that meant opening doors he'd locked a long time ago. Even if it meant going back to the time and place where he'd lost faith in himself. Picking up the phone, he called Anna.

He got her voice mail, but he couldn't say what he needed to in a message.

He hoped she hadn't written him off. He didn't know what he'd do if his stupidity at the wedding had cost him his shot at the movie that might help save Mulligans.

RINGING THE DOORBELL at Stephanie's house and waiting on the porch felt weird. He'd gotten into the habit of knocking and walking in. But with Anna there he was back to good manners.

She yelled from inside, "It's open."

So much for manners.

He opened the door and almost turned back around when the music hit him. She was unbelievable. No one's taste was that bad.

The walls of the small entryway were painted a bright lime green that made him think of the fairway on number eight in the afternoon sun. He knew Stephanie hadn't gotten around to painting before she moved out, so Anna must have painted. This wasn't what he'd have expected from a woman whose entire wardrobe seemed to be black and white. Well, except for one memorable T-shirt.

Most of Steph's stuff was gone. All that was left in the living room was the blue couch and scratched coffee table. His footsteps echoed in the empty space. The place was familiar and strange at the same time. He leaned against the doorway to the living room and looked at

Anna stretched full-length on the floor, facing the bookcase built into the corner.

He didn't know what to say. He hated asking for help. Had no idea why she was lying on the floor. And at the moment, Anna's music was making it impossible for him to think, let alone beg.

"Can you please turn off the freaking John Denver?"

She turned her head. "Mason. What a surprise. I was sure you'd left the country." She turned back to looking at the empty bookcase.

He crouched down and poked at the volume on the iPod speakers on the floor near the doorway.

"Turn that up. He helps me think."

"He makes me vomit," Mason answered. She didn't seem to be paying attention, focused as she was on the empty bookcase. It was as if the messages she'd left never happened. As if she had no interest in why he'd suddenly appeared or in the two films hanging over them.

"What did Stephanie have in here?" she asked. "Just books?"

"Books. Pictures. A music box Brian gave her for her birthday. A music box which did not play John Denver because no one likes John Denver and that would have been a sucky birthday present."

She didn't even blink.

"I need books." She contemplated. "And pictures. For my shelves. Why are you dressed like that?"

He looked down at his navy pants, blue-and-white striped dress shirt and red V-neck sweater. What was wrong with the way he was dressed?

"I was going golfing."

"Dress code. Of course."

A headache was beginning behind his temples. "Are you lying on the floor for a reason or did this crappy song cause an aneurism?"

"You can't change my mind about John. Many have tried. None succeeded. 'Annie's Song' is plain and simple gorgeous."

"It's plain and simple. That's the problem. Some guy at Hallmark could have written it."

"If you stop making fun of my music I'll tell you why I'm lying on the floor."

He wanted to talk about the movie but if this was what she wanted... Besides, what the hell was she doing on the floor? "Deal."

"I'm decorating."

He looked around again. There was the iPod. Stephanie's couch and table. A vase or statue or something on the coffee table. He thought it was supposed to be a tulip but the colors were wrong, as if it had been painted in the dark. Maybe it was an eggplant. On the floor near the chair a pair of knitting needles skewered a tangle of orange yarn.

"The green is nice," he said. "Stephanie doesn't mind if you paint?"

"She said as long as I let her approve the colors, she's happy. She took the place off the market while I'm here."

"So for decorating, don't you need furniture?"

"First you plan. You see the room from as many angles as possible to know what will work." She crossed one foot over the other knee. "I'm at the visualizing stage."

"Annie's Song" had ended, but unfortunately the next song was Dionne Warwick complaining she couldn't find her way to San Jose. It was wrong that any song could make him wish for more John Denver.

He lay down on the floor next to her. She was clearly not interested in talking about the movies. "So what am I looking for?"

"The lines of the room. What it wants. Stuff like that."

"I think it wants some Bose speakers and this turntable system I saw on eBay."

She pushed his leg with her foot. "Boys. You're all alike."

"Jake has a turntable?"

"Bought it before they bought a kitchen table."

"I knew I liked him," Mason said.

"You didn't call him back, either."

Apparently now they were talking about the movie.

"I've been…"

She pushed herself up on one elbow, lacing her fingers in her curls to hold them off her face. She was so close he could see the dark ring around her lighter-brown irises.

"Don't you dare say you've been busy."

He shut his mouth.

She lay back down. "I'm sorry about talking to Christian," she said. "I would never have told him if I thought he didn't know. I understand if you want someone else to do the Mulligans movie. I just wish you'd tell me. You gotta get that thing going before these pod people who live around you get the upper hand."

"I'm here now," he said. "Ready to go when you say the word."

"Word," she said quietly.

He was pretty sure they were good again. Pretty sure it was him and Anna lying on the floor of her house with the movie settled between them. He felt surprisingly content. He missed Stephanie and Brian—having someone to talk to was comforting.

"I don't think the room wants that vase," he said. The songs had shifted again and thank God now the Black Crowes were on. That was a band he could get behind.

"I'm pretty sure no one wants that vase," Anna agreed. "I bought it kind of accidentally. It's so ugly I feel bad for it. I can't bring myself to throw it away."

"You're not very good at this decorating thing. I hired someone to do my place."

He could have sworn she actually shuddered. "Absolutely not. I grew up in a *decorator* house. Never again."

"Well, what's the rest of your stuff look like?"

"I don't know."

Mason sat up. This conversation was making his head hurt. "You know, I ask you perfectly ordinary questions and your answers are so weird it's like we're not in the same conversation."

She rolled her eyes. "I've never lived anywhere that was mine. I have this storage space in Jersey City—which is mostly for Blue Maverick, but I have a few things. I have to wait until Rob borrows his boss's truck to take me over."

"I have a truck," Mason offered before he really thought about what that would mean. Spending time with her that wasn't necessary.

She sat up, too. Her eyes were sparkling as she clapped her hands. "You want to go to Jersey City?"

"Absolutely not," Mason answered. "But I'll take you if you want to go."

She reached for her boots, which had been lying on the floor next to her. He watched her tug the laces tight, the slender bones in her wrist twisting as the supple muscles in her forearms tightened. He shoved his hands in his pockets, wishing that a less sexy award-winning filmmaker had shown up outside the zoning-board meeting that night.

He picked up the vase on the way past the table. She noticed and raised an eyebrow. "If that thing matches the decor in your house you better ask the decorator for your money back."

"The kids make stepping stones every spring. We're always looking for ceramic stuff to break up to use for the mosaics."

"I'm not positive it'll look better in small pieces, but please, feel free to try."

She pulled the door closed behind them and then gave an extra tug while she turned the key in the lock. She was so at home already the door trick was automatic for her. He wondered what she'd say if he pointed that out. Her nomadic lifestyle seemed pretty important to her. But if that was true then what the hell were they doing going to Jersey City to pick up her stuff?

CHAPTER NINE

"THIS IS IT." Anna pointed to a driveway on the left. "Sorry about the neighborhood. I guess this isn't the nice part of Jersey City."

Mason pulled into a space next to a Dumpster and put the truck in Park.

"Jersey City doesn't *have* a nice part." He eyed the former warehouse. "Maybe I should put it on my list of potential new towns for Mulligans. We couldn't be worse neighbors than this place."

"Kick-butt movie, Mason. Mulligans isn't going anywhere now that Blue Maverick's on board. Got it?"

He nodded and pocketed the keys. "I got it. Hearts and minds." Rounding the back of the truck, he popped the lock on the tailgate and lowered it. The duffel he kept on hand was tucked in behind the toolbox on the left. He sat on the tailgate and started to unlace his shoes.

"What are you doing?"

"Changing."

She stared at him.

"What? You didn't think I was going to move your stuff in my golf clothes, did you?"

"You have a 'get stuff out of storage' outfit, don't you?"

He took the sweater off and then unbuttoned the shirt.

She let him get it unbuttoned all the way and off one arm before turning her back. He wished he didn't feel so stupidly happy that she'd sneaked a peek.

She muttered half to herself, "I hope no one thinks we've pulled in here for a nooner."

His head was tangled in the T-shirt he'd pulled out of the duffel and he choked on his laugh. When he got loose he said, "No one would come here for a nooner. This is where people come to dispose of bodies not to have affairs."

"Still, you are practically naked."

"I'm dressed now," he said. Was he mistaken or did he hear a small sigh before she turned around? Whether she sighed or not, whether she peeked at his chest or not, none of it should matter because he wasn't about to get more involved with her than was absolutely necessary. He just wasn't.

Inside they signed the visitor log and rode the elevator to the tenth floor. Anna led him down the long rows of individual storage spaces, each chain-link enclosure securely padlocked.

"I love looking in these things. There's one full of hunting trophies. Like sport fish and deer heads. The stuff people are spending money to store, you know? Makes you wonder," she said as she slid the key into her lock. She opened the gate and stepped to the doorway. "Huh."

Quickly scanning the rectangular space, Mason felt uncomfortable. Two-thirds of the floor was filled with neatly boxed and labeled video and filmmaking equipment. The rest was the craziest mishmash of crap he'd ever seen outside a junk shop. Did Anna know?

"Look at what *I'm* paying money to store," she said.

Yep. She knew. "But this is your stuff. I mean, it means

something to you, right?" Although how the collection of mismatched furniture, a good third of it flat-out broken, could mean anything to anyone was beyond him.

"Not really," Anna said as she walked farther into the enclosure. "People gave me stuff or I picked it up and then when I'd move, I'd put the stuff here. I thought when I had a house sometime I'd want it."

He managed not to ask *why*, but it took some effort. "What's first? You want to make a pile and I'll start hauling stuff down?" he asked.

She didn't answer. Her back was to him but he saw when she put her hand up to her face. And then her other hand.

Oh, no. She wasn't crying. Anna wouldn't do that to him. They'd just worked things out so they could talk to each other again. *No, no, no.*

He edged a step closer, listening carefully. "Anna?"

She sniffed.

Not crying. He was trained in crying for Mulligans, but this was different. This was Anna.

His every instinct screamed run, but he took another step toward her. He wanted to say, "There's no crying in Jersey City," but instead he reached back to his training and managed to say, "Is something…I mean, are you okay?"

She sniffed again. The thin cotton of her black T-shirt stretched across her shoulders as she hunched forward. "I'm not crying. I know you think I'm crying, but I'm not."

The last syllable came out on a sob. A sad, hiccupy, breathy sob. Just as he was getting ready to reach for her, to pat her or do something so maybe she'd stop "not crying," she straightened up. He stood close enough that their hips were touching. And their thighs. The side of his boot bumped the side of her boot. Not enough contact to mean anything except *I'm standing with you.* He hoped she understood. He hoped it was enough.

"I'm sorry," she said without looking at him. "I'm a filmmaker, right? I deal with images—I make people see things. So, in my mind, the picture I had of this stuff I stored was that it would be my home base. But it's junk. What does it mean about me that I thought junk was my home base?" She turned away again. "I'm *not* crying. Just give me one second."

"Maybe when you get it to Steph's it *will* look different to you. More like you remember."

She sucked in a quick breath as if she'd been stung by a bee. *Bad.* He'd made her start crying again. He leaned to the side so their arms were touching, her wrist gently rubbing his. He wanted to put his arm around her and he would have if he hadn't been stupid at the wedding. That dance had been so hot there was no pretending it hadn't happened or that he hadn't almost kissed her. He wasn't stupid enough to think he could touch her again and have it come out any differently. Hot wasn't comfort so he stuck with leaning.

"I can't take these things to her house. I don't want to be the person who brings *that*—" she gestured at a lamp with a wagon-wheel base and an imitation-leather shade complete with a faux branded horseshoe "—into Stephanie's home."

Mason tried to concentrate on what she was saying but he thought it was possible she'd moved her knee closer to his. And that her fingers were turned toward him, just enough to touch the back of his hand. "So we'll get new stuff."

Her face lit up. "That's what I need. Forget this stuff. I'll FreeBay all of it—someone will want it."

Mason wasn't sure she was right about that but he didn't say anything. She wasn't crying anymore and he wasn't doing anything that might make her start up again. "Let's go, okay?"

"One sec," she said. She crouched down near a black plastic end table and pulled a cardboard box out from underneath. She piled a scrapbook and a framed picture and a lamp made from a Coke can on top. Then, after looking around one last time, she turned resolutely and walked out. He held the box for her as she put the lock back on.

"So, is there a Goodwill around here?" she asked.

Mason snorted. "Come on, Anna. You're going shopping at Goodwill? In Jersey City? What the hell would you find there that would be better than that?" He gestured back at the storage space.

"You're right. I need a classy Goodwill. Montclair?"

They were at the elevator and Anna leaned against the wall after she pushed the button. He leaned next to her, balancing the box on his hip. "I don't mean to tell you what to do, but if you're going to suit yourself, why shop someplace where the stuff's been thrown away once?"

"New?"

He nodded. The elevator opened and Anna got in ahead of him. Once they were started down, she looked brighter, maybe she felt better being farther away from that crap.

"All right," she said. "Let's do it." The way she said it, all bright and determined, like it was a *job* but she was going to take it on, made him smile. Most women would have leaped at the idea of shopping and here was Anna, so smart and driven about her work, who seemed to be taking on the enemy instead of heading to the housewares department.

"That's quite a lamp," he said.

She touched the stained white shade with one finger. "A friend made it for me in high school."

Her expression shut down and Mason guessed she wasn't really ready to joke around yet.

BACK IN THE TRUCK, with Mason behind the wheel, Anna was nervous. She never bought stuff. She'd never had her own place. Stephanie's house wasn't hers, but she seemed to be doing this anyway. Why? What was she thinking?

"Where to, boss?" Mason asked. "Ikea? Pier One?" She couldn't do it. Stepping into one of those huge spaces, confronted with all that stuff, the same stuff a million other people had, and then picking something, made her think of her parents and how everything had to match and nothing could stick out, certainly not a daughter who'd crossed the line one too many times.

Besides, she'd seen the gifts table at Stephanie and Brian's wedding. How did people know what kind of saltshakers they liked? Dishes, forks, an ironing board? Not that she owned anything that needed to be ironed, but people who had houses had ironing boards. Didn't they? *Ironing boards?* She was so screwed.

"Anna?" Mason said, interrupting her thoughts. "You still with me?"

"I can't go to those places," she blurted.

"What's the matter? Scared of dishes?"

"No. Not scared." She tried to backpedal. "I don't want to make this a project. I mean, I need a cup or maybe a chair, not a dining-room set." Mason must have noticed how petrified she sounded because he quickly shifted plans.

"No Ikea. We'll start small." He thumped the steering wheel. "You know what? I know just what you need."

She almost protested. Almost said they should forget it and go home, but then she thought *home* and so she nodded. Maybe Mason knew what she needed. Maybe she'd let him show her. Just about this one thing.

He took her to Goodies, two doors down from the shuttered Lakeland Cinema on Main Street. She'd walked past the home store a few times, but never gone in. Until now.

She followed Mason through the door, taking discreet, calming breaths all the way. She'd grown up on Long Island, recreational-shopping capital of the world, with a mother who shopped and decorated in the Martha Stewart tradition—each move made with deadly serious intent. She knew what she was supposed to do.

She was supposed to know what she wanted. But everything meant something, said something, and she was with Mason. Maybe on her own she could commit. She could say she was a person who liked dishes with enormous pink hibiscus on them or a person whose life wasn't complete without a silver tray full of pillar candles in six sizes. But she didn't know any of that stuff about herself and she was leery of making any statement in front of him.

She wanted to be her blank-slate moviemaking self with him. She shouldn't have let him see Terri's lamp even. The lines were already too blurred.

He'd stopped in the doorway of a back room. "Come on."

She went but only because leaving would have made her look weird and she was sure she already looked weird enough.

"When someone new comes to Mulligans," he said, "I

bring them here to pick out a quilt. Since I know you're a bed connoisseur, I thought this might be a logical start."

She blushed. "You can't let that go, huh?"

"You were rolling around on my bed. How am I supposed to forget a visual like that?"

"I'm sure if you applied yourself, you could manage."

She moved past him to escape any more smart remarks but then stopped short. The room was full of quilts. Colors and patterns lined the walls. There were quilts stacked on shelves and chairs and others hanging from dowels on the walls.

She took a small step into the room. This was gorgeous. This was what she needed. Not a whole home, just one space.

As she moved around the room, touching the intricate stitching, letting the textures soothe her, she said softly, "When I got my first bed it was a big deal. No more crib, right? My mom bought me new furniture. She painted, changed the curtains, carpet, everything. She bought this silk quilt. It was pale pink and had ribbon roses embroidered on it. It was like something Barbie'd have in her town house."

She paused in front of a stack of white-on-white quilts, looking back over her shoulder at him, wanting to know if he was getting it. He nodded.

"She wouldn't let me sit on it. Every night before I went to bed she folded it up and put it on a rack and in the morning she'd put it back on the bed. When I was sick she took it out of the room. I used to stand next to it and bend over, to rest my head on it. I was terrified she'd find out I touched it but I couldn't not."

Mason's shocked expression was satisfying to her. "That's a horrible story."

"She's a piece of work, my mom. Everything in its place. Children are seen and not heard and never, ever messy."

That was when she saw it. Hanging over a wooden dowel, high enough on the wall that she hadn't noticed it right away, was a patchwork quilt. Not a Laura Ingalls patchwork, this was a grid of off-center squares and tilted rectangles in lush, glowing shades of yellow and orange with spikes of red. It was like the embers of a campfire, warm and cozy and wild all at once.

Stretching up on her toes, she ran her palm over the bottom row of patches. The tight quilting stitches swirled in freewheeling, patternless abandon. She smoothed the quilt again. Some of the patches were a sueded, velvety fabric.

Mason was next to her, head thrown back to see the quilt. "You like this?"

"I love this," Anna said.

"It's the one?"

She nodded. She didn't trust herself to speak. This really was the perfect thing. She didn't want to decorate, not the way her mom had. She wanted to nest. The quilt was perfect.

"Good start?" he asked, sounding unsure.

"Good start." She'd trusted him and he had known what she'd needed.

He reached up and lifted the quilt down, handing it to her gently. "Welcome home, Walsh."

At the register, Mason dragged his wallet out of his back pocket. "I got this."

She'd seen the price tag and had been perfectly willing to pay for it even though it cost as much as a very nice lens for her camera. She couldn't accept a gift like that from him.

"Thank you, Mason, but it's too much."

He pulled his credit card out and put it down on top of the quilt. "When I was a kid, wherever we lived, I slept in a sleeping bag. No sheets, no pillow, just this cheap, polyester flannel sleeping bag with Scooby-Doo on it. When someone moves into Mulligans they get two sets of sheets and a quilt from Goodies. You move out, you take those things with you. Let me buy this for you—it'll be like you're one of us."

She put her wallet away. She liked the idea of belonging with him.

THE NEXT TWO WEEKS were crazy for Anna and Jake. With Mason finally enthusiastic about the Mulligans movie, they were run ragged capturing the elements that would fill the screen and convert the people of Lakeland.

Anna didn't see how they could miss. Mason loved the idea of a family reunion. He'd given her that list of all the people who'd ever lived at Mulligans. Jake was in charge of contacting them and she was out in the field. She was getting fantastic material. The movie was practically writing itself because every person she spoke to hit the same themes, even if they used different words.

Chris surprised everyone with his enthusiasm for the reunion. He thought of a slogan—I Am Mulligans—and was making T-shirts. The slogan was on the front and individual names or organizations on the back. It had been days since she'd seen either him or Alex and Drew in anything other than their I Am Mulligans shirts with ACD printed on the back. The ones he'd made her and Jake and Rob said Blue Maverick Films on the back. He'd made window stickers and they were starting to pop up around Lakeland.

She suspected he'd engaged some high-school connections and the word was trickling up from kids to parents.

Today she was in the office of the Lakeland Cinema, interviewing Manny and his nephew, Stevie, who turned out to be the most cheerful person on the planet.

"I'm telling you, man," Stevie said, "I was, like, going nowhere. Then my momma died and when I couldn't make the rent, I was on the street." He patted his plump belly. "I got skinny. No food. No cable. It sucked."

Manny spoke up, saying "Normal folks would have looked for a job."

Stevie slapped his hand on his knee. "That's the thing, though. I didn't know. I never had no job before. My momma had her checks coming and she took care of me. When she was gone, I had nothing. I didn't know what I was supposed to do or how to get back to where I was living on the inside of four walls instead of on the outside."

Anna pulled the focus in close, framing his brown eyes. She'd seen this look on enough faces in the past few weeks that she knew what was coming next.

"I got picked up for shoplifting. Mason was there, in court, with someone else and he gave me his card. I almost didn't call him."

"God was watching out for you," Manny interjected. "Made you pick up the phone."

"I bet Momma had God by the ear. 'You send my boy a sign.'" Manny smiled again. "Mulligans, man, you learn stuff there that you didn't even know you didn't know. Like Mrs. Henderson, that old lady, *knows* stuff. I took this class with her and we made soup from a chicken—not out of the can. Bones and everything, you put it all in. Best damn soup you ever tasted. I learned all kinds of stuff there."

Anna was almost nodding along as he ticked off the familiar points. When Stevie finished, she packed up the camera while he and his uncle talked. "I love that film," Anna said, indicating the poster for *Cinema Paradiso* that was hanging on the wall near the door.

"It was the first movie I showed when I opened," Manny answered.

"What did you end with?"

"Nothing."

"What?"

"I brought in *The Sound of Music*. You be quiet," he said, pointing a finger at Stevie.

Stevie shook his head in mock disgust. "It's a movie for little girls."

"The projector shorted out. A tiny fire and the print was ruined." Manny sighed. "I had to give away free popcorn. It's a good thing I was already closing. No last movie. It just went *phhhht*."

"Huh." Anna considered Stevie and his uncle. "You wouldn't want to open for one more night, would you? Show a real last movie?"

The two men immediately guessed what she meant. Manny clapped his hands even before Stevie said, "Hot dog!" Then the older man frowned. "The projector is still broken," he said. "You don't want your movie to *phhhht*."

Anna patted his hand. "I can get someone to help with that. This is going to be awesome!"

WHEN SHE BROUGHT it up to Mason the next day over lunch in the dining room at Mulligans, he looked unconvinced. "The Lakeland Cinema? I thought it closed."

"Manny will open for one more night."

"Manny?" Mason said.

"He owns it. He—"

"I know Manny. I'm just surprised you do."

"I live here for the moment, Mason. I know people."

"Okay, but isn't that risky? Showing the movie right downtown where the people who hate us are most likely to be found?" She reached for the pitcher of water and topped their glasses.

"But that's exactly it. The Mulligans family reunion will be the Mulligans coming-out party and a Lakeland block party, too. We can march from here to there and then back for a party after the movie. You can introduce your baby to the rest of Lakeland and you'll do it right in the middle of the opposition's power. Take the fight to them."

"I hate this." Mason looked around the dining room where Mulligans residents occupied a few other tables. "I don't know why everyone needs to be inside our business. What do people care what we're doing here? We're privately funded for a reason."

"If they don't know what you're doing, they're going to make things up."

"Let them."

"Is that fair to the other people living at Mulligans? You can stay there forever, but the residents are supposed to move on, right? It's better for them if things are transparent."

"But we're not hiding anything."

"It *looks* like you are. Mason, when there's a mystery people fill in the blanks. It's the way we're wired."

Mason looked at her for a long beat but then dropped his gaze to the white tablecloth. "Are we talking about Mulligans or Five Star now?"

How could she answer if she didn't know, herself?

"It doesn't matter. The answer's the same. The truth is power."

"Sometimes the truth hurts more than it helps," Mason said.

"This isn't one of them."

He was quiet again, his lips tight. "Fine. Have your party. Let the world in."

She couldn't resist pressing just a hair. "And then?"

"After, Anna. I have to do this thing first and then we'll talk. I promise."

He took his plate and walked toward the kitchen. As soon as his back was turned, she clenched her fists. She'd known for a while that he knew something. But now he'd promised he'd talk to her. She felt that promise inside her, thrumming in her veins. Mason was a guy who didn't promise easily—he knew how hard it was to follow through. But now that she had his promise and the idea of telling Terri's story wasn't just an idea anymore, she was scared. Nervous she'd pushed something into motion she wouldn't be able to control. As much as she needed to know about Terri, she dreaded what that story might cost Mason.

CHAPTER TEN

ANNA WALKED OUT on the porch, dropped the rent check in the mailbox and lifted the flag. Stephanie had asked her how long she was planning to stay and Anna really owed her an answer.

She needed to figure that out.

Her cell phone rang and she ran inside to get it.

"Anna Walsh," she said.

"Anna! Colin Paige. How've you been?"

"Great. Good to hear from you."

Colin was one of Anna's film school buddies whose career had taken off just after hers. They'd both been shooting in San Francisco the year before and had shared a house in the Mission District.

"I heard through the grapevine that you and Jake are closing up shop."

"He bought a gallery." That sounded unfinished but what else could she say, really?

"Good for him, but better for me. Does this mean there's a chance you'd consider working with me on that project I told you about—the charter schools in Utah?"

"Don't tell me you got funding."

"PBS, baby!"

"Big-time, huh."

"You want in?"

She should have said yes before he'd finished making the offer. But instead of excitement, there was nothing. When she and Colin and Jake hashed this idea over last year, she'd struggled to hold back her jealousy that she hadn't thought of it first. With the coup of PBS funding, the offer should have been irresistible. Working on a PBS-funded film with Colin Paige should have been on her list of top-five goals. And yet…

"I have stuff to finish here," Anna said. "A couple months. What's your schedule?"

Colin launched into a conversation about the details and his plans. As he spoke, part of her was listening. But part was wondering why she wasn't out of her head with joy. And part was thinking about Mason and Stephanie, Jake and Rob so close in Hoboken, this house, and how much she didn't want to abandon what she was putting together here.

Colin sounded shocked when she told him she'd have to think about it. After they hung up, she dropped onto her couch and used Mason's lighter to light the candle on the coffee table. She sat back, holding the lighter open, flicking the wheel. Colin had just handed her the key to a very nice year. So why hadn't she said yes?

Nothing would ever be like working with Jake. But it shouldn't be impossible to work with someone else. She flicked the lighter again, remembering the first night she met Mason and how dangerous he'd looked even in his suit. Jake had asked about that "magnetic" thing the next day and she'd known exactly what he meant. She and Jake had spent their childhood communicating silently and with cryptic, half conversations as they went about the business of being children in a home where everything childish was frowned upon. Their instincts and reflexes were the same, but Jake was also her safety net. With him she could be herself and know he wouldn't judge her. He might mock her, but he wouldn't judge.

He also wouldn't lie to her. More than once in the past few weeks he'd said he was worried that her career had taken over her life. She flicked the lighter again, disgusted with herself. Jake should see her now. Her career apparently meant less to her than sitting on a secondhand couch lighting candles.

MASON STARED *at the forms. Paternity Testing for Child Support, Paternity Testing for Immigration, Discreet Paternity Testing. Where was the option for Paternity Testing that Makes Your Stupid Kid Take Your Advice From Now On?* Because that was the test he needed.

Any smart person would have done a test the second Chris's mom showed up. According to the *Discreet Paternity Testing* brochure, 1.6 million men were paying child support for children they didn't father. Bunch of idiots was the implication. Send in your discreet forms and your discreet check for $645 and your indiscretions can be discreetly denied. So what kind of fool was he? Chris's mom had handed him a child and a form to sign that said he was the dad. He'd taken the child, signed the form and never looked back.

He picked up the two plastic bags that came with the test. He would not want to open the mail at the paternity-testing lab. The list of "acceptable" DNA collection objects turned his stomach. Sweaty T-shirt was the most pleasant option. Unfortunately, Chris might notice if he stole a shirt so he was stuck with the second least disgusting choice.

Mason went upstairs to the bathroom Chris used. He took a hair out of the hairbrush. *Root intact? Check.* He sealed it into the bag with the Child label. Then he went into his own bathroom and repeated the procedure, sealing his hair into the bag marked Alleged Father.

He stood in his bedroom holding the sealed bags in his hand. He did not want to do this. He already had all the answers he needed. But Chris needed a piece of paper. Mason had chosen the discreet option—you didn't need to go to a lab to collect the samples—because he hadn't told Chris he was doing it.

He wasn't sure if he was ever going to tell Chris he'd done it. That was a deceptively attractive option. The danger was if Chris realized there was a way to do this without Mason. After all, the discreet test worked both ways. All Chris needed was his eighteenth birthday, a hair or a sweaty T-shirt and $645. Then he could get his own confidential answer, without any help from Mason.

The only way he was going to have any control over what his son learned and when he learned it was by doing the test himself. Mason dropped the sealed bags in the envelope and tossed it on his dresser to mail later. The brochure had promised his discreet and confidential results would be rushed to him in three days. *Perfect.* Couple days to get there and three more to get back. He had about a week before he'd have the results in his hands. More than enough time for him to straighten Chris out, for them to get their relationship back, for Chris to tell him to forget about the test. Maybe he'd even have some time left over to cure cancer.

She had the camera on Mason in his office, trying to get some of the lines she needed from him. He was supposed to be doing a narration for the film, and not just because she thought his delicious gravelly voice that sent thrills through her belly would sell the movie all on its own. She wanted Mason to put the words on the film that pulled it together and framed it. He was the driving force at Mulligans and she needed him front and center.

It wasn't working. The office seemed to be about a hundred degrees and the lights weren't helping. The air was close and she was jumpy and Mason sounded like a doll with a string in its neck spouting sayings programmed in at the factory.

Where was the man she'd come to admire over the past few weeks? The one whose quick mind and easygoing nature put everyone at ease? She hadn't seen this hesitant and withdrawn Mason since the end of the zoning hearing when he'd lost his confidence in the face of the neighbors' attack.

Anna realized she'd lost track of what he was saying. "I'm sorry, can we go back for a second?"

Mason threw his pencil on the desk. "No. I don't want to go back. I don't want to go forward. This isn't working."

No kidding.

"Maybe if we shift the location. Would you be more comfortable in the lobby or one of the meeting rooms?" She was so tired of this shot and hated the idea of moving the gear, but she'd do it if it meant they could finish.

He propped his chin in his hand, strong fingers cupping his face, framing his lips. If only he'd kissed her at the wedding. No way anyone could live up to the raging fantasy she'd built about Mason and his lips. No one's kiss could be the lush combination of strong and gentle she pictured every time she saw him. If she'd kissed him then maybe she could let go of this obsession. She could stop thinking about kissing him, being kissed by him, what it would feel like if...

She saw his lips quirk, those not-quite-dimples at the sides of his mouth flashing into view. "What are you thinking about?" he asked.

"Nothing," she denied quickly. "What the light is like in the lobby."

"Huh," Mason said. "You didn't really look like you were thinking about the lobby."

"I was. I think it'll work. Let's try it."

He stood abruptly, unfastening the lavaliere mic from his pocket. "Nope. I know what we need to do." He strode out from behind his desk, looking more like himself than he had all morning. She sat straighter. She hadn't said anything out loud about kissing, had she? He wasn't thinking about it all the time like she was. He wouldn't be coming over to her just to see if...

"You wait here," he said, dropping the mike in her lap. "I'll be down in a minute."

She was flustered. "You need a new outfit?" she asked. "For the new location?"

"Yes, I do," he answered. He paused in the doorway. "You don't happen to have a change of clothes with you, do you?"

"What?"

"Forget it. Dumb question."

She packed the equipment while he was gone, letting the familiar, mechanical work of breaking down the lights, stowing the camera and lenses, soothe her. This happened sometimes. A movie stalled until either she or the subject was able to jar something loose. She'd let Mason take the lead, do what he felt was best.

When he came back he was wearing golf clothes.

"You're joking, right?"

"You said change of location."

Forget letting him take the lead. This was ludicrous. "I'm not going golfing with you. We need to work."

He snapped his fingers and grinned. "Exactly. We need to work but we can't. Therefore, we go golfing. And—"

"What does golfing have to do with—"

"If you'd let me finish…and when we get back I'm so relaxed we get your footage in one take."

Anna knew when she was beaten. "Man logic," she said with disgust. "You can't argue with it because it doesn't make sense in the first place."

"Man logic," Mason corrected. "It doesn't have to make sense if you get to play golf."

He drove. Wouldn't let her bring her camera. Said they were relaxing, not working. She got so irritated that she didn't tell him she and her dad had been the Father-Daughter Tournament champs at their country club for four years straight. The last year she lived at home they hadn't played. Her father had still been furious with her for the gossip swirling around Terri and the concert. If they had played, though, Anna knew they'd have cleaned up that year, too.

She was so irritated with Mason, she almost didn't love riding next to him in his bad-ass Firebird on this sunny afternoon. Almost.

"How come you have this car?" she asked.

He looked at her as if she was insane. "It's a vintage Firebird. Who wouldn't want this car?"

"It doesn't really fit with the rest of your style, though. I mean, your golf clubs have matching head covers. Doesn't the Firebird think that's a little girlie?"

"First of all, it's a car, it doesn't have an opinion. And second of all, the head covers protect the clubs. They're essential, not girlie. And third of all, I thought about getting another car, but…" He shrugged and patted the dashboard with a crooked, half-ashamed grin. "She's been with me a long time. Couldn't stand to let her go."

Anna snorted. "Men." But she secretly loved that he'd kept something of his old self. She was impressed at all the changes he'd made to straighten out his life and his work with Mulligans. But the part of her that refused to play by society's rules loved that he hadn't gone all the way over to the dark side. Mason Star might live in the suburbs, but as long as he had that Firebird, she knew he was still himself.

When he went through the Lincoln Tunnel, she started to get an uncomfortable suspicion. "There's no golfing in the city."

"We're not going to the city."

"Mason, we're *in* the city right now."

"Passing through."

Which was exactly what she was worried about. The golfing you could get to if you went through the city was on Long Island. Long Island was a section of the country she avoided at all costs. It was where her parents lived and was at the center of all the worst memories of her life.

"Can I at least get a hot dog?" she asked.

"What are you, ten years old?"

"There's a guy right there." She pointed to a vendor standing on the next corner. She didn't expect him to stop. Jake would never have stopped. He would have known she was being confrontational because she was nervous, but Mason wrenched the wheel and double-parked. He looked at her, one hand poised on the door handle. "One hot dog. With everything, I suppose?"

He'd not only pulled over, he was buying, serving her?

"I can get it myself."

A taxi blared its horn behind them.

"You want a soda?"

Another taxi joined the beeping and a bike messenger skimmed past Mason's door with less than an inch to spare.

She twisted to see out the back window. Maybe she shouldn't have pushed him. "I don't think you're supposed to park here."

"Do you want a soda with your hot dog, Anna?"

He looked mad, his eyes focused and his forehead wrinkled as he enunciated clearly. But Anna felt a thrill. He was looking right at her, not paying attention to any of the chaos mounting outside the car. He cared about getting her a hot dog.

Maybe if she went to Long Island with him it wouldn't be so bad.

She sat back contentedly. "One hot dog, just mustard, and a Diet Coke. Please."

He grinned over his shoulder at her. "Chicks."

No other man in the history of men had looked so sexy buying hot dogs. That, she knew for a fact. His V-neck sweater emphasized the breadth of his shoulders and the flat-front khakis made his lean hips leaner and his long legs longer. He was dressed like every country-club brat she'd grown up with, but the costume couldn't disguise the innate sexiness in his swagger or the sense of danger from the shadow of stubble on his jaw.

When he reached in his back pocket to get his wallet, he lifted his sweater and she got a glimpse of his white shirt neatly tucked in and his black belt passing through the loops and never in her life would she have thought that would be sexy. But it was. What would happen if she pulled his shirt out, dragged his sweater off, unbuttoned those pants?

He had his change and her lunch and she had less than three seconds to compose herself. He handed a cardboard tray to her and then climbed in, narrowly missing being picked off by a passing produce truck. She hadn't quite managed to compose herself and she jumped when their hands touched. "Sorry," he said. "Did I spill something?"

"No. Nothing. Thanks," Anna managed to say.

"Don't say I never gave you anything."

"I won't," Anna muttered, thinking about the dreams she'd have that night of button-down shirts and Firebirds and Mason doing everything she told him to do. "I really won't."

He pulled off the Long Island Expressway in Blaine and wound through the residential streets. "You want to make a bet?"

"Sure." Anything to distract herself from the scenery outside her window. This town was too much like the one she'd grown up in. The one she avoided going back to.

"I get three tries to guess your favorite food." He took his right hand off the wheel and stretched it across the back of the seat behind her. "If I get it right, you have to do something for me. I get it wrong, I have to do something for you."

If she hadn't been so distracted by his hand, hadn't been concentrating so hard on not leaning back to let it brush the nape of her neck, if she hadn't already started thinking about him and the things she'd make him do, she might have noticed he seemed too confident. She might have made a counteroffer. She might have refused to play. But she was distracted. And she was greedy to have him under her control, so she agreed.

"Hot dogs," he said.

She shook her head. If she asked him to take off his shirt, he'd think she was pervy. If she asked him to let her take off his shirt, he'd think—"

"Carrots."

"Duh. No. Who would have that as their—"

"Rob's grandmother's secret-recipe gnocchi."

She stared at him, speechless. "You set me up," she finally protested. "You knew the answer."

"Why would I bet if I didn't know the answer?" he asked, as if she was the one being unreasonable.

"Man logic. You all stink," she said, even as she wondered what he wanted her to do. If he even hinted at kissing, she was going to demand he let her out of the car.

Right after she kissed him.

No. That was bad, wrong, unprofessional, seductive and hot and so very, very right. *Oh, my.* Anna attempted to settle in her seat, waiting not very patiently for Mason to claim his prize.

HE KNEW she thought the bet had been a cheat and yeah, it had been. But he didn't really care. This whole day was strange. He almost felt as if the rules he'd been living under since he got sober were lifting. As if if he stuck with

Anna he would stop feeling so nervous all the time about fitting in and just be himself.

He knew he'd surprised her with the stupid hot dog. But she never asked for anything. He'd never met a woman so unwilling to be helped. So, yeah, she asked for a hot dog and she only did it to be irritating but, hell, he'd take it. He'd surprised her. He thought he'd made her happy. He'd take it.

But this bet? This was all about him.

"I can't believe you think I'm going to let you buy me a golf outfit just because of that bet. You cheated." Anna looked around the club's pro shop with disgust.

"I didn't cheat."

"You didn't guess. You said 'guess' my favorite food."

"I won. Stop whining." He held up a very short skirt.

"That's a tennis skirt."

No one who'd seen Anna's ass would blame him for trying.

"I'm not letting you dress me," she said. "If they won't let me play in jeans, that's their problem."

She really thought that was what he was doing. But that wasn't it. If he'd wanted her dressed right because of the course dress code, he'd have swung by her place and let her change. Nope. This was about Anna in something he bought for her.

"Do they have a bikini section?" he asked innocently. He loved the way she punched him, loved that it actually hurt. Anna didn't pull her punches, not ever. That was comforting. Even if it left a bruise.

Anna crossed her arms. "I'm not changing. They can either let me play or lose my business."

"But if you can't play, I can't play. If you can't play, I

can't relax. Remember the relaxing? Thus—" he pointed at the rack of shirts "—you need a new outfit and I get to pick it."

"No."

"Keep pouting and I'm picking one of those things that's a skirt in front and shorts in the back."

The look she gave him promised a whole lot of things that left him turned on even though he thought she'd probably meant to scare him. Mason was having a good time. A really good time.

"What happened to trying the things your movie subjects like? Getting to know me from the inside out?" he asked.

"You wear women's golf clothes?"

"That's not what I meant."

"I took up smoking for you."

He gave her points for sounding honestly aggrieved about that. As if she were in danger of lung cancer after that one drag.

"Here." He handed her a navy blue, pleated golf skirt. He guessed it would be about knee length, which was fine. She'd be comfortable and his imagination could fill in the rest. "It's almost black. That should make you feel comfortable."

She didn't reach for the skirt. Instead, she studied him. He had the uncomfortable feeling she'd figured out some way to weasel out of the bet, or worse, turn it back on him. He jiggled the hanger, hoping she'd take the skirt.

"No, thanks. If this is what you want, we're doing it right."

Her hands flew across the hangers, clicking through each one. He needed to do something to get back in control but he was out of his league.

"Perfect!" Anna exclaimed as she pulled out a bright orange scrap of fabric that might have been a bandanna but was no way big enough to be a whole skirt. Mason swallowed hard, trying to get his suddenly dry mouth to work.

"What are you doing?" he croaked.

"Helping you with your prize. The point is to get me out of my usual clothes, right? *This* is different."

He was speechless, even when she grabbed a white sleeveless shirt from the rack and swept the silky fabric across his arm on her way to the changing room.

"I'm a six and a half in shoes," she called over her shoulder.

He bought her blue-and-white spectator-style golf shoes just to prove it had all been a joke and didn't mean anything really. When she put them on and her smooth and gorgeous legs went all the way up under that should-have-been-illegal skirt, he knew he'd been beat. The only thing he could do now was sit back and try to enjoy his prize.

CHAPTER ELEVEN

MASON JAMMED his club back in the bag and threw himself into the driver's seat of the cart. *She was a ringer.* If Anna wanted to quit making movies she could have a nice fallback career as a golf pro. She didn't need that skirt to distract the other players. Her crushing drives and precision putts were enough to make him crazy.

"You didn't tell me you knew how to play."

She climbed in beside him and put her new shoes up on the dash. "Did you ask? Because I'm pretty sure this expedition was more ultimatum than invitation."

He turned the key and started down the fairway to find his ball. He hoped it was at least somewhere reasonable. On five he'd hit his ball in the water three times. Three times in a row. And he bet they were stacked one on top of each other at the bottom of the pond because they'd gone in at exactly the same spot.

"Where'd you learn to play?" he asked her.

"A stuffy country club very similar to this one about twenty miles down the expressway."

He glanced at her. "I wouldn't have guessed you grew up rich."

"Yeah, well, I never really fit in and by the time I left

I was on bad terms with my parents and pretty much everyone I knew back then."

He parked near the bushes where he thought his ball had landed. Hers was clearly visible another fifty yards ahead, smack in the middle of the fairway.

"What happened?" he asked as he kicked through the underbrush looking for his ball. She was quiet, sitting in the cart. He stopped looking for the ball. "Anna?"

"Sorry. Bad judgment. I was a wild kid, pushing back against the boxes towns like these and parents like mine want to keep you in. But I…I made a bad mistake. Someone got hurt. After that it felt like I wasn't really welcome anymore."

He spotted his ball about five feet away, snug against the roots of a pine tree. He went over and kicked it out, measured the position with his club head, sighted down the course.

"They kicked you out?" He had to work to keep the resentment out of his voice.

"No. They'd never have done something as obvious as that. They just…stopped looking at me. Like I was so distasteful they couldn't stand me anymore. It was a big story and everyone was talking, but the things they said about my friend were awful and not true. My parents hushed it all up. In their world, not talking is better than talking about something upsetting."

He lined up his shot and hit the ball, watched as, through some miracle, it actually landed near the green. When he got back in the cart, she had her arms wrapped around her. She looked like the teenager she might have been when her world stopped making sense.

"I don't know what to say. It must have been awful. I can't imagine not talking to Chris."

"Yeah, well, you seem like a decent dad, Mason. He's lucky to be your kid."

She sounded so sure. Alone out here with Anna, he wanted to tell her, just have the words out there and see what she thought.

"Chris isn't positive he is my kid."

She swiveled to look at him. "Not positive about what?"

"He asked me to take a paternity test."

The words cut him but he needed to say it.

"I'm sorry to be obtuse. Didn't his mom…and you…?"

"If we did, it was one time and I didn't exactly keep a diary."

She didn't say anything for a second. He hoped she wasn't disgusted by what he'd said. He was trying to be honest, but God, was it ever hard. He hated admitting that he couldn't remember if he'd slept with Chris's mom.

When she spoke again, it was back on point. "But why is he with you? Where is she?"

He rested his hand on the steering wheel and looked out. One of the reasons he liked golf was you could see where you were going and the hazards were all written on the map on the score sheet. If you kept your cart on the path, you'd be all right.

"She died. Overdose in Florida when he was eight. But he's with me because she got sick of him around the time he turned seven. I didn't know about him before that. She showed up one day out of the blue. Had him in the car. Anna, you should have seen him. He was tiny, skinny as a blade of grass and about that sturdy. His eyes were…not what you want to see on a kid. She said he was mine and the smart reaction is the same as yours, 'prove it,' right?"

She nodded.

"But I looked at him and he was lost. He needed somebody to hang his hopes on. I'd just opened Mulligans—I was ready to start helping. So he stayed."

"And you never—"

"This sounds stupid but I honestly never thought about it again. He's my kid. My son."

Anna had tears in her eyes. She looked away and he was glad to give her a moment to compose herself. He didn't know what he'd do if she cried.

"Like I said. He's lucky to have a dad like you."

He put the cart in gear and pulled out. "I have the envelope with the test results at home. I didn't open it. I can't decide what to do with it. But the odd thing is, if it is negative? I don't have the slightest idea how to stop being his dad."

"That's not odd, Mason. Odd is people like my parents who cut me loose when I got embarrassing. I know what I say isn't going to make a difference because I just met you guys, but Chris loves you. He's mad at you and he asked you for something he shouldn't have. But I don't think he'd have asked you to do that test if he didn't feel absolutely sure he could count on you no matter what." She smoothed her hands down her thighs. "I never would have asked my parents to prove I was part of the family. I'd have been too nervous they'd tell me to get lost."

He didn't realize how much he'd wanted to talk to her about the test until after it was out.

"Thanks," he said.

She shrugged. "It's just facts, Mason."

She got out and chipped her ball onto the green. He matched her and the two of them walked together up to the hole. She was farther away so she walked over to line up her shot first. She crouched to check the line of the green. He looked at her legs. What would it feel like to slide his hand up that smooth skin? What would it feel like to turn her and feel her arms around him? He hadn't forgotten a single second of their wedding dance. Hadn't stopped wanting to hold her again.

He couldn't, though. He was letting her in and letting her know him. He heeded to focus on keeping some distance if he wanted to throw her off the scent of the bus crash story.

IF SHE'D SAT DOWN in the morning and made a list of things unlikely to happen today, she couldn't possibly, not in five million years, have come up with this. She was wearing a skirt Mason bought her in a pro shop, playing golf at a country club very similar to the one she'd worked so hard to get banned from that last awful year at home. She'd told him things she didn't tell anyone. He'd told her things she'd never even have guessed at.

She was so off balance, she didn't know one thing that was true.

Actually, that wasn't quite true. She did know one thing.

"I thought you'd be better at golf."

"Kick a man when he's down, why don't you." He moved around the cart to drive but she headed him off.

"I'm driving. We have things to talk about."

He looked flustered, which turned her on for some reason. He was tall and broad and she'd knocked him for a loop. And the beautiful thing was, Mason wasn't the kind of guy who'd ever swing back if she knocked him sideways. He had that enormously gentle strength that let him give and give and never ask for a break. Some random woman dropped a kid off on his doorstep and he took the kid and raised him. His son demanded a paternity test and he was hurt and confused but strong enough to take the risk that it might help. She asked him to do this movie that was so clearly driving him crazy and he was doing his best to get it done because it mattered to the people he cared about.

He was a person you could count on. A person who'd stick with you even if you'd done something wrong or made a horrible mistake or couldn't quite explain what had happened on the worst night of your life.

She clapped her hands. "Hop in, Mason."

He slid into the cart next to her. "Um, just to let you know, I'm not all the way relaxed yet. Maybe we should hold off on the questions."

"I want to talk about golf."

"Golf?"

"Were you always this bad?"

He laughed. "And there's the famed Walsh honesty policy."

"Answer the question."

"I can drive the ball but it doesn't go where I want— never has. I used to be able to putt."

She smiled. And then she took a risk. She patted his leg. Just a quick pat and it was over. But it was big for her. She'd wanted a connection with him. His thigh felt nice. Firm. Which immediately had her thinking about his bed.

Bad, Anna. Golf. Concentrate on golf.

"So how come you play?"

"It started out as camouflage."

"Camouflage for what? Middle-class white guys?"

"Exactly."

Anna's story instinct kicked in. He was getting ready to tell her something that he usually didn't share. His voice had deepened and roughened enough that she knew he was forcing out something hard.

"After rehab you're supposed to avoid all the places and people that might make you backslide. So I couldn't go back to the party scene. Five Star was done with me. And I couldn't go back to living like I did when I grew up, either. I wouldn't have, even if I could. So I went to the suburbs. But I had no idea what I was doing. There are all these rules."

"I know about the rules," Anna said.

"I didn't. I was desperate to fit in so I watched what other people did and faked it. Golf seemed like the perfect cover. Nothing scary about a Saturday-afternoon game at the club, right?"

"Depends on how you define scary."

"You know what I mean."

And she did. Her heart broke a little for him. He'd finished rehab at about the same age she'd been when she graduated college. She'd been running hard from her old life, eager to chase her dreams on film. He'd been running just as hard but with no eagerness. All he'd been trying to do was fit in.

"All right," she said. "Lucky for you, I'm here to make your Saturday game much more enjoyable. We'll fix your long game first." She jammed her foot on the gas, getting the cart up to its top speed. Her dad used to let her drive when they played—she'd loved feeling so grown-up with him.

"You're kidding me." Mason gripped the roof of the cart as she went around a turn too fast. "*You're* going to fix my *golf* game."

"I let you dress me up like a country-club wife. The least you can do is let me give you some pointers."

"I've taken lessons, Anna. I appreciate the thought but—"

"You've got nothing to lose, do you?"

He didn't look convinced.

"If you don't find my lessons helpful, you can delete any five songs you want from my iPod."

"And you won't reinstall them as soon as I walk out of the room?"

"They'll remain music non grata for six months," she said as she pulled up to the next tee.

He got his club and set the ball on the tee before looking at her expectantly. "'Annie's Song' is on the block, Anna. Make sure I know what you're doing."

"Okay, first lesson. See those trees on the left, halfway down?"

She pointed to a clump of pines that were clearly out of bounds. He nodded.

"Aim for them."

He waited for the punch line. But she gestured impatiently.

"Let's go. You've been hitting it long all day, you've got the power to reach them."

"Anna, those trees aren't on the fairway."

"If you argued with all your instructors it's no wonder lessons never helped."

He turned back to the ball and lined up—aiming straight down the fairway. If she thought he was going to start hitting balls out of bounds on purpose, she was insane.

Anna cleared her throat. "It doesn't look like you're aiming for the trees."

"I'm not. That's the stupidest piece of golf advice I've ever heard."

She pulled their scorecard out of her pocket and studied it. "So the man who's shooting forty-nine thinks he can ignore advice from the woman shooting—"

"Real golfers don't brag."

"Aim for the trees or I'm taking off my shirt."

He stared at her. She put her hands on the hem. He kept staring. She lifted it half an inch and he got a peek of skin. "I never wanted to wear it in the first place," she threatened.

"Anna, I'm only allowed on here because the pro is a buddy of mine. Cut it out." Even as he spoke, he watched carefully to see if she might be goaded into raising it a little more. Maybe he could get a hint of what kind of bra a woman like Anna wore.

"Golf pros don't intimidate me. You can call my dad's club and ask why I'm banned. Public nudity was just one of the charges."

He weighed his options. He wanted to see her naked. She would have her shirt off if he waited a minute or two more, the wicked gleam in her eyes left no doubt of that. But this wasn't the time or the place. He and Anna would be kicked off the course so fast he wouldn't even have a chance to admire the view. But God, did he ever want to.

He turned back to the ball and smacked it hard. The ringing crack of the ball as it hit a tall pine in the clump Anna had indicated startled him. The ball had actually gone where he wanted it to go. It must have been a fluke.

He looked at Anna and she looked entirely too satisfied with herself. He stepped up close, knowing he was crossing the lines they were so careful to keep between them, but needing to get some control back. "Next time I'm going to let you take your shirt off."

She took a step forward, closing the distance even more. "Next time it'll be the reward, not the threat."

He almost dropped his club.

For the next three holes she set up stupid targets, left, right, backward, into the water hazard on an adjoining hole. He had never in his life yelled "fore" as often as he did on those three holes.

At first the clubs were uncomfortable in his hands, the grips small and slippery. He broke three tees just trying to get them in the ground. After he hit the ball onto the adjoining hole, he had to bend over and breathe before his stomach would settle down. He felt obvious and nervous and as if he were being watched by a gallery and not just his crazy documentary filmmaker/golf coach.

They were going to get in trouble. He hated to stick out like this. It got so bad on the eleventh hole when she told him to hit it on the ground across the cart path into some bushes, that he almost couldn't swing the club.

He'd gotten more dirty looks in the past half hour than in the previous ten years of golf. He was down to two balls, the rest were lost.

On the other hand, he hadn't missed a single one of the screwed-up targets. Anna had quit playing entirely and was lounging in the cart thinking up new challenges like some demented mini–golf course designer. If there'd been a windmill on this course she'd have told him to aim for the propeller and he'd have hit it dead on. He closed his eyes and swung, opening them to watch as the ball skittered across the path and into the bushes Anna had pointed out.

She gave him an enormous, goofy smile and a double

thumbs-up. He didn't know if it was the shot, the smile or the combination of both, but he felt slightly better.

By the time they got to the fourteenth he wasn't exactly enjoying himself but he had stopped sweating and the clubs' grips seemed to have shrunk back to their normal size.

"Where to?" he asked over his shoulder.

"Down the fairway, lay up in front of the first bunker."

He looked where she'd pointed. "But that's a real shot."

"Don't argue with me. Just do it."

He hesitated, looking down the fairway. If he put the ball there he'd be in perfect position to make par. Maybe even birdie.

"Do it," she repeated.

He got in position over the ball again but couldn't swing.

She got out of the cart and stood off to the side. "Mason, you've hit it someplace stupid eighteen times in a row. It can't go farther out of bounds, farther into the water, farther onto someone else's hole than you've already hit it. What's the worst that can happen this time? Line it up, trust yourself and do it."

And he did.

The club met the ball, sweet spots kissing, and the ball soared out in a long, high arc before dropping in exactly the spot Anna had called. He was dumbfounded. How could that have worked?

When he looked over his shoulder at her she raised her hands in a "what can you do" gesture. "You worry too much about screwing up. Now you know the world doesn't end if you're out of bounds."

He scooped up the divot his club had dug in the tee box and stepped on it to press it back down. He was off kilter. Hitting his ball all over the course had made him incredibly nervous. That last shot felt so natural he was incredibly pumped. Anna figuring out what was wrong with him left him incredibly scared. He couldn't afford to have her see him that clearly.

"You want to head out?" he asked.

"We didn't finish our round."

"I'm good."

She nodded. "Okay."

The sun was starting to go down and the light picked highlights out of her curls. She must've felt him watching her and met his eye, shoving her hair back off her face. The sleeveless shirt exposed the gorgeous sweep of her bicep, the vulnerable pale underside. He cupped his hand around her arm, rubbing his thumb along the muscle and watching as she went still, letting him touch her but not encouraging anything else.

At the wedding he'd needed to feel her close to him, needed to press into her and feel her press back. But now, despite all the reasons he knew he should keep away, he wanted her to know she mattered. That she was important to him.

He kept his hand on her arm, squeezing gently as he kissed her. He lingered, brushing her lips with his own, feeling her mouth open with surprise or desire, he didn't know. He dipped his tongue in, and he was suddenly, achingly hard.

He pulled back. She opened her eyes again, and her pupils were dark, wide with desire. She'd felt it, too. He filed that information away for another time. "I didn't buy you that outfit because I wanted you to fit in. I just wanted to see what you look like in a skirt."

She blushed.

"You're one hot golf pro, Walsh."

He slid his hand up and into her hair. The thick curls clustered around his fingers and it was all he could do not to tug her forward and plunge his other hand in. He leaned in and kissed her again, longer this time, and then he stepped back.

"Thanks for this day, Anna. It was just about perfect."

She touched her lips, the silver of her ring sliding back and forth as she rubbed. Then she smiled at him. "You're welcome. Anytime, Mason."

THE RIDE HOME was quiet. Anna was still in shock over that kiss. The way he'd kissed her.

She'd felt caressed even though he'd only touched her arm and her lips and, briefly, her hair. She'd felt seen, even though her eyes were closed. She'd felt loved, even though it was her and Mason and love wasn't supposed to have anything to do with that.

The kiss had made one thing clear, though. She'd understood what she needed to do to finish the Mulligans movie. So she concentrated on that while the Firebird carried her home, away from Long Island and back to Lakeland, back to Stephanie's house that she was starting to think of as hers. Back to her work and her story that she finally knew how to tell.

When he stopped in front of Stephanie's, she heard him roll down the window. She turned and caught her breath. He looked perfect, dark hair in devilish spikes, white smile, framed by that inky, bad-ass car.

"See you tomorrow, Walsh."

She nodded, not trusting her voice. She'd never, not once in her adult life, taken comfort from knowing she'd be in the same place, doing the same thing, the next day. But having Mason to look forward to had changed that.

She lifted a hand. "See you."

Later that night, when she was finished with the film, there wasn't a narration.

Of course not. That wasn't Mason.

What there was, was Mason in the background of almost every scene. He was either there in person physically fixing things or arranging things or helping solve problems. Or he was in the stories the people told.

Mason said, come on home with me.

I didn't know what I was going to do until Mason said he had a place.

We were so scared—we didn't know what would happen to us or our kids until Mason worked it out.

When I felt like I couldn't take it anymore, Mason was there. He took me out on the porch and he sat with me until I was ready to get back in and try again.

They went on like that. He was the heart and soul of Mulligans, but not in the way she'd imagined with the narrative. He was the belief system, the support structure, the guiding principles. He'd never be the person who put himself forward or took the limelight or claimed the glory.

When the movie was finished, she watched it through. It would be impossible to watch that film and not know who was at the heart of it. The only person in the entire movie who didn't say a word.

SHE WAS STILL in bed the next morning when her cell buzzed on the nightstand. She pushed back her patchwork quilt to answer it.

"Hey," Jake said. "I'm on the porch. Let me in."

Anna got up and went to the front door. Jake looked relaxed, Anna thought as he passed her and went into the house. His more settled life agreed with him.

Jake turned a circle in the living room, examining everything she'd done, and then lifted an eyebrow. "Mom would be proud."

"Shut up. She'd hate this," Anna answered.

Jake sat on the couch and put his feet up on the coffee table. "You're right. You know why? Because it's what she could never do—make a place people could live in." He leaned forward to look into the dining room with its freshly painted pale turquoise walls. "Who knew you, the queen of black and white, had such a color fetish?"

Anna sat next to him and put her own crossed feet on the table, something she'd never have done in their mother's house. She wouldn't have dared. But the living room at Stephanie's house was entirely different. She'd made sure of that.

During a few long evenings, Anna had painted it a warm but muted orange, one step away from the deepest yellows on the color wheel.

The knubby yarn she'd bought was currently posed in a wooden bowl with the bamboo needles still spiked through it. Turned out she wasn't a person who could sit around and do nothing but move her fingers. The yarn was a good color, though, so she kept it, tangles, split ends and all.

A creamy oval shag rug and the simple gauzy curtains Helen Henderson had helped her make softened the edges of the room. The bookcase wasn't exactly full, but she'd put some books in there and a framed photo Stephanie had given her from the wedding, of her and Mason standing near the dance floor.

She didn't know who'd taken it and she wasn't sure she liked the intimacy she read in their closeness. But she put the picture in the bookcase and every once in a while she looked at it. Just looking didn't do any harm.

She liked this room she'd made. She liked knowing she'd done this, decorated a space and made it her own.

"Whose is this?" Jake leaned forward and picked up Mason's lighter from the table where she'd left it next to the candle she lit in the evenings.

"What? That?"

"Yes, Anna, this very masculine lighter with the initials MPS." Jake flipped the cap open and hit the flame. "What's his middle name?"

"Patrick." Too late she realized she'd just admitted whose lighter it was.

Jake snapped the lid back down. "I hope you know what you're doing."

"I hope so, too," she said as the memory of Mason's lips ghosted across hers.

Jake sighed. "Way to be reassuring." He patted the pocket of his shirt. "I'm sticking with my objections to digging up the Five Star crash, but just to prove my good faith to our partnership, I brought you a present." He handed her a folded piece of paper. "David Giles called. He wants you to come to Nick Kane's place."

Anna sat forward. "Why? What do they want?"

"All I know is he said they have something they need to film. Big-time. Nick's farm is outside Princeton. Said you won't want to miss this."

Princeton was a few hours away—they could be there by noon easily. Was it possible David had decided to talk at last?

"When can we go? Can you get away today?" Anna had planned to meet Mason but she'd have to reschedule. He'd probably be glad for the day off.

"He said just you."

"What? Why?"

"I don't know, Anna. These guys haven't been straight with us since we started, so if you don't want to go, I'll tell him. It's your call."

There wasn't one doubt in her mind what she was going to do. "Did he give you his address?"

CHAPTER TWELVE

WHEN ANNA CALLED TO say she'd be gone for the day, Mason had had a moment's panic. She hadn't said where she was going, just that she'd be back by the next morning at the latest. He hoped the kiss hadn't spooked her.

He'd gotten used to seeing her every day, filming Mulligans. Obviously, it was hilarious to watch her tackle the buffet. And, okay, he'd made lasagna for tonight because he knew she liked it. But lots of people liked lasagna. So, all in all, he was absolutely not feeling bummed about missing her today.

Mason opened his office door and yelled, "Brian!"

Brian poked his head out of the office next door. "Do we need a reminder about inside voices?"

"When we wrote the budget this year did we include money to build a miniature golf course?"

Brian closed his eyes. "That's it. I knew the day would come. Someone call the ambulance—Mason's flipped his lid."

Mason pulled his door shut behind him and started toward Brian's. "I'll take that as a no. Do we need to revise the budget or can we just start building? I'm buying."

Brian darted into his office and attempted to shut the door before Mason got there. "No. I'm not getting involved. Just because you're crazy doesn't mean I have to be part of it. Build your own golf course."

Mason got a foot in the door and wedged his shoulder in the opening. He gave a shove and Brian backed up a couple inches. Not enough for Mason to get all the way in, but enough to slide more of his shoulder through.

"We can make it educational."

"What, number the holes in Spanish?"

Mason beamed at Brian as if he were a particularly well-behaved puppy. "That's an excellent idea. Write it down. But I meant, physics or science."

"I have to work." Brian pushed back on his side of the door, pinning Mason's shoulder.

"Ouch. Back off," Mason grunted. "Besides, this is an order. Your boss says you need to build a golf course."

"How come you're only my boss when you're being irritating?" Brian asked. "Where's Anna, anyway? I bet she'd love to play with you."

"She had an appointment out of town. She won't be back until tomorrow."

"Oh." Brian eased up on the door unexpectedly and Mason stumbled into the room. When he straightened up, Brian was looking superior. "That explains the insanity."

"I don't know what you're talking about." He smoothed the front of his shirt and pretended he really didn't see a connection.

"So you didn't cook up this idea to distract yourself from the fact that you miss her?"

Mason gave himself big props for managing a slightly outraged look. He made a mental note to hire someone less astute the next time Mulligans needed a supervisor.

Brian pressed on. "Don't pretend this isn't about Anna,

buddy. I'll go with you to the lumberyard but I'm not going down De Nile."

Mason groaned. "You did not just say that. That was almost bad enough to make me leave you at home."

"Only almost. Shoot." Brian said. "Let me think. A horse walks into a bar…"

Mason punched him on the shoulder. "After all these years, I'm impervious to your bad jokes. Resign yourself. We're building a golf course."

They took the Mulligans truck. Mason let Brian drive so he could use the laptop to look over the miniature golf course plans he'd downloaded. When they were about six blocks away from the lumberyard, Mason's cell buzzed in his pocket.

He took it out and glanced at the caller ID. *David Giles*. The phone buzzed two more times in his hand while he fumbled, trying to turn it off. He didn't get it in time to prevent the call from going to voice mail.

"Something wrong?" Brian asked.

"No."

Brian seemed to accept that answer because he looked back to the road. The new-voice-mail icon flashed on Mason's phone. He tried to concentrate on the laptop but his enthusiasm had dried up. They'd been calling off and on all summer. David mostly. Nick Kane a couple times. He'd managed to avoid them thus far, but now… Glancing at Brian, Mason punched the button and put the phone to his ear.

David's voice came across the line, sounding pretty much the same as he had when they were touring together.

"Mason, I wish you'd call me. You didn't used to be such a jerk. Heard you met Anna—she's something, huh?

Anyway, call me. We need to talk. If you don't call, then we're coming to you. If Mohammed won't visit the water…or you know what I mean. Five Star reunion! We're gonna make this happen."

Mason's stomach pitched and he thought he might be sick. He hadn't heard David's voice in years. Hadn't been in a room with all of them since that last day in Chicago. Why was David talking about Anna? Had they talked about the crash? What had David said? They were coming here?

Brian turned into the parking lot of the lumberyard.

"Pull over, pull over," Mason said. As soon as the truck was stopped, he jumped out and doubled over, retching into the bushes. Brian was at his side, clearly worried.

"Are you okay?"

"Not feeling well, Mason?" Roxanne Curtis asked from directly behind him. He spun around.

"Unbelievable," Mason said as he tried to catch his breath. "What are you doing here?"

"Buying mulch," she snapped. "Is that alcohol I smell?"

Brian's eyes flashed. "Don't be ridiculous, Roxanne."

She pushed her tinted blond hair behind her ear. "Too bad the zoning board couldn't see you like this. It's exactly what we've always expected. But last I heard we had all the votes we need to shut you down for good, so I guess it doesn't matter. See you, boys."

Mason pushed himself up and went after her, Five Star forgotten. "Wait, Roxanne. Can we talk?"

Brian was right with him. "Mason, this is not a good idea."

She paused, but she held the strap of her purse close across her chest. Did she think he'd try to steal it or was she just that uptight?

"Why are you doing this?" he asked. "You know Mulligans isn't a problem."

"Mulligans *is* a problem. The kind of people who live there are not the kind of people who live in Lakeland. Not anymore."

She stared at him, chin tilted, sun glinting off that high-end haircut, and then he knew. She was scared. Scared if Mulligans was still there that the new people who came in would always have a reminder of what Lakeland had been, what kind of people lived there before it became gentrified.

"You're trying to kick us out so you can blend in."

She didn't flinch. He'd give her that. But her eyes flickered away and back and he knew he'd hit home. He couldn't believe it. He'd thought it was about money…or revenge for turning down her overtures…but it was deeper than that. It was about who she was and who she'd been. If Roxanne was going to reinvent herself and her neighborhood, she couldn't have Mulligans staring her in the face.

"Mulligans is a drain on the local resources. The tax loss alone is enough to—"

He held up his hand and she did flinch then. God, she was actually afraid of him. What kind of life had she lived? "I've read your pamphlet. I think we're always going to disagree. I figure people like you and me who make it up and out, we have to turn around and give a hand to someone coming behind. But you want to close the door, make sure all that nasty stuff stays buried."

Brian put his hand on Mason's chest. "Let it go, buddy."

Roxanne sneered. "You think you know me, but you're wrong. I have the best interests of this community at heart. Long term, people like you just don't fit in."

She spun, still clutching her purse, and walked away.

"Hey," Brian said. "You okay?"

"You mean besides the fact that I'm having decapitation fantasies about a suburban housewife? Yeah, Brian, I'm peachy."

He walked back to the truck.

"You can't let her get to you, Mase. She's not going to win. Thank God, we've got Anna and her movie on our side."

After David's phone call, Mason wasn't sure that was even true. He was starting to think Anna wasn't on anyone's side but her own. What really got him, though, was the idea that he was still a liability. *People like you.* His past and his bad decisions could be the thing that blew Mulligans's chances. How long did he have to hide before people would let his mistakes go?

"I have stuff to do. Miniature golf is a dumb idea anyway, especially if we don't know if we're still going to be in Lakeland."

"Mason."

"Don't, Brian. Let's go home."

Mason stared out the window on the way home and thought about Five Star and Roxanne and Mulligans and how everything he'd ever tried to do turned out wrong. Which got him thinking about Chris. At least he hadn't lost that battle yet. It was one he couldn't afford to lose.

NICK KANE WAS a rock star. He might as well have had a stadium marquee over his front door. His house was so ostentatious, crammed full of tributes to himself, that Anna almost wished she could show it to her mother just to see the horror on her oh-so-proper face.

Nick ushered her into the sunken living room where the rest of Five Star—David and Chet Giles and Harris Coleman—were sprawled in uncomfortable-looking steel and webbing sling chairs.

"Anna!" David exclaimed. "Thanks for coming."

She hadn't expected all of them. What was going on?

"Nick?" she asked the man next to her.

"I thought David told you. We're going out on tour. David wants you here to film this since it's, like, our kickoff."

"Film what?" she asked just as the doorbell chimed again.

David stood up and crossed to her. "You brought your gear, right?" His eyes were lit up. She didn't think he was drunk, but it was possible. "This is big. Historic."

"I brought my stuff. I need to set up…" Her voice trailed off when she saw Nick come back, followed closely by Christian. "Chris?"

"Anna. Hey." He managed to sound close to normal even though the tips of his ears were flushed with embarrassment.

David looked put out. "You know each other?"

"Yeah," Chris said. "She's—"

"We've met," Anna said abruptly. "What's going on?"

Chris shook hands all around as everyone ignored her question.

Finally David clapped his hands. "You better get your camera, Anna, before we have our historic signing."

"Your historic what?"

Nick shook his head ruefully. "I didn't think he could do it, but David convinced Mason to come back. And Chris's band is going to open for us. Five Star is going back on tour."

"David convinced Mason to come back?" Anna asked, looking at Chris. "Is that true?"

"It's not finalized," David said quickly, "but this is the first step. We sign Chris and we'll have Mason. Anna, get your stuff, why don't you."

Anna looked at each of them, the four aging rock stars, all past their prime, and the boy who was so eager to jump-start his career. She couldn't let Five Star have what they wanted, not from Mason's boy, when Mason had been trying so hard to protect him. But she liked Chris and wouldn't embarrass him if she could help it. She'd been like him once, knew what it felt like to want out so badly you were willing to do just about anything to get there.

"I wish you'd told me what you were planning before we all made the trip out here. I can't film Chris."

"What?" David said.

"I need a release before I can film anyone."

"Well, have him sign it," Chet said. "I have a pen."

"He's a minor," Anna said, with some steel in her voice. She might not want to embarrass Chris but she didn't want these other jokers to miss how serious she was. "You'd need his father's consent. Which I'd be very surprised to find you have."

"Anna," Chris protested, "this isn't about him."

He was so young. ACD might have talent, but Chris was the only one in the room who didn't know Mason was the only reason Five Star had called him. At least Chris hadn't known that until Nick opened his mouth.

"I thought we were clear this was all about Mason," he said to David. "I told you I wasn't coming back without him. The kid is fine, but I said Mason or no deal."

"Right, that's right," David soothed.

"So where is he? Why'd he send his kid and not show up himself?"

"Nick," David said.

"No. What the hell is going on here?"

Anna glanced at Chris. He was scowling at the ground, fists bunched at his sides.

"Listen, Nick, I don't know what David has told you, but I don't think Mason agreed to any of this. You should check with him. In the meantime, I think I'd better be going. Chris?"

But then suddenly she wasn't going anywhere because Nick had launched himself at David. The two of them landed with a heavy thump on the floor and then David's head snapped back with a crack.

"What the hell, Nick!" Chet exclaimed as he tried to pull the drummer off his brother. Harris took a step forward but didn't move to help. Anna started edging around the still-thrashing pair toward the door, herding Chris ahead of her.

"I can't believe you're doing this again!" Nick yelled. "You said he was coming. I don't know why I believed you. Of course he's not coming and doesn't want his kid here. You screwed him over so many times, he'd have to be an imbecile to come back for more."

Chet had finally wrestled Nick upright. David got up slowly and dusted himself off. Nick pulled himself away from Chet and stood, chest heaving, and glared at them. "I want you out of my house, David. Take your brother and Harris and don't come back. I'm done."

David shook his head as if to clear it and then pointed his finger at Nick. "You're fired. As of now, you're out. Don't come crying back. Ever." He spun on his heel and walked out, Chet let go of Nick and he and Harris followed David. The heavy front door slammed so hard

Anna felt the floor shake. Chris, standing next to her, looked as shocked as she felt.

Nick rubbed a hand over his face, his eyes. "I'm such an idiot. I really thought he'd gotten in touch. Mason probably wouldn't even talk to him. He hasn't taken any of my calls. He never talked to him, did he, kid?"

Chris shrugged. "My dad doesn't talk to me about you guys."

"Yeah, well, he's got solid reasons."

"Come on, Chris," Anna said. "We should go."

"Did you know David slept with Mason's mom?" Nick said suddenly.

No. No, she did not know that. From the look on Chris's face he hadn't known that, either.

"Yeah. We were booked in some bar she was working and our singer quit. Split for L.A. in the middle of the night with some chick. Mason's mom had been hooking up with David. She said her kid could sing. David set him up with an audition and Mason blew us away. He was just a kid. Looked like you, Chris. Tall and skinny, his hair all over and those crazy eyes. If he wasn't so tall, I'd have thought he was twelve. They lied about how old he was—said he was eighteen."

Nick's mouth turned down, his graying stubble making him look older than he was.

"When we found out he was sixteen, she was supposed to get him a tutor or something for the GED but she never did. She was a real, flat-out bitch."

Anna listened to him speak and she found her brain disengaging the way it did sometimes when she was working with material that was too painful to listen to: Her mind drifted to the gentle, single-minded care she'd

seen on Mason's face when he was tying Christian's tie.
How did a person learn that if they came from what Nick
was describing?

Chris. His expression was confused and full of pain.
She needed to get him out of here, away from this mess.

"Nick, we have to go."

He didn't acknowledge her, lost in his memories.

Anna took Chris by the elbow and steered him out of
the room. Nick suddenly looked up and came after them.

"The kid should hear this. David's setting him up the
exact same way. Mason never asked for anything except
to be in the band, you know? He loved David. And David
screwed him over. That crash. If only things went different that night."

"Nick, please," she said with a gesture at Chris, who
stood by the front door, wide-eyed. A chill swept over
her, knowing she was closer than she'd ever been to
Terri's story and instead of pursuing it, she was hoping
she could get out the door with Chris before Nick said
anything else.

But it was like someone had flipped a switch for Nick
and everything was pouring out. "The last day David said
we were doing an intervention. But it was a massacre.
Even his mother piled on. We ripped Mason to shreds and
kicked him out."

She pulled the door open and held it, pushing Chris
through. Nick stood where she'd left him in the gaudy
foyer, surrounded by mirrors and memorabilia. As she
watched, he leaned toward the door calling to her, "Tell him
I said sorry. Won't matter to him, but tell him anyway?"

Anna nodded. She suspected that when she delivered
that message, Mason, with his enormous capacity to

forgive and to offer second chances to everyone except himself, just might call Nick to tell him it was okay.

ANNA WALKED Chris to his car and tried to figure out some tactful way to ask him what the hell he was thinking, but there really wasn't one. She supposed this wasn't the time to berate the kid anyway. He looked shell-shocked.

"Not what you were expecting, huh?"

Chris shoved his hands into his pockets. She heard the frustration and held-back tears in his voice as he muttered, "They said they'd heard us play. They never said anything about Dad."

"You heard Nick, David is not a nice guy."

"He won't talk about them. He never talks about them."

"I guess he has his reasons," Anna said.

"Yeah." Chris waited a beat. "Are you going to tell him?"

Her heart went out to him. He sounded like a little kid who'd broken a window.

"I won't if you promise you'll talk to him."

"I can't, Anna. You don't understand what he's like."

"Chris," Anna said, "I won't get in the middle of you and your dad. I saw what went on here and I can't keep it from him."

"God," Chris half moaned. "I wish I knew that stuff before I went there. He doesn't tell me anything. Those guys know all this stuff that he did and I don't know any of it."

"Chris," Anna started but then stopped, unsure of what to say. Then she realized she did know. She knew exactly what to tell the hurting boy. "Your dad loves you so much it makes him nuts. He'd do anything for you. If you explain how important it is for you to know about his past, he'll talk to you. But you have to be honest."

Chris wiped a hand quickly across his eyes. "I'll tell him. But it's the reunion tomorrow. I don't want to mess him up."

"You have to tell him or I will. I won't lie for you."

Chris nodded.

She stood in Nick's driveway and watched until Chris made the turn back out toward the highway. *Wasn't that just a huge barrel of laughs?*

Later when she walked in the front door of Stephanie's house, she felt as if she was taking her first easy breath since Nick started talking. She really loved this little house. It felt like home.

She'd brought all her equipment upstairs to the second bedroom she used as an office. She sat at the desk and pulled up the Five Star footage she'd shot back before she met Mason. It hadn't been that long, a couple months ago, but it seemed like forever. The urgency in her voice as she asked questions seemed foreign now. On the way home from Nick's, she'd been grateful she didn't get any of today's debacle on film. That scene would have devastated Mason.

She continued watching, moving more quickly through the recording sessions and the footage from the band hanging out together. Her eyes were bleary by the time she'd seen everything she wanted. Usually when she ran through tape like this she'd have a million ideas pushing at her. But now she felt very little.

Mason had been betrayed by his mother and the guys he'd looked at as his family. He'd been so young. Certainly he'd made mistakes, but he'd needed help and support, not the abuse he'd gotten.

She was amazed he'd been able to get over that. But then she thought about the Mason she'd gotten to know.

How hard he worked to fit in and appear normal and she knew he hadn't. He was constantly looking over his shoulder, waiting for someone to come along and tell him he didn't belong again. Someone like the zoning board telling him he was no longer welcome. Someone like his son asking him to prove their relationship. Someone like her, forcing him to reach back to the worst time of his life.

He'd needed someone, and her reputation must have been attractive, but she was holding the Five Star movie over his head. Somehow he'd found the courage to say yes to her because it might help save Mulligans.

Oh, Mason. She wished he was there or that it wasn't the middle of the night. She wanted to hold him and tell him he didn't deserve any of the things that had been done to him.

She wanted to tell him she wasn't doing the Five Star movie.

Huh.

She tested that idea. She'd thought about that movie for so long, since film school really, but even before that she'd wanted to know what happened to Terri. She'd been thinking about that for fifteen years.

There was a part of her, she supposed, that would always wonder. But she didn't need to know anymore. Not if it meant more pain for Mason. She could live the way Nick Kane had, knowing something happened, but not knowing the details. That would be better than putting Mason through the trouble that would come from pawing through his past. Whatever he'd done, whatever had happened, Mason was a different person now and he'd more than made up for his mistakes.

Anna dragged each file one by one to the trash can. Then she turned off all her equipment. She didn't want to be in the room with it anymore. If it weren't so late she'd have called Mason. She considered calling Jake, but he didn't really need to know. If they didn't do the Five Star film, he would just start his new life sooner.

Anna felt that familiar twist of panic again when she thought about Jake and the gallery. Blue Maverick was over. She'd turned down Colin Paige. The Mulligans movie was truly her last film. She went down the stairs and outside. She'd take a walk, burn off some energy and clear her mind.

As she walked, she played the Mulligans movie in her mind. It was a good film. It wasn't a bad way to go out.

She ended up downtown. It was eerie with just the streetlights for company. Almost like a movie set. Manny had hung a banner advertising her film on the front of the cinema with a spotlight trained on it. It was the brightest spot on the street and she sat on the bench in front of the post office to check it out.

The Lakeland Cinema was a solid building in good repair. Manny had taken her through it one day. He'd cleaned it all in preparation for the showing of the film and he'd wanted her to see it. A friend of hers from the NYU film school had come out and fixed the wiring problem that had caused the fire in the projector.

Now, sitting across the street, an idea started to form. She swiveled and looked up and down the street. Some of the stores still had Lakeland Neighborhood Association signs, but there were I Am Mulligans stickers in more windows. She saw Lakeland differently than Mason did. She had hope that the people were ready to embrace Mulligans. If only he'd let them in.

She leaned back again and crossed her arms. If a person had a small movie theater this close to the city, she could stay connected to the part of the business she loved the most, sharing stories with other people. It wouldn't be her stories anymore, but she could find the ones that meant something or that had a particular beauty or joy and she could help those stories make their way to an audience.

Yep, Anna thought, if a person had a small movie theater and maybe a small shingled house, that person might be well on her way to a life. If that person were especially lucky she might even get to share that life with someone special. Someone brave and wounded and sexy and in desperate need of her help on the golf course. Someone with a big, firm bed who liked to dance and liked to tease her about her music. Someone who knew how to wear a tuxedo and liked her in her jeans but wouldn't mind if she wanted to test out some other kinds of clothes once in a while. A person could be happy here, Anna thought. Really, truly happy.

CHAPTER THIRTEEN

MASON COULDN'T CATCH his breath. He'd been off balance and out of sorts all day, ever since Chris had woken him up that morning at quarter to seven. That right there had been enough to practically give him a heart attack. Chris hadn't been awake before him since he turned twelve and developed the nocturnal lifestyle common to all teenagers.

But this morning the door of his room banged open and Chris was there, next to his bed, already showered and dressed in his I Am Mulligans shirt. Chris tugged the covers. "Dad, get up."

Mason tugged the covers right back where they belonged over his face. "Go away."

Chris tugged harder and the cool air of the room hit Mason's shoulders. "Dad, it's the reunion. You have to be downstairs when people start to come."

He knew when he was beaten, so he sat up and stretched. Chris looked happy. Cheerful, even. "You know it might be a bust, right? It's possible no one's coming."

Chris stared at him. "What are you talking about?"

"Well, just because you invite them, they might not come. We don't have any way of knowing…"

Chris threw a shirt at him. It was a royal blue I Am Mulligans shirt and when it unfolded in his lap, Mason saw that the back read Mulligans and under that Head Honcho. "Where have you been the past month?" Chris said impatiently. "Didn't I tell you I was making shirts? Didn't I give you a bill for the shirts and the printing?"

Mason remembered that but he'd stuck it in a stack with a bunch of other bills, waiting for the end of the month when he did his books. "Um, I guess."

"But you didn't look at it, did you? You have no idea what it said?"

"No?"

Chris flopped down on the bed next to him. "I'm amazed this place stays in business if this is the kind of leadership it has. Dad, I bought three hundred shirts. People are coming."

"But just because you bought shirts, that doesn't mean—"

"They're custom shirts, Dad!" Chris was almost shouting. "They say stuff on the back like what group you're with. The two hundred and fifty-three people who told me they're coming ordered custom shirts for their groups."

"Two hundred and—?" Mason was distinctly unclear about whatever it was Chris was saying. "You don't have any coffee around here, do you?"

"Dad! Get up."

"You really had orders for all those shirts?"

"Yes." Chris tried to adopt his normal sullen tone but he couldn't keep the excitement out of it. "There's people coming from the school district, and Stevie has a county group, and I made one bunch for, get this, the Lakeland Downtown Business Owners. I think Manny had some-thing to do with that."

Mason lay back down. "So people are coming?"

"Yes," Chris said. "Get. Up."

Mason got up but he never really got his balance back. He couldn't understand where all these people were coming from or why. He knew Chris must have worked some kind of magic but he didn't understand how. When he was showered and dressed in a white, long-sleeve thermal with his Head Honcho shirt over it, he cornered Stephanie.

"This was a bad idea. I count on you to tell me when I have bad ideas. Why didn't you tell me this time?"

"This isn't a bad idea." She turned around. "Did you see my shirt?" Hers said The Law under Mulligans. Mason nodded. Not because he thought she was right but because he knew it was way too late to stop the event. He should have followed his instincts and stayed underground. He should not have exposed his friends and his place to the town. But it was done now. He felt as if some horror show was coming down the road toward him and he had no idea how he'd head it off.

ANNA SMILED at the symmetry when they parked on the street in almost the same spot they'd used for Stephanie's wedding. Rob and Jake walked ahead, just the way they'd done that day. She watched them, but instead of feeling as alone as she had at the wedding, she felt anticipation. She'd be seeing Mason in a few minutes. She had no idea how she would start to tell him everything she was thinking about, but she'd figure that out. She wanted to spend this day with him and then tomorrow and then next week. She couldn't wait to get started.

She hustled up to Rob and Jake and the three of them went through the gate together.

She didn't see Mason right away. She met Chris just inside the yard. He was working at a registration table, checking people in and handing out shirts. "Anna!" He beamed at her. Which was shocking because Chris wasn't exactly a beamer and their parting yesterday had been tense. But he beamed at her now. Alex was sitting next to him, three pencils stuck in his ponytail, and the other kid from the band, Drew, was behind them, digging shirts out of boxes as Chris called for them.

She smiled back at Chris and then leaned over the table. "Did you talk to your dad?"

His face flushed red. "Not yet. But I'm going to, Anna. I swear. I just didn't want to fight with him today. He's…I don't know, acting flakey. Like he's not into it or something. You're not going to tell him, are you?"

"I can't keep it from him, Chris. You can't ask me to do that."

"I'm not. Just today. As soon as the party's over, I'll tell him."

He looked so sincere and happy behind the table with his friends and his shirts, Anna decided that it wouldn't hurt anything if he waited. Besides, he was probably right. The last thing Mason needed today was a fight. "Okay. But you promise you'll tell him tonight?"

"Swear."

She looked around. Everyone was wearing the I Am Mulligans shirts. She estimated there were close to two hundred people milling around the grounds preparing for the march from Mulligans to the theater downtown. Probably more people would be at the theater. "This is really happening, huh?"

Chris continued to beam even as he nodded again. It felt

like she was in an alternate universe. "The shirts look great," she said. "Hey, did I ever tell you what we named the film?"

He shook his head.

"I Am Mulligans."

What was the word for something brighter than beaming?

"That is so cool," he said. "Thanks."

She started to walk away. "Make sure you take care of that thing, right?"

"Tonight. I swear."

She saw Stephanie and Brian and shook a million hands but nowhere did she see the tall, sexy man she was looking for. If she were a person who tended toward paranoia, she'd have thought he was avoiding her. But there was no reason to think that way. He was probably incredibly busy—as many people as she'd met, he must have met more. And some of them, many of them, knew him and had traveled here for him. It made sense that he was spending his time with the people who mattered.

They had time.

She'd brought her camera with her. She'd decided that she would film the celebration today and cut it in with *I Am Mulligans* so Mason would have the whole story together. Turning the camera on, she started to wander around, trying not to look for Mason even while her every nerve was waiting for him.

About forty minutes later, the march started to get organized. She worked her way toward the front and fell in next to Jake and Rob. "Have you seen Mason?" she asked.

Rob lifted his eyebrows. "Anna, it's unseemly for a lady to sound so desperate."

"Don't you think it's strange that he's nowhere around?"

"We saw him," Jake said. "He looks stressed, but it's a lot of people. He's around somewhere."

So. It was her then.

Stop it, Walsh.

No paranoia. No need. She'd find him sooner or later.

HE'D SEEN HER the second she walked through the gate. He'd started over when he saw her stopping to talk to Chris. But something had stopped him. There was no point. She'd done the Mulligans movie. Now he owed her the Five Star one. And once she heard that story everything would change. So for today he'd focus on the people who were here for Mulligans and then he'd worry about the rest of it when it happened. But he wouldn't torture himself by seeing Anna. Enough was enough, even for him.

During the march, Stephanie kept pointing out I Am Mulligans stickers. A bunch of houses had homemade banners hung on the porches, with slogans promising their support. When they turned the corner onto Main Street downtown, it was even stranger. Practically every business had some kind of sign or poster in the window. The banner on the movie theater was waving in the breeze and Mason watched as the crowd, most wearing I Am Mulligans T-shirts, streamed inside. Manny was standing at the ticket window, a big smile on his face. "Never had this kind of crowd when I was running the place," he said.

Mason wasn't sure how to answer that. He pointed to the Sold sign in the window. "You found a buyer?"

"This morning," Manny said. "Gonna be good."

"Congratulations," he answered before he got swept inside with the crowd. When he got in the theater, Chris was down in the front, waving for him. "Dad! This way."

He was so floored by the idea of being summoned by Christian in public that he didn't even notice the other people in the row. Stephanie and Brian stood to let him in and he climbed over Christian to slump into the empty seat. He sensed her before he saw her, his arm prickling with awareness. When he turned, she was smiling at him.

"Head Honcho, huh?"

"Chris made them."

"I know." She touched his arm. His skin went hot then cold then hot again. "He did a great job. So did you. Congratulations."

"Nothing's settled yet."

"Not officially, maybe. But I think you got your hearts and minds even without the movie, pal."

She stood up then and looked toward the back of the theater. Manny was in the entrance, and he waved when he saw her and then disappeared back into the lobby.

Anna put her fingers in her mouth and whistled. The crowd slowly settled down. "Hi. I'm Anna Walsh. My brother, Jake, and I are glad to see so many people here." She pulled Jake to his feet. "We took this project for a lot of reasons, none of which had anything to do with Mulligans." The crowd laughed at that. "But by the time we were finished, we knew without a doubt that Mulligans is a place worth being part of." She pointed to her shirt. "I am Mulligans," she said. "I think before you leave today anyone who's not already one of us, will be ready to join."

Jake started clapping. "Let it rip, Manny!" he called.

The lights went down and the movie started even as the crowd was still clapping. Anna sank into her chair. When she leaned over to whisper in his ear, her breath raised the hair on the back of his neck. "This is for you, Mason. No more deal. No more questions. It's from us for you."

He wasn't sure what she was talking about but he couldn't ask because the opening scenes started to play and the theater was dead silent.

Mason watched it unfold scene by scene and for forty-five minutes he forgot about everything except what was happening on the screen. He was blown away. He knew Mulligans inside and out. It had been his idea in the first place. But seeing it new, through Anna's eyes…. He fell in love with the people and the ideas all over again.

Chris was too thrilled to keep still. He poked Mason and cheered, and at one point Mason was pretty sure he heard some suspiciously sniffy breathing. It had been a long time since he'd shared something like this with his son. One more gift Anna had given him.

By the time the final scene played, Mason was overwhelmed. The guy in Anna's movie, Mason Star, director of Mulligans, was very different from him. Was that how Anna saw him? Was it possible that's how he really was?

What would happen if he told her about the crash? The whole story. He'd never talked about it with anybody, not even David. After it happened, he'd sealed it up and he'd had good reasons. But it had been inside him so long, the memory was getting heavier each year. In the way of his relationship with Chris. Definitely in the way of any chance he had at a relationship with Anna. And, he was starting to understand, it was also in the way of him being himself.

When the screen went dark, Manny turned on the lights, and the crowd was on their feet, cheering, stamping and yelling. He couldn't hear himself speak as he leaned over, caught her hand and said, "Thank you."

She squeezed his hand and smiled and he knew. Things were going to be okay.

He got pulled away in the other direction. Larry Williams was in the aisle, shaking hands with Stephanie. Chris stood next to Mason and listened as the zoning board chairman congratulated them on being a catalyst that pulled the town together, a shining example of community in action and the recipient of a fifty-year zoning waiver that the board had voted on in an emergency session held in their seats as the credits rolled.

Chris raised his arms and whooped. Mason was dumbfounded, but he managed to shake Larry's hand and stammer out a thank-you.

"Wait here," Christian said to Larry. He darted back into the row of seats and emerged with his backpack. Reaching inside, he pulled out a stack of shirts and handed them to Larry. "I made them up, just in case."

Larry shook one out. The familiar logo was on the front and the back read, Lakeland Zoning Board.

"That's the kind of optimism we need around here," Larry said as he slipped a shirt on over his dress shirt. Mason grinned at Chris. His boy was something else.

Chris looked serious all of a sudden and then he pulled Mason into a hug. "Congratulations, Dad. You deserve this."

Mason wasn't sure what had changed, but whatever it was, he'd take it.

Walking back to Mulligans in the midst of the boisterous crowd, Mason was happy. Really happy for the first time in months. He still had stuff to work out with Chris. He hadn't even started to work things out with Anna. But he had hope. And when there was hope, there was a chance.

On the grounds at Mulligans, the party got going immediately. The dance floor was back in the same spot it had been for Stephanie and Brian's wedding. ACD was setting up to play before a DJ came in later. Long tables groaned with food, some made in their own kitchen, some in Tupperware with masking-tape labels identifying the owner, and even more in silver pans from the local deli and pizza place.

And then it all went to hell faster than he could say Five Star.

He saw David, that unmistakable mane of blond hair so obviously out of place. He made a beeline through the crowd straight for Chris.

"What the hell?" Mason muttered. There was no way he wanted David anywhere near Mulligans, near Chris, near his life.

The yard was so crowded he would have had trouble walking even without people grabbing him and trying to talk to him. He fought to make headway and all the while he watched David near the soundboard huddled with Christian, Alex and Drew.

He was almost there when he glimpsed Anna. She had her handheld camera and was scanning the crowd. Why would she be filming? Had she known David was coming? Did she set him up to get a scoop for her movie?

His blood chilled. He needed to get to Chris. Maybe David didn't know who he was. How could he? It was possible he'd only stopped to talk to Chris coincidentally.

But as soon as he was close enough to hear, he knew he was wrong. David not only knew Chris, it sounded as if they'd been talking together for weeks.

David was leaning in, his voice impatient, as he punctuated his point by slapping a hand on the soundboard.

"Chris, I need to talk to your dad so we can bang out the details for the tour."

"What tour?" Mason towered over him. He bit off the words. "Who in hell told you you could talk to my kid?"

"Dad—"

"Mason." David jumped in. "It's good to see you." He actually looked as if he was going to try for a hug.

"What *tour?*" he repeated.

David looked confused. "Chris didn't tell you? We asked him to open for the Five Star Reunion Tour."

Christian didn't even look at David, his attention on Mason. "Dad, I can explain."

He was going to kill them. He was going to kill every one of them. First Alex and Drew because friends don't let friends do dumb things. Then Christian, for a whole mess of reasons. And finally, when he was finished killing the boys, he was going to kill David Giles. Rip him apart with his bare hands and feed the parts of him to the pigeons downtown.

"Get inside, Chris. Right now. This meeting is over."

"Dad!" Chris had switched from anxious to rebellious.

Mason grabbed Chris by the front of his shirt and pulled him up close. "I swear to God, Chris. I know you wish I wasn't your father. And I know you can't wait to make tracks away from here for good. But for these next few months, until you turn eighteen, I'm in charge. You're my son. David is a jackass and the only way you're going on tour with him is over my dead body." Mason gave him a shake to emphasize his point. "Now get inside and wait till I come for you."

Christian's face had gone pale. He wiped a hand over his mouth, unable to meet Mason's eye. He'd never laid a hand on his son and he wasn't planning to start now, but it looked as though Chris wasn't sure of that. When Mason dropped the front of his shirt, Christian sagged and then he backed up and ran for the house. Alex and Drew melted back into the crowd and he was alone with David.

David and Anna. No one else seemed to have noticed what was going on. She was standing close, still holding her camera, her gaze steady on his face.

The last time he'd seen David, Mason had been desperate and scared and heartbroken. He was surprised that he didn't feel any of that now.

"That's it," he said, anger making his voice low and harsh. "I don't want to see either of you near my kid again. Let's get done what we need to do and then you can get out of here. You want to talk to me?" He pointed at David. "Let's talk." He pointed at Anna. "Bring your damn camera. I'll tell you your story and then you can leave with him."

She flinched as if he'd slapped her. He didn't know how they made it through the crowds, but once they were in his office, he twisted the lock on the door.

"Turn on the camera, Anna. It's story time."

She didn't move to lift the camera. "Please, Mason, you're hurting right now, but you don't have to do this. Let David leave and we can talk."

He'd expected to feel something if he ever saw David again. He'd been so important to Mason, and then when Five Star kicked him out, he'd missed them like a part of his body. But he didn't feel anything but rage.

Anna had laid the camera on his desk. So he picked it up, turned it on and propped it on top of the file cabinet.

Anna had no idea what to do. She couldn't stand the

way Mason looked at her; he was on a rampage. She decided to try one more time.

"Please, Mason. Don't."

"No. It's time. You want the truth. You got it." He looked to David. "Feel free to jump in when we get to the good parts."

Turning back to the camera, he started to speak. "The night of the bus crash, I was drunk onstage. By that point, I was usually drunk onstage, offstage and everyplace in between. My memory cuts out right after "Dirty Sweet" and doesn't come back until after the show. Even then, parts are hazy. But here's what I know. I brought a girl back to the bus. Terri Nixon. She came up onstage during the show and was hanging around afterward. She didn't want to come with me but I needed someone. She was there so I turned on the charm and she came."

Anna's heart was pounding so hard she was surprised David and Mason couldn't hear it.

"We got on the bus and drank some more and she started to loosen up with me in the lounge in the back. Everyone went to bed in the middle sleeping compartments. Everyone except me and David and the girl. She was just a kid. We started kissing… Everything was fine. We ran out of booze at some point and I got up to go find some. That's one of the things I can't forget. If I hadn't needed more whiskey, I wouldn't have left her alone."

"Mason," David said sharply.

"What?" Mason spat. "What do you have to say to me?"

"Turn off the camera."

Mason crossed his arms on his chest. "Not today."

Anna couldn't listen to any more. "Please, Mason. You don't have to do this."

He ignored her.

"I had to go up to my bunk to get the whiskey. I stopped in the bathroom on the way. The spins were bad by then. I got the whiskey and took a minute to talk to Joey, the driver."

Anna crossed her arms, pressing her hands tight against her body to stop herself from reaching for him.

"I could hear her. I don't know how long it took before I realized she was shouting. David was all over her and she didn't want it. I remember thinking that the sounds, her voice, didn't sound right. But I was so wasted. I don't know—I didn't go see. That's the second thing I can't forget. If I hadn't been that drunk, I'd have known. I'd have heard that something was wrong, and I'd have gone back there."

Anna put her fist to her mouth. She'd hoped, somehow, that when the crash happened Terri had been asleep, passed out even.

David moved toward the door but Mason got in front of him. "You can leave. You will leave. But not before I tell this."

He went on. "She got away from him. I don't know how. She ran out and came up to the front of the bus and she was crying. I offered her a shot. That's the third thing I can't forget. She was panicked and I offered her a shot like that would help."

"Then—" Mason's voice hitched as if he was trying to keep it steady but having trouble "—she freaked. She tried to get Joe to pull over, but he was laughing at her. David was coming up from the lounge and she panicked. She grabbed the wheel. Joe tried to get the bus back under control but she wouldn't let go. The bus slid sideways…and you know the rest. Terri, Joe and the couple in the pickup we hit died. The cops came around asking questions and I did what I was told. Kept my mouth shut and pretended I had been asleep. That's the fourth thing. I never told what David did. I spent the next two years nonstop drunk, trying to forget it. But I'll always remember. I'll always know that my drinking was the reason it happened. If I hadn't been that guy, that stupid drunk asshole, it wouldn't have happened."

Anna was crying, for Terri and for Mason, who'd been carrying the weight of that guilty secret all these years.

"You wanted your truth," he said. "There it is. She was a kid. David told me it was better for her parents if they didn't know she caused the crash. I…I thought it was better if they didn't know she was attacked. Maybe they could mourn her easier if they thought she died having fun. How screwed up is that? Like there's a good way to mourn your dead teenager."

He paused finally. David was looking from Anna to Mason to the camera on the cabinet.

Anna shook her head. "Her parents had it bad. Everyone talked about Terri—terrible things about why she would go on the bus and she was drunk and…you can't imagine. It was awful."

Mason turned angrily on her. "How do you know that?"

"She was my best friend. We went to the concert together and I dared her to get up onstage. She was scared and I teased her until… The last time I saw her, she was running onstage."

Mason's face had gone pale. "That's why you're making this movie? Is that the thing that turned your parents against you?"

"What happened between me and my parents was

going to happen anyway. Terri's death only made it come sooner."

"I'm so sorry," Mason said. "I'm so sorry."

Seeing him, knowing him, loving him, another piece snapped into place. She crossed the room and picked up the camera to turn it off. Then she faced David.

"Nick Kane said the same thing the other day. He was sorry for how you all treated Mason. How you kicked him out instead of trying to get help for him. This was why, wasn't it? You knew Mason. Knew how he'd feel about this. Knew if you could screw him up enough, he'd blame himself and keep his mouth shut."

David crossed his arms. "You're crazy."

"You would have been in serious trouble, David, wouldn't you? Terri was seventeen. You were what? Twenty-eight? Twenty-nine? Your career would have been over."

David shook his head and started for the door. "I'm out of here."

Mason was staring at David like he'd never seen him before. "Are you kidding me?" he said. "You kicked me out to keep this quiet? You didn't trust *me*?"

David's lip lifted in a sneer. "You were so damn easy, Mason, so ready to take the blame. You did all the hard work yourself."

Mason was across the room in three strides and then he had David by the neck up against the wall. The veins in his forearms stood out as he pressed the smaller man backward. "That's it, David. That's the last time. All the crap you gave my mom and me, and that poor girl. It's over. I'm ending it here. You come near me or my family again and I'll kill you. Got it?"

David tried to speak but he couldn't get any air.

"Mason, stop!" Anna said.

He stepped back and David slumped away from the wall.

"You're nuts," he sputtered. "You've finally lost your mind."

Mason opened the office door and stood with his heels planted, arms crossed. "Wrong. I finally know exactly what I'm doing. You have five seconds to get out of here before I go out in the yard and find one of the many Lakeland police officers who are eating my potato salad to come in here and arrest you for trespassing."

David eased past him and when he shut the door, the air seemed to go out of the room.

Anna looked down at the camera in her hands. She wished she'd never dug at this story. Terri was dead and all the trouble that had caused was in the past.

"I'm so sorry, Mason. I don't know what to say."

"There's nothing to say," he replied. "I screwed up. I get that you can't forgive that."

Anna lifted her head. He was leaning back on his desk, his shoulders slumped. "Forgive you? For what?"

"For not helping her. For being so wasted. For not taking care with everything I'd been handed. For being such a stupid idiot. For not telling the cops what David did."

"Don't," Anna said. "You're not responsible for her death any more than I am."

"But now that you know, you can't trust me. I understand."

"Mason, didn't you watch that movie? Who you are is the guy who had the vision for Mulligans and put his own money up for it. The one who makes a place for people society doesn't want. The one who said yes to Brian; and the Hendersons; and Maddie and her kids; and Chris. And me. The man you are is the man I love."

Mason rocked back, taking some of his weight with his arms. "What about the man I was?"

She crossed the room, one slow step at a time. Finally she was in front of him and she wrapped her arms around his waist and rested her forehead on his chest.

"You're not him. You won't be him. You have your life here, your friends, your work, everything you've learned. You beat it. This is your second chance."

He stroked her hair. "You have your story now. You can do what you want with it. I'm okay if you tell what happened."

Anna shook her head. "I erased everything I had last night. I'll erase this right now." She rested her hand on the camera. "You matter to me, Mason. More than any story. I tried to tell you in the theater but maybe you didn't hear me."

He put his hands gently on either side of her face and lifted her chin. He was looking at her like he'd never seen her before. He slid his arms down to her waist, clasping his hands behind her. "You gave up your story for me? That's what you meant when you said 'no more deal?'"

She nodded.

He lowered his lips closer to hers. She pushed upward, pressing herself against him. Before their lips met, he murmured, "We good?"

Her mmm of assent was swallowed in their kiss. This was the kiss she'd been waiting for. Her hands roamed up his firm back and down over his jeans. He pulled her against him and then slid a hand in between them to cup her breast, kneading through her T-shirt with desperate pressure.

It was a wild kiss, even with all their clothes on. She moved against him and he slid himself around until they fit together perfectly.

Just when she was starting to think maybe, finally, she was going to get a chance to test out his bed, she remembered something. Someone.

"Chris," she said, her lips moving against his.

"What?" he mumbled.

She pulled away. "Chris. He's waiting for you."

"Oh God," he groaned.

"You need to talk to him."

He nodded, arms still wrapped around her. "He wasn't going with them," she said, "He was going to tell you but was waiting until tonight."

"How do you know?"

"They were all at Nick's yesterday. That's where I went. Chris didn't want me to tell you, so he promised he would."

He leaned his forehead on hers, and she hoped he could take comfort from the closeness. "I'll find him. But you'll be here, right?"

"I'm not going anywhere."

He kissed her again, briskly and thoroughly, before reaching for an envelope on his desk. He pulled the door open but came back to her for one more kiss, this one deep and lingering. "This might take a few minutes. But you better be here when I get back. I know there's a buffet outside and it's going to be hard for you to resist. But I have stuff—" he cupped her ass and pulled her in for another kiss "—stuff I want to do with you as soon as I'm done."

Anna shoved him toward the door and sat in the desk chair. "Quit stalling and go talk." She crossed her feet on the corner of the desk. "I'll be here."

"Holy hell, Anna. Don't look at me like that."

"Go," she said.

"I love you," he answered and then he went. But she knew he'd be back. She was looking forward to that very much.

CHRIS WAS in his room, belly down on his bed, staring at Peek. He didn't look around when Mason came in. He wasn't sure what to say, but then he thought of Anna and her confidence in him and he figured he could do this.

"I'm sorry I grabbed you like that. I shouldn't have done it."

Christian lifted his left shoulder in a shrug.

"You want to talk about this?"

Chris flipped over and Mason saw tears on his son's face. "Yes, Dad, yes. I want to talk about it. I want to know what you know. I want you to tell me about it. I...I don't want to hear your life story from some random guy."

Mason eased onto the bed. "Okay," he said carefully. "I was talking about the part where you were going on tour with Five Star. But if you need to hear about the rest of it, I'll try. It's hard for me. But I'll try."

Chris wiped his forearm across his eyes. "I told them no, Dad. Yesterday."

"I figured," Mason said and then he realized it was true. Chris was a smart kid. Much smarter than Mason had been. He wouldn't have let himself get suckered by David. "I was thinking, if you want to, we can talk to the Shreds again. Not touring, but maybe you can pick up a few dates. A couple weeks out of school won't kill you."

The tightness in Mason's chest loosened when he saw his son's grin. "That would be awesome. The best." Chris sat up. "Thanks."

Mason shrugged. "You were right. I don't trust me. But I do trust you."

There was a second of silence. "Listen, Anna's waiting for me downstairs—" Mason answered Chris's smile with one of his own "—I know. Got to catch her before she wises up. But I...I had that test done. I didn't look at what it says. It's yours, if you want it."

He held the envelope out and Chris took it carefully. "You didn't look?" the boy asked.

"I don't need to. I know."

Chris hefted the envelope a couple times and then dropped it back into Mason's hand. "You keep it, Dad. I'm set."

And if that wasn't the best thing his kid had ever said to him, he didn't know what was.

Mason leaned in and hugged Chris. He held him tight and then released him, knowing the anti-emotion meter must be just about ready to explode. He stood and stretched and then started for the door.

"Don't wait up," he said.

Peek hit him in the back of the head. "No details, dude. That's disgusting."

He was grinning as he swung down the stairs two by two on his way back to Anna.

LATER, MUCH LATER, so much later Anna was confident it was already tomorrow, they walked downtown together. She'd told him she wanted to show him something. At the Lakeland Cinema, she dug in her pocket and came up with a key ring holding two keys. When she unlocked the door and stepped back to wave him through, he looked confused. "Does Manny know you're doing this?"

"Manny," Anna said as she led him into the theater seating area, "doesn't own the cinema anymore."

She pushed him into the middle seat of the middle row. They sat down and she put her head back on the velvet cushion. Mason entwined his hand in hers.

"I don't suppose you're going to tell me what we're doing here."

"Enjoying the view. And I'm also inspecting the ceiling for water stains. If Manny lied about the roof not leaking I'm asking for my deposit back."

"Anna, did you buy this theater?"

She nodded smugly. "Yes, I did. I think I'm going to have Chris add Real Estate Mogul to my shirt."

His voice was hesitant when he said, "So does that mean…?"

She nodded. Leaned in to kiss him. "I'm staying. If you'll have me."

Mason grabbed her and swung her onto his lap facing him. "Oh, I'll have you, Walsh. I'll have you as long as you want."

"You want to see my other key?"

He nodded. She dug in her pocket again and came up with the key ring and his lighter. He couldn't believe she was carrying it around. She flicked the wheel to get a flame to see by and then separated the keys. "This is the theater," she said. "And this is my house."

"Your house? You mean Stephanie's house."

"My house," Anna said quietly. "I mean, there's paperwork and stuff to do. But I put a deposit on the house this morning, too. Looks like Lakeland better make room for me."

She slid the keys and the lighter back into her pocket

and then rested her palms against his firm chest and sighed. "Good thing I never wasted any money on spare blouses."

He was finger combing her hair, his strong, confident fingers sweeping through her curls.

She leaned back, savoring the feeling. "You know what sucks, though?"

"What?"

"Every time I think I'm going to get a chance to test out your bed something happens. Now we're alone and, well, your bed is back at Mulligans."

"My bed?" Mason laughed.

"It's a very nice bed," Anna said primly.

"I believe you told me that before."

She put her hand on his bicep and squeezed. "It's firm. Which is so very attractive."

He shifted under her, groaning. "Let's head back, then, before the bed gets a complex."

Anna rocked and pushed against him. "We don't want the theater to get a complex, either, though. Do we?"

"I always knew you were very wise," he said, before laughing and capturing her mouth with his.

Anna sank into the embrace, completely comfortable and eager to see what else Mason Star had in store for her.

* * * * *

THOROUGHBRED LEGACY
*The stakes are high when it comes to love,
horse racing, family secrets
and broken promises.*

*A new exciting Harlequin continuity series
coming soon!
Led by* New York Times
bestselling author Elizabeth Bevarly
FLIRTING WITH TROUBLE

Here's a preview!

THE DOOR CLOSED behind them, throwing them into darkness and leaving them utterly alone. And the next thing Daniel knew, he heard himself saying, "Marnie, I'm sorry about the way things turned out in Del Mar."

She said nothing at first, only strode across the room and stared out the window beside him. Although he couldn't see her well in the darkness—he still hadn't switched on a light...but then, neither had she—he imagined her expression was a little preoccupied, a little anxious, a little confused.

Finally, very softly, she said, "Are you?"

He nodded, then, worried she wouldn't be able to see the gesture, added, "Yeah. I am. I should have said goodbye to you."

"Yes, you should have."

Actually, he thought, there were a lot of things he should have done in Del Mar. He'd had *a lot* riding on the Pacific Classic, and even more on his entry, Little Joe, but after meeting Marnie, the Pacific Classic had been the last thing on Daniel's mind. His loss at Del Mar had pretty much ended his career before it had even begun, and he'd had to start all over again, rebuilding from nothing.

He simply had not then and did not now have room in

his life for a woman as potent as Marnie Roberts. He was a horseman first and foremost. From the time he was a schoolboy, he'd known what he wanted to do with his life—be the best possible trainer he could be.

He had to make sure Marnie understood—and he understood, too—why things had ended the way they had eight years ago. He just wished he could find the words to do that. Hell, he wished he could find the *thoughts* to do that.

"You made me forget things, Marnie, things that I really needed to remember. And that scared the hell out of me. Little Joe should have won the Classic. He was by far the best horse entered in that race. But I didn't give him the attention he needed and deserved that week, because all I could think about was you. Hell, when I woke up that morning all I wanted to do was lie there and look at you, and then wake you up and make love to you again. If I hadn't left when I did—the way I did—I might still be lying there in that bed with you, thinking about nothing else."

"And would that be so terrible?" she asked.

"Of course not," he told her. "But that wasn't why I was in Del Mar," he repeated. "I was in Del Mar to win a race. That was my job. And my work was the most important thing to me."

She said nothing for a moment, only studied his face in the darkness as if looking for the answer to a very important question. Finally she asked, "And what's the most important thing to you now, Daniel?"

Wasn't the answer to that obvious? "My work," he answered automatically.

She nodded slowly. "Of course," she said softly. "That is, after all, what you do best."

Her comment, too, puzzled him. She made it sound as if being good at what he did was a bad thing.

She bit her lip thoughtfully, her eyes fixed on his, glimmering in the scant moonlight that was filtering through the window. And damned if Daniel didn't find himself wanting to pull her into his arms and kiss her. But as much as it might have felt as if no time had passed since Del Mar, there were eight years between now and then. And eight years was a long time in the best of circumstances. For Daniel and Marnie, it was virtually a lifetime.

So Daniel turned and started for the door, then halted. He couldn't just walk away and leave things as they were, unsettled. He'd done that eight years ago and regretted it.

"It *was* good to see you again, Marnie," he said softly. And since he was being honest, he added, "I hope we see each other again."

She didn't say anything in response, only stood silhouetted against the window with her arms wrapped around her in a way that made him wonder whether she was doing it because she was cold, or if she just needed something—someone—to hold on to. In either case, Daniel understood. There was an emptiness clinging to him that he suspected would be there for a long time.

* * * * *

THOROUGHBRED LEGACY
coming soon wherever books are sold!

Thoroughbred Legacy

Launching in June 2008

A dramatic new 12-book continuity that embodies the American Dream.

Meet the Prestons, owners of Quest Stables, a successful horse-racing and breeding empire. But the lives, loves and reputations of this hardworking family are put at risk when a breeding scandal unfolds.

Flirting with Trouble

by *New York Times* bestselling author

ELIZABETH BEVARLY

Eight years ago, publicist Marnie Roberts spent seven days of bliss with Australian horse trainer Daniel Whittleson. But just as quickly, he disappeared. Now Marnie is heading to Australia to finally confront the man she's never been able to forget.

The stakes are high when it comes to love, horse racing, family secrets and broken promises.

A new exciting Harlequin continuity series coming soon!

www.eHarlequin.com

Cole's Red-Hot Pursuit

Cole Westmoreland is a man who gets what he wants. And he wants independent and sultry Patrina Forman! She resists him—until a Montana blizzard traps them together. For three delicious nights, Cole indulges Patrina with his brand of seduction. When the sun comes out, Cole and Patrina are left to wonder—will this be the end of the passion that storms between them?

Look for

COLE'S RED-HOT PURSUIT

by USA TODAY bestselling author

BRENDA JACKSON

Available in June 2008 wherever you buy books.

Always Powerful, Passionate and Provocative.

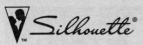

Romantic
SUSPENSE

Sparked by Danger,
Fueled by Passion.

Seduction Summer:
Seduction in the sand…and a killer on the beach.

Silhouette Romantic Suspense invites you to the hottest
summer yet with three connected stories from some
of our steamiest storytellers! Get ready for...

Killer Temptation
by Nina Bruhns;
a millionaire this tempting is worth a little danger.

Killer Passion
by Sheri WhiteFeather;
an FBI profiler's forbidden passion incites a
killer's rage,

and

Killer Affair
by Cindy Dees;
this affair with a mystery man is to die for.

Look for

KILLER TEMPTATION by Nina Bruhns in June 2008
KILLER PASSION by Sheri WhiteFeather in July 2008
and
KILLER AFFAIR by Cindy Dees in August 2008.

Available wherever you buy books!

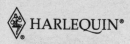

HARLEQUIN
Super Romance®

COMING NEXT MONTH